THE WHITE BUTTERFLY

THE WHITE BUTTERFLY

*A Novel About One Woman's Quest
to Chase Her Dreams*

The Second of the Claybourne Trilogy

MARY CHRISTIAN PAYNE

Published by TCK Publishing
www.TCKPublishing.com

**Sign up for the newsletter to get news, updates
and new release info from Mary Christian Payne:
http://bit.ly/MaryChristianPayne**

Lily Barton and Kit Claybourne were over-the-moon. It had ended. Peace had finally come. After four years of horror – of blood soaked battlefields in France and across the globe – of brutality beyond the imagination and of brave, courageous men reduced to pitiful creatures, crying out for their mothers, the 'War to End All Wars' was over. At the eleventh hour, on the eleventh day, of the eleventh month of 1918, the fighting ceased. It was reported that officers held their watches, and soldiers waited, with the same brave composure with which they had fought so valiantly. As the time reached eleven o'clock, there was an expected silence, and then an eerie rippling sound that those who were far behind the Front likened to the sound of a soft wind, from the Vosage Mountains to the sea. It was the reverberation of thousands of soldiers cheering.

For Lily, it meant that the nurses with whom she had toiled in the Causality Clearing Station at *Aubigny,* in France, would be coming home. Her great friends, Maddie, Poppy, and Gena had completed their mission, and they would be returning to England. The Doctors whom all of the nurses had worked with, side-by-side, would be close behind them. Her friend Dr. John Garrett, a *Sandhurst* graduate, who had known Kit during their school years, would come to *Claybourne-on-Colne* for a visit, and soon he and Gena would marry. There was even a strong possibility that they would settle in the quaint, Cotswold village that Kit and Lily called home. John had written and said that he was ready for peace and tranquility, after the horrendous sound of artillery fire all of his years in France. That meant a move to the English countryside.

Lily had kept in touch with her V.A.D. chums via post and she'd been thrilled to learn that the romance between John and Gena, which had begun in France, when they'd all enjoyed a three-day furlough to Paris, had developed into an engagement. For Kit, the end of the war meant the return of his trusted valet, Michael Richmond, who had survived the bloody trench warfare, and, by the grace of God, so had most of the chaps he'd fought with at *Etaples*. That included Tom Holiday, who had saved Kit's life. Some, of course, wouldn't be coming home. They would lie forever in cemeteries scattered throughout France.

For both Kit and Lily it meant that a watershed moment would occur. It was finally time to plan their wedding. Eleanor, Kit's deceased wife, had been gone since the previous December, and it would be over a year by the time Lily and Kit tied the knot. Even though Kit had wanted his wife out of his life long before her death, he would never have wished that she be murdered. The past year had been truly gruesome, what with Eleanor's murder and Kit's arrest on homicide charges. To Lily's amazement, her intuition had helped solve the crime. It was all behind them now, and soon Lily would be the Countess of Gloucester. She'd marry an Earl and become a step-mother to his three-year old son, Win, whom she had adores since his birth. They could look ahead to a well-deserved, happy future, watching Win grow, and, hopefully, adding other children to the nursery at Claybourne Court, Kit's ancestral home in the town named for his family *Claybourne-on-Colne*.

All England was overcome with delight. The war had been a ghastly nightmare. An entire generation of young men had been lost. Estimates of the total numbers of deaths world-wide ranged from nine to over fifteen million. In Great Britain the total death toll was nearly a million. The figures were astonishing, and most believed that the war had solved nothing. It might even have set the stage for the world to be back at war someday, due to the harsh treatment accorded Germany at the Treaty of Versailles. But, for the moment, joy was abundant.

Even in their tiny hamlet, too many lives had been lost, and too many men had returned with ghastly injuries. Kit, himself, had lost an eye; Lily's brother, Jordan, had been killed; Lily's step-brother, David Morris, had lost a leg; Kit's younger brother, Sebastian, had died when his car crashed into a tree, due to overwhelming fear caused by his dread of conscription, which was about to be put into effect. His inability to live with being branded a coward was what had really killed him. Each time he went out of the house, he feared running into one of the radical zealots who wandered about handing out white feathers to men who looked to be of fighting age, but weren't in uniform. The feathers were meant to brand a young man as a coward and humiliate them. They accomplished their goal with Sebastian. Sebastian would have liked to declare himself a Conscientious Objector, but his mother, The Lady Cynthia, Dowager Countess at Claybourne Court, would never have condoned such action. It would have brought dishonor to their ancient, English family. So, Sebastian died instead. That brought sympathy.

Lily rang her mother and step-father, Elisabeth and Will Morris, the moment the news was received that an armistice had been agreed upon. The Morris' were also wild with happiness at the war's end. Kit's mother, Lady Cynthia, immediately planned a small, family celebration at *Claybourne Court* the night of November eleventh. Included were Lilly and Kit, Lily's mother and step-father, Elisabeth and Will Morris, Will's son David and his bride, Susan, and needless to say, Win, Kit's three and a half year old boy, along with the Morris's little girl, Melinda. A lovely dinner was planned in the grand dining room, with fires roaring in both the dining and drawing room fireplaces. It was a raw, windy, November day. Although it was still a bit over a month until the anniversary of Eleanor's death, everyone decided that mourning was officially over. They could bring out colorful clothing for the evening. Mary, the cook, planned a lovely dinner with Mrs. Briggs, the housekeeper. Although there was still rationing in effect, Mary knew she could work within the guidelines, and still produce a delicious dinner. They didn't want anything exotic anyway- just a simple, conventional meal. Not everyone present would be of the aristocracy, and it was not Lady Cynthia's intention to cause any awkwardness with unfamiliar foods. Court bouillon, a simple green salad, baked chicken, potatoes, and green beans would be more than sufficient. She sent Halsey, the butler, to the cellars to select several bottles of his best white wine, and champagne for dessert – English Trifle. It was meant to be a celebration, and Lady Cynthia had every intention of making it one.

Mrs. Briggs used white linen table covering, with red napkins and dark blue and white Wedgwood china. The theme was the United Kingdom, so the colors were very appropriate. Everyone was asked to dress in one of the colors in the English flag. Lily choose a winter-white cashmere dress, quite plain, but very chic. With long sleeves, and a rounded neckline, it was calf length, with pleated skirt and a dropped waistline; Lady Cynthia choose a dark blue suit, of merino wool; Elisabeth Morris also wore dark blue, a simple day dress in navy print with white dots. Jane Marshall Morris, having given birth seven months previously, was enjoying having a waistline again. She choose a red silk, bell-skirted tea gown, with a velvet sash and long sleeves. The gentlemen all wore navy blue suits, with white shirts and red ties. The children looked adorable. Win wore his navy Eton suit, with a white rounded-collar shirt, and a small, red silk handkerchief folded in his breast pocket. Tiny Melinda Morris wore a bright red and navy baby dress with white collar. She was seven months, having been born the previous May, and she had David's dark hair and brown eyes. It was perfectly obvious that she was the light of her parent's lives.

Everyone arrived at close to the same time and all settled in the drawing room, where cocktails were served. Kit had told Lily, shortly after their engagement, that as soon as they were married, he wanted her to undertake the redecoration of Claybourne Court. It had been quite some time since there'd been any renovation, and Lily was terribly excited at the prospect. Kit felt it only right that the house be made to reflect Lily's tastes. Any remnant of Eleanor's past presence should be erased. Lady Cynthia heartily agreed. So, as they sat in the drawing room on that November evening, Lily told the ladies of her thoughts regarding color changes, drapery modification, nursery transformation and other updates.

One of the first things that Kit was insisting upon was that the gazebo, or summerhouse, be torn down, and replaced with something else. That was where Eleanor had been sitting the night she was murdered. They did not want any reminder of such a sordid piece of the past. Lily had her heart set on a walled, brick garden, with a high wooden gate and benches, where she could read on summer days. Perhaps even a fountain. Kit had agreed with her plan, and the landscape architects were already drawing up blueprints.

The women's conversation naturally turned to Kit and Lily's wedding plans. Lily had been living with her mother and step-father, since Kit's release from prison for the unjustified charges placed upon hm. She still acted as Win's nanny at Claybourne Court during the daytime hours, until she and Kit became husband and wife. She acted strictly in that capacity, and there was no pre-marital, inappropriate lovemaking. Of course, when two people are in love, it's difficult to be under the same roof and not yield to temptation, but Lily was a strong girl, and she'd vowed to save herself for marriage. Kit didn't make it harder for her. He shared her values, and they both knew not to put themselves into tempting positions. A kiss, or a hug, was fine, and long walks on the grounds of Claybourne Court was one of their favorite things to do. Win usually accompanied them. Often, Lady Cynthia joined them too, which gave Kit an opportunity to discuss business matters with his mother. Most times they took their little St. Charles Spaniel, Ginny, on a lead. All of this company minimized tantalizing situations. If they were totally honest there was something rather titillating about waiting until marriage for any intimate contact. It heightened their desire for one another, and brought about even more desire to be husband and wife.

They'd discussed a date to be married, and both agreed that it would not be until the war ended. Now, that day had finally arrived. Neither wanted a winter wedding. Their marriage was to be a new beginning for everyone - including Win. Lily loved springtime. It symbolized a fresh, start to everything- new flowers in bloom, baby birds chirping in the lacy green leaves, pristine lawns and, new-born woodland animals everywhere. They both agreed that it would be a perfect time to begin their new life as husband and wife. Finally, they settled upon Win's birthday, April Fifteenth, 1919. Kit and Lily's marriage would mean a new beginning for the little boy too, so the date of his birthday was a good way to signify such a change. It would be his fourth birthday, but the first with Lily as his Mummy.

Just before the guests gathered on that November night – the first night of peace in four, long years - Kit presented Lily with a sapphire ring, surrounded by small diamonds and rubies, to signify an end to the war and a lovely beginning to their new and joyous life. Her wedding ring would be a band of diamonds. So, as the entire family gathered, she proudly and joyously showed off her engagement ring to all who were thrilled at her happiness. Kit scarcely removed his hand from around her waist the entire evening. It was clear to anyone who looked at the couple that they were on cloud nine. In her white cashmere dress, her cheeks glowing with contentment, Lily was beyond beautiful. Her long, auburn hair had been cut to a shorter length, with soft waves surrounding her face. It was a drastic change for her, but so were a lot of things that were happening in her life. She'd never dreamed that she would marry an Earl, and live in one of the most splendid homes in all of England. At first the prospect frightened her, but she'd spent enough time at Claybourne Court to learn that it was the people who lived in a house that made it a home. There wasn't a single person in that exquisite mansion whom she hadn't grown to love. Everyone at Claybourne Court felt the same way about Lilly and she looked ahead to a blissful, warm, happy household.

Eleanor had been a terrible Countess – thinking only of herself, and never making any attempt to show appreciation to the staff, or to the residents of *Claybourne- on-Colne,* the quaint Cotswold village where the great house was located. It was those people who made it possible for the Claybourne family to live such an opulent lifestyle. Lily wanted the entire village to feel that it was their home too, and she already had plans to do so. Outside of the lovely cottages that dotted the landscape surrounding the village, there were numerous small tenant farms, which were still beholden to the Earl for whatever they had in life, and in turn paid him a tithe. Eleanor had ignored those tenants abysmally and even spoke of them in derogatory terms. Unlike Eleanor, Lily had great tenderness in her heart. She planned to pay regular visits to each and every home. There would also be picnics on the lawn, with croquet for the villagers, entertaining country fairs for all to enjoy, a continuation of the Christmas Eve Gala, and events at the stables, such as equine shows which the villagers could take part in. It was the beginning of a new age and with it would come a new inclusiveness at Claybourne Court. She hadn't discussed those plans with Kit yet, but she knew he would be very grateful that his wife cared about the people who lived on his estate.

Neither Kit nor Lily had any desire to send Win off to boarding school at a young age. She learned that *Eton* did not even take boys' until age thirteen. So, they planned to send him as a day student to *Beaudesert Park School,* a preparatory school for *Eton,* and other fine, English boarding schools, such as *Harrow. Beaudesert* began to take students at age four. A child could either board there, or attend as a day student. They'd decided that he would start at *Beaudesert* in the fall of 1919, and continue there until the time came for him to enroll at *Eton* at age thirteen. *Beaudesert Park* was wonderfully near *Claybourne-on-Colne.* It was located *in Minchhaven, Gloucestershire.* Lily chatted about the school with her guests that evening, and learned that Jane Marshall Morris was quite familiar with it. She was a teacher in the village, and was familiar with most of the private schools in England. Jane felt that *Beaudesert* gave excellent preparation for *Eton.* Lily made a mental note to make certain that she and Kit drove over to take a peek at the school, taking Win with them.

After what everyone agreed was a delightful dinner, the men retired to Kit's library to enjoy cigars and brandy. The women found themselves back in the drawing room, sipping tea or coffee and resuming their comfortable pre-dinner conversation. In the library, the men were discussing the after-effects of the war. Kit said that he expected the U.K. to be hit by a post war recession. The country had never really recovered from the poor economy that was in effect before the nightmarish war began in 1914. The Government had promised 'Homes for Heroes', but returning heroes were not treated well. Hiring people for domestic work became difficult. The young military men knew they could earn more in other positions, and they wanted more from life. The same was true of women, who had done war work outside of the home, in offices and factories, and liked it much more than polishing floors and scrubbing pots and pans. Claybourne Court was fortunate, as all of their long-time employees stayed on during the war. The only man who'd enlisted was Michael Richmond, Kit's valet. The other men were either not of an age to serve, or had some sort of medical difficulty.

Kit said that he was anxious to dive back into improving Claybourne Court. He had plans to plant more land into saleable commodities such as wheat, corn, oats, and barley. He also intended to expand into raising sheep, since wool prices had skyrocketed and were only expected to grow higher.

He liked the idea of raising sheep for their wool, because there would be no need to slaughter those gentle animals. It seemed foolish to Kit to have so many thousands of acres of land put aside for ornamental purposes. He felt that a sizable amount could be put to use in a more productive manner. Raising sheep would cut down on the need for maintenance of large portions of land which otherwise needed regular care. There was also the germ of an idea to bring the Claybourne name into the business arena, by building a Mill and producing fine woolens In *Claybourne-on-Colne.*

David Morris said that he and his father, Will, were going to expand their Chemist shop on the High Street. The town was expected to grow, and many returning veterans were in need of medication to help them cope with shell shock symptoms and other various and sundry medications for war wounds. There was talk that *Claybourne-on-Colne* might be getting a new physician, which would be a windfall to the chemist's business. The last resident physician had been Lily's father, Dr. Tom Barton. Now people in need of medical care had to travel to someplace larger, such as Gloucester.

Back in the drawing room, the conversation turned to Lily's wedding.

"I'll be a first-time bride, and I would like fuss and frivolity," Lily said. But, I don't want to do it up too big, as Kit was married before. It's not improper for a first-time bride to have an over-the-top wedding, but it would just make me feel a bit uncomfortable. I'm glad Kit's first marriage was in America, so there won't be a duplication of guests. I really don't want a terribly big wedding, anyway. I grew up in this small village and I've always been a country girl. I'd like to keep that in mind when planning our wedding. I intend to have three bride's maids and one matron of honor. That reminds me - Jane, I want you to be matron-of honor," she smiled.

Jane looked stunned. "Me? You want me?" she replied, obviously surprised.

"Lily, I never expected such a thing. Please don't feel the need to do that, just because I'm married to your mother's step-son."

"Don't be silly, goose," laughed Lily. We've grown very close. Whether you were married to David or not, I'd want you to have a place of honor. Now, no more of such talk," Lily continued.

Jane reached over and hugged her. "Thank you so much, dear Lily. What fun this will be."

"All right. Then, my other three attendants will be my friends from the V.A.D., whom I met while in France. You've all heard of them. Maddie Brooks, Poppy Paulson and Gena Weatherford. I'll have to write to them at once, but since its five months away, I should think that they can put it on the calendar easily enough. I also hope that some of the doctors I worked with will have a part. One of them is a good friend of Kit's – John Garrett. He's engaged to marry Gena. They could even be married by the time of my wedding. I hope so. Anyway, I believe Kit wants him to serve as Best Man. I haven't spoken to Kit about any firm plans yet. We firmly vowed not to think of marriage till the war was over, but now the time has come."

"What colors, sweetheart?" asked Lily's Mum.

"I haven't any idea. I'll have to think that one over. I'll have to get some swatches from the dressmaker. I'll need to think about the colors of everyone's hair, and the season. I do love pastels, so I imagine something soft and feminine."

"Lily dear you'll make the most beautiful bride. I'm going to be the happiest mother on earth when you walk down that aisle," smiled Lady Cynthia. "You are precisely the sort of girl I have always wanted for Kit. I'm sorry we had to go through so much upset, but Kit never should have married Eleanor."

"I couldn't agree more," added Elisabeth Morris, Lily's Mum. This is the sort of thing a mother dreams of when her little girl is still in the pram."

"Gosh, Mum, I'm sorry I made you wait so long," Lily giggled.

"No", Elisabeth smiled. "It's been well worth the wait. I couldn't have dreamed of a finer son-in-law than Kit."

"You won't get any argument from me on that point," Lily responded.

Mrs. Briggs brought a fresh pot of tea and set about pouring. In the meantime Jane asked if Lily and Kit were planning a wedding trip.

"Well, I suppose. But, the entire world is so scarred from the war. I'm not certain where we'd go. I think that will be Kit's responsibility. He's traveled much more than I have and probably has better ideas. Wherever he chooses will be splendid, I'm sure."

Their conversation was interrupted by the men, who had finished their brandy and cigars. One-by-one, they were wandering into the drawing room.

Kit was carrying Win on his back, and David Morris was doing the same with Melinda.

"Now there are two proud Daddy's," Lady Cynthia smiled. "I remember your father carrying you the same way, Kit."

"Yes, I remember it too. He said he was 'taking me for a horseback ride'." Kit held his son close to his chest, and it was so clear that he utterly adored him. Then he sat down on the sofa, with Win on his lap.

"If you two have any idea about additional children to the household, I'm not sure little Win will be too terribly thrilled," David chuckled.

"Oh, David, you don't think that Kit has spoiled Win, do you?" laughed Lily.

"Well, David's not one to speak," Jane smiled. "Melinda has it in her mind that she's a princess."

"She is Jane. Surely you know that by now," David answered, smiling.

They all broke into laughter. Lily did hope that she and Kit would have many babies. She was nearing twenty-six years, so she felt that if they were going to have children, they would have to dispense with any precautionary measures and start adding to the family as soon as they married. There was just so much to look forward to in their new life.

2

Not only was the annual Christmas Eve Gala at Claybourne Court scheduled for 1918, it was to be an even happier celebration than usual. John Garrett and Gena Weatherford decided to pay their first visit to *Claybourne Court* for the occasion. John's parents were both deceased and Gena's were not on amicable terms with hers, who were still holding a grudge about her decision to join the V.A. D. Now, apparently they were more irritated because they had announced their engagement before they'd even met him. Gena did try to make arrangements for them to meet, but her parent's always gave her one excuse or another and kept putting it off. Gena knew it wouldn't have mattered whether they'd met him or not. They were utterly foolish people. John was a second son, so although he came from a titled family, his older brother would inherit the title and family estate in Wiltshire. Gena's family was also titled, and her parents had always planned for her to marry an eldest, so that she would live out her life overseeing a lovely country estate. None of those things meant a fig to Gena, nor to John. She decided that if her parents wanted to attend the wedding, and be a part of their married lives, they were welcome, but otherwise, she was not going to have them bring heartache and upset to her wedding day. She and John were very excited about seeing Lily and Kit. John and Kit had been friends at *Sandhurst Military Academy* when they were younger, and then John met Lily in

France at the Field Station where they were both assigned - *Aubigny*. Lily's best friend at the Field Station was Gena, so it almost seemed meant to be that Gena and John would fall in love. Lily couldn't wait to hear all of their wedding plans.

Kit's first wife, Eleanor, had been killed at the Christmas Gala in 1917. At first, there was some consideration regarding the appropriateness of celebrating Christmas Eve in the very home where Eleanor had lost her life. But, after much consideration, Kit made the decision that Eleanor had already brought too much heartache and grief to his ancestral home. Canceling the annual Christmas Eve party would only bring sadness to a village that looked forward all year to such a meaningful event. Most of those in the village had not even known Eleanor. Those who had were less than fond of her, so it seemed senseless to give up something joyful, when there wasn't any grieving taking place.

Lily and Lady Cynthia began to plan for the gala event. That year, Lily took over the task of addressing the engraved invitations to all inhabitants of the village, asking them to come to Claybourne Court on Christmas Eve. It was to be a grand celebration of the joyous holiday. After the mistake that had been made the previous year, when they'd hired an unknown woman, who turned out to be Eleanor's murderer, to watch over the small children and entertain them, this year one of the kitchen workers, Cissy, offered to assume that responsibility. Cissy had seven brothers and sisters, all younger than she, so she had plenty of practice with youngsters. One of the receiving rooms was set aside as a place for them to play. A gorgeous fir pine tree was again brought from the property, and stood in the massive drawing room, decorated with all of the ornaments that the Claybourne *family* had collected through generations past. As usual, Lady Cynthia searched the shops and bought gifts for each resident of the village and then moved on to selecting a perfect gift for each child. It was her favorite task. Lily wrapped each in pretty paper and tied fancy ribbons on them, penning the name of the recipient on a separate card.

The kitchens below stairs were in a flurry of activity. Lovely cakes, cookies, special pies, and puddings were spread across the long, wooden table as they were removed from the ovens. The holiday feast of rib roast and Yorkshire pudding was prepared, and as always, Mary never failed to make the delicacy perfect. Since there were so many guests, Mary had to prepare several roasts and side dishes to accommodate everyone, as well as a giant bowl of English Trifle, which would sit in the middle of the dining table. Stacks of fine china, sterling silver flatware, teacups, crystal wine glasses and champagne flutes adorned the other end of the table. Guests were able to help themselves, buffet style, and then were served the roast beef, au jus, Yorkshire pudding, carrots and potatoes by one of the footmen. The other footman circulated about the rooms, carrying trays of champagne, eggnog, and water. Children were given hot cocoa, or cranberry juice mixed with plain soda water.

The house was decorated with pine swaths and red bows wrapped around the banister of the massive stairway, winding over the archways that led from room to room. The mantles of the fireplaces were also decorated with pine and holly sprigs. The wireless played carols in the background. It was one of the most festive Christmas Eve's that Kit could ever remember. He and his mother stood at the doorway, welcoming everyone, while Mrs. Briggs took their coats. It had been discussed as to whether Lily should stand in the receiving line with them, but she refused to do so. She felt it would be inappropriate to present herself as a member of the Claybourne family, before it was actually a *fait accompli*. It wasn't long after guests had begun to arrive that Lily spotted John and Gena making their way through the doorway. Lily nearly ran to the entrance, and put her arms round Gena. They both screamed, laughed and cried as they held on to one another.

"Oh My Gosh I wondered if I'd ever see you again. Let me look at you," cried Gena, as she stood back from Lily, and examined her. "You look so posh, Lily. What've you done to your hair" I never thought you'd cut it. It looks so chic."

"You look wonderful too. Just glowing. Let me see your ring," Lily asked.

Gena held out her left hand, and there sparkled a quite large Sapphire solitaire, surrounded by diamonds and set in platinum. More importantly, next to it was another platinum band, which signified that she and John had married.

"Gena! Are you and John already married?" Lily exclaimed.

"Indeed, we are. As of last week. We decided to marry before we came to visit you. When we arrived back from France, we took the train from Dover to London. We stayed there for a few days, and decided to get married at St. Martin-in-the Fields in London. It was all simply spur-of-the-moment. Just the two of us. So, it's a done deal. I'm Mrs. John Garrett."

"I can't believe it. I wish you'd rung Kit and me. We would have taken the train to London, and been there with you."

"I know you would have, Lily. But, truly, we wanted a quiet, no fuss wedding. Yours will be the posh one," Gena laughed.

Speaking of . . . Lily held her hand out to show Gena.

"Oh my goodness. What a sensational ring. Sapphires, diamonds and rubies. Is that to represent the end of the war?"

"Yes. He gave it to me on the night of the armistice. It seems very appropriate, don't you think?"

"Absolutely. And really, really gorgeous. So, have you two set a date?" Gena asked.

"Yes. On Win's birthday, April fifteenth. In the chapel here at Claybourne Court, with a reception back at the house."

"It will be perfect. You wrote and asked me to be a part of it, and of course you know I'm thrilled. Who else will be participating?"

"You, my step-brother's wife, Jane, Poppy and Maddie, Lily answered.

"Oh, Lily. How perfect. Almost as much fun as Paris was, only a much better time of year." Gena laughed. "Also, this time you'll have your own man with you."

While visiting Paris on a weekend furlough during the war, they had been stranded in a fierce snowstorm. Now they could laugh about it, but they certainly didn't laugh that night. Lily had never told the story to Kit. Something inside of her knew that he wouldn't have approved of four girls and four men traveling to Paris and staying in the same hotel, albeit in separate rooms. She whispered to Gena that Kit didn't know of their Paris adventure. She put her finger to her lips to motion that she wanted it to be kept a secret. Gena quickly understood and signaled the same motion back to Lily.

At just about that moment, both Maddie and Poppy came through the door, where Lily and Gena were still standing. There was another round of hugs and cries of excitement, along with oohing and aahing over Lily's ring and Gena's marriage. Maddie was a bit of a shock, in a just below the knee, red fringed, sleeveless dress, and a matching headband.

"My God, Maddie. You've become a flapper," exclaimed Gena.

"Yes. I'm just enthralled with the new look. I guess I'm one of those girls they're calling 'Sweet Young Things'," Maddie laughed.

"And do you perform all of these odd new dances? The Charleston and the Black bottom?" Lily was amazed.

"Oh yes. I even have a cigarette holder. You need to come to London and see what the modern world looks like. But, Lily you're as gorgeous as ever. I don't really think you're the flapper type," Maddie smiled.

"It's a good thing, too, or I don't think she'd be marrying Kit," Gena said, teasingly.

"No, I probably wouldn't be," Lily laughed. "But, you look darling Maddie. So do you Poppy," she added.

"So, the wedding is on for April?" Maddie commented. "I'm so excited. When do we get to know what our dresses will look like?"

"I hope you remember that I have red hair," laughed Poppy.

"That will all be taken into account, I promise. I'll be looking at fabric swatches after Christmas. I'll need your measurements, so remember to leave them with me before you depart tonight."

"I love spring colors. I'm sure you can find some really pretty fabrics," Maddie commented.

"Yes. Spring is my favorite season," added Lily.

"We plan on staying past Christmas, if that's all right. John is quite serious about setting up a medical practice here. We both want a peaceful, country village. From what we've seen, this is ideal," said Gena.

"Oh, it would be Gena. Plus, we really are in terrible need of a physician. My father died the summer of 1914, and we haven't had anyone since. We've had to rely on physicians from other surrounding villages. But, now the Claybourne family is going to build a new hospital right in the center the village, which will make it an attractive place for a physician to practice. Of course you can stay as long as need be."

"Splendid. I'll need to tell John about the hospital." Just as she said the words, John Garrett arrived at their sides. He put his arm round Lily and gave her a big kiss on the cheek. "How really wonderful to see you again. I almost didn't recognize you without your V.A.D. uniform. I must say, I prefer what you're wearing now."

Lily was dressed in a red and white striped taffeta dress, in the new shorter length with a pleated low slung skirt. She wore her mother's pearls. Gena looked equally lovely in a sleeveless simple, crimson wool dress, with a pin tucked bodice over a straight skirt. "Kit tells me that you two have set a date," John smiled.

"Yes. We're so happy, John. We'll be married on April fifteenth. I'm hoping that you'll decide to set up a medical practice here. It would be so lovely. Just imagine - our best friends living in the same village."

"Well, we're going to spend some time looking around the next couple of days. If I can find something I feel is suitable, I feel fairly confident that we'll set up shop here. I also want to make certain that Gena can find the house of her dreams."

"What sort of house are you looking for, Gena?"

"My favorite is Victorian. I don't know if there are any like that here. I've seen a lot of cottages, that are precious, but I'd like something a bit larger."

"I'll go with you to look the day after Christmas. I can think of several that might be perfect. We do have a lot of cottages, but there is one section that's filled with Victorian. Very posh too."

"Not too posh I hope! In other words, we can't afford to live the way you and Kit will be living."

"Gena! My situation is very different. I'm just extremely fortunate, I know that," Lily remarked. "I wouldn't lead you to anything like *Claybourne Court*. No, the houses I'm referring to are old, Victorian townhouses — bowed fronts and all that– this village is not full of enormously wealthy people – middle class, and very nice. I think the homes I'm thinking of would definitely be within a doctor's price range. Come to think of it, I wonder if John might be interested in buying or leasing my father's old cottage for his offices. We used to live there too, but I think you want something larger to call home. The cottage would be perfect for an office, and it's fully furnished with all equipment. My father had just added an X-ray machine, before his death. Mum wants to sell the cottage, or she's willing to let it. What do you think John? Would you like to take a peek?" Lily asked.

"What a smashing idea, Lily. That would keep me from having to pay for all new equipment, which can be a bloody fortune. Absolutely, I'd love to see it."

"Do you plan on nursing too?" Lily asked her friend.

"Perhaps at first. I'll help John get established. But, I think I'd like to stay home and start on babies." She laughed, and poked Lily in the arm.

"You know the whole time we were in France, I was certain that I'd return to England and go on to medical school. That was always my life's ambition – to wear a white coat and be called Dr. Barton. Kit said he would support me in that dream, if I wanted to follow it, but, I so dearly love little Win, and would like to have some babies - at least one of my own. So, I think I'll be a homebody for a while. Perhaps someday, I'll still pursue my dream. Who knows? France changed a lot of things, didn't it?" Lily murmured.

"Indeed it did. If I were to nurse again, I'd want to specialize in something happy. No more of the atrocities we saw in France," Gena answered. The other girls nodded.

"Yes, I know what you mean," Lily replied. Well. Let me take you around and introduce you to others, and then on the twenty-sixth, we'll go house hunting. What fun?"

Before the night was over everyone knew Gena and John and loved them. The news spread quickly throughout Claybourne Court that John might be the new doctor in their village, so there was great excitement over that prospect. Lily introduced Gena, Poppy and Maddie to her mother and Will, as well as David, Jane and their little girl, Melinda. Elisabeth immediately understood the deep friendship that the girls had formed at the V.A.D. Causality Clearing Station in *Aubigny*. She had heard about all of these girls since Lily's return. She knew Lily adored all of them, but the Gena was considered her best firend.Lily explained it by saying that once in a while, someone comes along in life who one knows will be a friend for life. That's what happened to Gena and Lily. They might go months without speaking, but when they did it was as though there'd never been a separation. Lily was so pleased that John and Kit's friendship was the same sort. From their boyhood days at *Eton*, and on to *Sandhurst*, they had formed a deep, special bond. How lovely that they would be married to girls who were equally close. There seemed little doubt that John would be setting up a medical practice in *Claybourne-on-Colne*. It was one, good, thing to had come out of the war

The Christmas Eve Gala of 1918 went off without a hitch. Unlike the year before, the feelings shared between friends and families were filled with love and meaning, and a sense of renewal, because they all knew that the war was over. Naturally there were moments of sadness, when someone mentioned the name of a loved one who would never be coming home again, but there was a general feeling that all had done their bit for King and Country. The Allied Forces had prevailed, and now it was time to move on.

Ralph Poindexter, Kit's barrister during the time he'd been held on charges for Eleanor's murder, brought his wife to the party. It was nice for everyone to meet her, and to be able to thank Ralph again for all he'd done on Kit's behalf. Lily hurried up to him and they chatted for a good while. She was interested in knowing the most recent news about Clara Thornton, the woman who had murdered Eleanor in a jealous rage.

"Has she been brought to trial yet, Ralph? The last I heard was that her barrister was asking for a change of venue." Lily inquired.

"It was granted. I agree with that ruling. *Claybourne-on-Colne* is awfully tiny and I'd be willing to bet that there are few, if any, people living here who don't know about the case. In addition, Kit's grown up here and everyone seems quite fond of him."

"Where will the trial be, then?" Lily asked.

"Probably over in Gloucester. It's larger, but still not a great distance. I still suspect that they're going to work out a plea deal. There's no way a jury will find premeditated murder. Clara is a pitiful creature, and Eleanor did everything in her power to denigrate her. Frankly, I hope they go easy on her."

"Shall I be called upon to testify?" Lily wondered.

"You might be, if a plea isn't reached. But, don't worry about it. Just tell the truth."

Right then, their conversation was interrupted when little, Win Claybourne appeared. Ralph had seen him once before, on the day that Kit was released from jail, but he was only a toddler then. This time he was able to see Win in all of his Christmas finery. He was growing into an exceptionally good-looking little chap. His silky, blonde tresses, had darkened a bit, to a taffy color, and his eyes had taken on the blue of Kit's, with flecks of green. One could already see that he was going to be a very handsome young lad. Although he spoke lovely English at nearly four years, he still held on to his nickname for Lily, 'Ba', and it didn't seem that would ever change. Kit joined Lily, Ralph, Ralph's wife and Win and they all went to the drawing room to admire the Christmas tree. The family would be rising early on Christmas morning, and after a sumptuous breakfast, they would proceed to gift exchange. Although the stores were not back to full capacity, everyone knew this Christmas would be more bountiful than the last.

Everyone slept rather late on the 26th, after a full day of gift opening, the day before, playing with toys, and eating another of Mary's delicious family dinners on Christmas Day. The Christmas Eve party had lasted until about midnight, and by the time everyone was tucked into their beds, it was close to two o'clock a.m. Then had come Christmas Day itself, filled with activity. As each guest woke, dressed and descended the staircase, on that day after Christmas, they found a wonderful, traditional English breakfast set out on the sideboard in the Dining Room.

Lily made plans with a local real estate agent to show John and Gena houses for sale that day. Elisabeth Morris was going to run over and unlock the door to the cottage, so that they could also take a look at it. As they ate their breakfasts, they thumbed through some of the photos of houses that Gladys Kemper had dropped off for them to look through. Gladys was the realtor whom Lily had contacted. Gena already had her heart set on an amazing Victorian detached family home. John told her that no matter how much she loved it, they would absolutely have to look at a few others, just to be certain. Gena and Lily rolled their eyes at one another, but agreed.

After breakfast was over, Edward Luther, the Claybourne Court chauffeur, picked them up in front of the house, and they headed out to explore *Claybourne-on-Colne*. The visited several homes that were for sale and most were lovely. Gena particularly liked one Georgian colonial, set back from the road, with bay windows, a twenty-five foot drawing room and lovely gardens in the rear. They sat in the car after viewing it and talked for quite a while about the possibility of making an offer. But, Gena still wanted to see a Victorian, so they continued their search. Finally, the car turned into 'Summer Lane', and Gena gasped. There stood a remarkable late Victorian house named 'Summer Meadow.' It was dark red brick, with large bay windows on the right and left, both upstairs and down. Mrs. Kemper gave them the history as they strolled through it. It was built in 1890 and retained many interesting period features, including high ceilings with cornicing's, fireplaces and original windows. It was laid out over three floors with elegant, well-proportioned, spacious rooms, perfect for family living and entertaining. It was probably much larger than they needed, but they loved it so much. There were six bedrooms, 3 reception rooms and four baths. The gardens were glorious. At first they told themselves that it would be foolish to purchase something so enormous, but then, they began to think more, and decided that if they were to have four children, which they hoped would happen, the house wouldn't be at all too large. The receiving rooms could be used in a variety of different ways. Gena loved flowers, so the gardens were a giant plus for her. They had Edward drive them back to *Claybourne Court*, where they went to their rooms, and spent a good deal of time thinking about what to do. They'd begun the day looking at Dr. Tom Barton's former cottage, which would make a perfect surgery. John thought it would fit him to a Tee. The Victorian House, on 'Summer Meadow" wasn't a long distance from the cottage. It was on the outskirts of the village, so there was a lot of privacy and acreage to accompany it. A guest house and stables added to its amenities. Finally, they decided to make an offer. John rang Mrs. Kemper and within an hour the seller rang her back and accepted the deal. Gena was-over-the-moon. When Kit returned home from a dashed trip to London on business, he, Lily, and the Garrett's jumped back into the auto, and Edward drove them over to 'Summer Meadow'. Mrs. Kemper met them there, with papers to sign and the key, so that they could have another look about. Lily was mad for it, and Gena already had a slew of decorating ideas. John and Kit looked at one another with wide eyes, and sighed. "I hope I have a busy practice," smiled John.

3

Lily and Gena were terribly thrilled at the thought that they would be living so close to one another. Most of Lily's friends from her younger days had either married or moved away from *Claybourne-on-Colne,* in order to find better paying jobs than could be found in their small village. Lily had been left with her mother, and of course her step-brother's wife, Jane. She was happy to spend the majority of her free time with them, and with Win, Kit and Lady Cynthia, but sometimes she caught herself longing for a chat with a longtime, dear girlfriend, after never-ending access to female companionship during her V.A.D. days. Now, Gena would be living close-by. Not only that, but she was married to John, a long-time friend of Kit's, so they made a perfect foursome.

During the next few months, the girls planned Lily's wedding. Gena and John moved into their new home in the middle of February, and John opened his medical practice. Everyone in the village was delighted to have a physician again, and they all took to Dr. Garrett immediately. Gena assisted at the office a few days a week. Both she and Lily helped organize everything. Right after Gena's move, Poppy and Maddie came for a visit, staying at *Claybourne* Court, and they excitedly made plans for the wedding in April. Both Poppy and Maddie were living in London, nursing at St.

Bartholomew's, and sharing a flat. They were-over-the-top with the reunion taking place at *Claybourne Court*. After sorting through unimaginable amounts of fabric samples, all of the bridesmaids settled upon a soft, floral print, designed with rosebuds, sprigs of lavender, pink lilies, and violets scattered over a white background. Green leaves were interspersed with the blooms. The fabric was a dainty muslin, feminine and perfect for a spring wedding. Next came the design. The newest look was sleeveless, with a tank-type top, which fit snugly to the body, over a dropped waistline, flaring out into a knife pleated skirt, ending at the calf. The dress was designed with a sash at the low-slung hipline, with a delicate flower at its middle. The maids would carry baskets of the same flowers in the fabric – roses, lilies, lavender and violets, and on their heads they would be wearing wide-brimmed garden party hats, swathed in white gauze. That was perfect, but they all felt it should have a small jacket that could be removed at the reception. Wearing bare arms to church was still not considered proper.

Next came the choice of a wedding gown for Lily. It was designed specifically for her in Paris. It was made of ribbons, rosettes and hand beading over white Alencon lace, with cap sleeves, and a tiered, floor length skirt. A lace train attached to the back. It fell from the waist and stretched several yards behind her. On her head she would be wearing a band of organdie, with attached rosebuds, and she would carry white roses, lilies, and white violets.

Kit chose an equal number of men to act as ushers. John Garrett was to be his best man. Next, was David Morris. The last two were Tom Holiday, who had saved Kit's life in battle during the war, and Charles Hunt, an old friend from Oxford. Tom and Charles had settled in London after the war. Each had come from the suburbs, so a move to London was almost like returning home.

By March first, 1919, all of the guests were gone from Claybourne Court, and there was only a little over a month before the wedding day. Lily's mother, Elisabeth, and Lady Cynthia planned the decorations for the chapel and talked over the menu for the wedding breakfast, which would follow the ceremony. The reception would be at Claybourne Court. Elegant engraved invitations were sent out to nearly one hundred people, some from London, but many from towns and villages where friends from the war now lived.

Lily's time was taken up with afternoon teas, and both she and Kit attended evening parties held in their honor. They were overcome with happiness, and it was hard to imagine that there'd been a time when they hadn't known if they would ever be together.

Kit worried over where they would go for a wedding trip. The majority of Europe was ravaged by war, and the thought of traveling abroad wasn't pleasant. Finally, he reached the decision to simply visit London for two weeks. Lily had never been to London, and although he knew the city well, and even owned a home there, Kit thought it would provide a fine place to begin their married life. He made reservations at the Savoy Hotel, requesting the bridal suite.

Kit and his mother were enjoying lunch on the terrace. It was a splendid April day, and the wedding was only a week away. They'd maneuvered dates on the calendar, and even cancelled appointments, in order to make time for one, last chat and some alone-time together before the big event. They sat at a wrought iron table, under a large, old oak tree, drinking white wine and awaiting a light meal of chicken salad and warm bread.

"Kit, I don't need to tell you how extremely happy I am to know that you and Lily will be husband and wife soon, and that Win will be settled with a mother who loves him. Perhaps as important, I can't put into words the joy I feel knowing that Claybourne Court will once again be consigned to a Countess who is a lovely, elegant lady. She'll restore the dignity of this home," Lady Cynthia remarked to her son.

"I know, Mother. I feel the same way. Lily has an enormous capacity for caring about others. She'll be a fine steward for this incredible home that I've been fortunate enough to oversee. Of course, I'm delighted that you're here to help Lily with the finer details of becoming a Countess. Unlike Eleanor, Lily won't mind being taught the things she doesn't know, or isn't certain about. I believe the first thing that attracted me to her was her obvious lack of selfishness. She always puts others ahead of herself. Just look at what she did for me – running back from France to make certain that if she could help me, she would"

"Yes, Lily is what I call a 'rescuer'. From the moment she stepped into this house, her calm demeanor set a different tone. My goodness. Even Eleanor took to her at once. The only thing I've never understood about Lily is how she could run off so impetuously, and join that gruesome V.A.D. I can't imagine her in one of those ghastly field hospitals in France."

"Well, Mother, that was a very unusual act for Lily. She was shocked and frightened that I still cared for Eleanor, when she loved me so much. I think she just acted without thinking. You have to remember how young she was and so very innocent. But, as I said, you saw how fast she came back to me when she knew I was in danger. She's still very young, of course. But, the V.A.D. taught her a lot. Her temperament is such that she won't mind be molded into the elegant, but still unworldly woman I want her to be."

"Did you know that she once had dreams of becoming a doctor?" Lady Cynthia smiled, as she took a sip of wine.

"Oh, the silly things young people dream, "Kit answered. "I think that came from her father, whom she adored, you know. She had an image of seeing herself in a white physician's coat. I'm surprised her father encouraged such thoughts. Surely he knew that female doctors aren't considered decent. Perhaps he thought she would move on to other goals as she matured. Of course, both of her parents had to know she'd marry. She's such a beautiful creature," Kit continued.

"That she is. You two make a handsome addition to the gentry. How I wish you had waited until she came along," his mother signed.

Molly interrupted their conversation with a serving tray holding two exquisite plates of Wedgewood china. The blue of the porcelain matched the glorious sky above them. She set their places and spread napkins, asking if there was anything more they needed. Lady Cynthia told her it looked marvelous, and Molly disappeared to let them continue their long-awaited chat.

There was silence as both sampled the delicious salad, and took bites out of the warm, buttered bread. Kit drank some more of his wine.

"You know, one of the things I admire most about Lily, is that she hasn't allowed herself to become influenced by this new breed of women who march about the streets of London waving banners and making spectacles of themselves, crying out for more rights. I abhor that sort of woman."

"Goodness, Kit. Can you imagine women being allowed to vote? I suppose it's only natural that the war had an effect in that regard. Women went out of the house and worked, and now they've gotten into their heads that they're no different from men. For the life of me, I cannot imagine why any woman would want to be treated as equal to a man." She shook her head in wonder.

"I'm of the belief that such women are quite unattractive, Mother. They've never had any attention from men, so they're bitter. They're also usually from the bigger cities. Still, Lily could have been caught up in such hoopla, what with the people she was associated with in France," Kit answered.

"What was your opinion of the girls who were here on Christmas Eve?" Lady Cynthia asked, tilting her head as the sun moved nearly straight into her eyes.

"They seemed like nice girls. I was a bit taken back by the one who dressed like a flapper. What's her name? Maddie, I believe. But, she seemed like a decent sort. Not a bit like Lily, but they say opposites attract. I liked Gena the best. Of course, she's married to my old friend John Garrett. I'm glad they'll be here in *Claybourne-on-Colne*. I didn't get to know any of her chums very well. None of them seemed like suffragettes, thank God," Kit laughed. "Lily is an old-fashioned girl in many ways. Regardless of her pipe dreams about wanting to be a doctor, her true calling is that of wife and mother. She's had her little adventure in France, and having been there myself I know how horrendous it was. I can assure you that Lily wants nothing more than to be my helpmate and a proper Countess for *Claybourne Court,*" Kit remarked.

There was silence as the two continued to eat their lunch. A soft breeze ruffled Kit's tawny hair, and he brushed it aside, smoothing it. As the silence lengthened, Kit sensed that his mother was going to move on to a subject that he knew he didn't want to discuss. He was right.

"Kit, it really isn't any of my business, and I know it's been a long time, but do you ever worry about that episode when you were at Oxford?" Lady Cynthia asked.

"Mother, that was sixteen years ago. Dad took care of it. It's completely in the past. I scarcely think it's anything I'd need to be concerned about now.

Of course, Lily doesn't know. Nobody, to my knowledge does, except you and Dad, and that's the way it will stay. I was a young fool, you know that. But, I seldom think about it anymore."

"All right, Kit. I sometimes worry that the past comes back to haunt people. But, I'm sure you're right. Your father was a master at making problems simply vanish. The Claybourne family must always stay free from any sort of scandal. Eleanor's murder was quite enough."

"Money does talk, doesn't it? I certainly had that on my side. So, please stop fretting about something that happened long ago and is over and done with," Kit encouraged his mother.

"Yes, dear, I shall. Also, I wanted to ask if you've heard anything from Eleanor's parents. I know they wrote to you directly after learning she'd died. I also know that you contacted them when you were released, and Clara was arrested. But, you've never mentioned them since. It's hard for me to believe that they've simply vanished from your life."

"No, they haven't and I don't believe they will. Yes, I've heard from them. They've indicated that they plan a trip to England in the summer to meet their grandson. Passenger ships will be speeding back and forth across the Atlantic now that the war is over. Having them pay a visit will be a tricky situation. Of course, they have every right to see Win and to get to know him. But, I'm certainly not about to send him to America on any regular basis when he's so young. They' have to come over here, at least until he's much, much older. I hope we don't disagree on that. Also, I have no idea what they know about Eleanor's and my relationship - whether she ever wrote and told them that we'd been separated – they never said a word about that to me," sighed Kit.

"Well, just wait until they're actually here. They probably won't be pleased that you married again so quickly. Do you intend to tell them the truth about everything?"

"Indeed, I do. If I must. It would be foolish to let them think that Eleanor and I were happy. I have no wish to hurt them, and won't tell them of her vile remarks to me, but I'll make it clear that we were estranged."

"I don't look forward to their arrival," Lady Cynthia frowned.

"Nor do I, Mother. It's another of those things in life that have to be reconciled after one makes a mistake. I seem to have a propensity for that," Kit laughed ruefully.

While Kit and his mother were lunching on the terrace at Claybourne Court, Lily and her bridesmaids were also having lunch at a quaint teashop on High Street. It was the last time they would all be together before the wedding, and Lily had a gift for each of them. Of course they all looked forward to a long chat filled with gossip. They were seated at a round table. Each girl had just unwrapped a lovely box and was lifting the lid. Inside lay a sterling bud vase, with tiny rose's climbing up the base, carved out of the exquisite silver. Naturally, everyone was delighted. Thanks and hugs were given to Lily, as each placed the wrapping on a vacant chair. The waitress arrived with a pot of tea and a luncheon menu, and took away the discarded wrapping paper. Each girl studied the offerings and ordered. Then, they settled in with their cups of tea and began to talk about Lily's wedding.

"Lily, are you at all nervous yet," asked Gena?

"No, not really. I have moments, I suppose every girl does. I worry that I won't be all of the things a Countess should be. There are so many tasks one is expected to perform. Kit doesn't really understand my anxiety, because he was raised always knowing the proper way things are done in a great house. I've a lot to learn," Lily answered.

"Lily, you'll be a marvelous countess. You have the most important elements – kindness, thoughtfulness, and a ladylike approach to life. You were born to fill this role," said Maddie.

"Oh, thank you, Maddie. I'll just take a day at a time, and I suppose it'll all come together. To tell the truth, if I'm concerned about anything, it's how much I've grown and changed since I worked at Claybourne Court. I'm not certain Kit really understands that. I'm afraid he still thinks I'm a totally naïve, innocent, little creature. After the war, that would be an impossibility. You know, I always had ideas that were somewhat advanced for a woman, anyway. Especially my dreams about wanting to attend medical school. Can't you just see me in a white coat, with Lady Claybourne written on it?" She laughed. "Since I've seen and done all of the things that women are capable of while I was in France, I'm even more convinced that a women can achieve anything she wants."

"Lily! You haven't turned into a suffragette have you?" asked Jane.

"Well, I don't think I'd want to march around, waving flags, carrying posters, and such. But, honestly, I don't see what's so awful about a woman having the right to vote. We're treated like ornaments, and made to feel that we haven't a thought in our pretty, little heads except for fashion, party-planning, and caring for babies. I knew girls at *Cheltenham Ladies' College* who were planning on becoming barristers, chemists, and even business owners. Someday, when my child-rearing days are behind me, I might return to my medical ambitions."

"But, do you think Kit would approve of that?" asked Maddie.

"No. Not right now, he wouldn't. But, times change. The world is transforming rapidly. I believe that if I give him the support he needs for the coming years, he'll support any endeavor I wish to undertake at a later time," answered Lily.

"John would support me in that sort of goal. He has no problem with my wanting to assist in his medical practice. I fully intend to do so until children come along, "said Gena.

"That doesn't surprise me," said Lily, as she took a sip of tea. "John worked side by side with women in the Causality Clearing Station. He knows that we have the same stamina and intelligence that men have. In fact, I think John will be a good influence on Kit in that area. All he really has is his mother as a model for what a woman should be like," Lily smiled.

"His mother seems like a pretty strong woman herself. I can't see her letting a man run all over her," Poppy remarked.

"No, she isn't that sort. But, she does believe in the man being the complete head of the household. That's the generation she comes from. So does my Mum for that matter. I guess every generation has to pave the way for the next. The war speeded things up enormously. Don't you think that once women went out to work it was a giant awakening? I don't think things will ever go back to the way they were. I'm not sure Kit has grabbed onto that yet," Lily laughed.

"And you aren't afraid that could cause difficulties for the two of you?" asked Maddie.

"I'm not expecting it to. Change takes time. I know that. I don't intend to leap into marriage with the idea of changing all of the old ways at Claybourne Court. Things will progress. Kit is a kind, understanding man. He knows that I'm a bright woman. He'll listen to my ideas. I'm just sure of it."

"Are you wanting to have babies right away?" asked Jane. "Of course, David and I did."

"Pretty quickly, I hope," said Lily. "I'm getting on toward twenty-six. I don't want to wait too long."

"Oh, you old thing," giggled Poppy.

Lily swatted her on the arm. "No, I'm not old, I know that, silly. But, I love babies, and I'm ready for them. I think Win should have another child in the nursery. He's been an only child, without the companionship of other children. I don't want him to grown up without any understanding about sharing."

"Sharing? What's that?" Gena teased. Since she'd been an only child, she could identify with Lily's comments.

"Okay, Gena. You understand what I'm saying. How did you escape being a spoiled brat?"

"Because my parents pawned me off on the nanny, and then to boarding school. There was nobody to spoil me," Gena retorted.

"Gosh, that's sad," Jane exclaimed. "My parents were so loving. I don't understand why people have children if they don't want to spend time with them and love them."

"It's the 'done thing'. People look askance at you if you don't procreate," Maddie said.

"Procreate? What a clinical word. It makes it sound like there's no love involved," Lily laughed.

"Don't be too sure there always is," Maddie said, rolling her eyes. "Look at Kit's first wife. Anyway, now that we're on the topic of 'procreation', Lily are you ready for your wedding night? I know you're still an innocent," she added with a smile.

Lily snorted. "Oh, gosh, Maddie. Well, I guess I am – an innocent I mean. But, after seeing everything I was exposed to in France, I don't think I'm a *total* innocent. Does anybody have any advice for me?" she prodded.

"What sort do you need, Love?" asked Gena.

"Um, well – honestly now – am I supposed to do anything – you know? Or, do I just lay there, and let him do everything? Mum gives me the impression that it's the latter," Lily giggled.

"Oh, Lily. Really. This is the Twentieth Century. Women are supposed to enjoy it too," Gena laughed.

"Yes, but what if Kit thinks I'm not acting like a lady? Mum says that ladies aren't supposed to like it."

"Lily! Your Mum is way behind the times. I can tell you beyond any doubt that men like it when you enjoy it. John would hate it if I just laid there and thought of England."

Lilly tipped her head back and laughed. "Well, yes, but that's John. Aren't all men different?" she asked.

"I suppose," Gena answered. "But, Gosh would I ever hate the thought of going through life having to pretend I didn't like making love with my husband."

"Well, I guess I'll just wait and see how Kit acts. Will I be able to know what he expects?" Lily wondered aloud.

"I certainly hope so," Poppy chimed in.

"You'll know," added Jane. "Just don't be concerned. Kit will explain everything to you, I'm sure."

"All right. I'll be fine. I love him so much, I just think everything will come naturally," Lily smiled.

"Good girl. That's exactly how you should think," added Maddie.

"Lily, not to change the subject, but do you think you'll ever get down to London after you're married? Maddie and I would love to go out on the town with you. Or, Kit and you," said Poppy.

"Kit has a house in London, so I'm sure we'll be spending time there. It was destroyed by a Zeppelin attack during the war, but it's been totally rebuilt. I've never seen it, but I'm anxious to."

"How very posh of you," Poppy laughed. We just have a tiny flat, but it *is* in Nottinghill, which is quite nice. Where is your townhouse?"

Lily thought a moment. "It's on Dower Street in Kensington, think.-Yes, that's right. Number 17, Dower Street."

"Very, very posh. Kensington, no less. I think we'll be visiting you," Maddie said, rolling her eyes, and winking at Poppy.

The chatter went on for another hour, and when they left, everyone was ready for the wedding just a week away. Lily was glad she'd had the chance to speak with friends her own age, so she knew a bit more than she had about what to expect from married life.

4

She scarcely sleep a wink the night before her wedding. All of a sudden every fear she'd had came roaring to the surface. She didn't even know Kit. That was the plain, simple truth. She'd met him at the end of September, 1914, and within just a few days, he'd gone off to war. The next time she saw him it was June, 1915, when he came home from France, injured. Eleanor was so ghastly to him then, and Lily's heart ached, as she witnessed the manner in which his wife demeaned and belittled him. On top of that, he lost his brother Sebastian to the car wreck right after his return. Then, after Eleanor was sent away to London, Kit had turned to Lily for affection, and of course she'd responded. What girl wouldn't have? He was gorgeous, and an Earl, with a fine education as well as a kind disposition. She'd truly believed that he and Eleanor were going to divorce, and that he was going to marry Lily. But, Eleanor had returned when the townhouse was struck by a Zeppelin. Lilly stayed at *Claybourne Court* until September, when she caught Kit with Eleanor in the nursery, practically making love. From September, 1915 until September, 1918 she hadn't seen hide nor hair of him, since she'd sought shelter at her Mum's house, and then in France with the V.A.D. She raced back when she learned that he was in trouble and saved him from a murder charge. The next thing she knew they were engaged.

Who was she marrying? She didn't even know who *she* was anymore. She remembered a conversation she'd once had with Eleanor, back in the beginning, when they'd first met. Eleanor had said something very similar. 'Who is Eleanor Claybourne?' she'd asked. Who would Lily Claybourne be? She'd wanted to be a doctor. Where did all of those dreams go? Her heart was beating quickly, and she knew that she was experiencing an anxiety attack. She got out of bed, and sat on the little window seat in her mother and Will's cottage. She made herself take deep, regular breaths, and soon she could feel herself calming.

Perhaps all girls felt like this the night before they married? Was that why everyone kept asking her if she was afraid, worried, or nervous. She'd been too busy with planning the wedding to have such feelings. But, now, suddenly, she realized that at the same time tomorrow, she would be the Countess of Gloucester, Lily Claybourne. She was moving into a different world. It was one thing to work as a ladies 'maid, nurse or nanny in such an environment, but in one day she would be expected to oversee that great house. Was that really the life she wanted? Were all of the adventures in her life over? Had her instincts to rescue others been what got her into this situation?

If she thought back on it, it was rescuing her mother from money worries that had first brought her to Claybourne Court. After that, it was the sadness she felt for Kit while he was fighting in France. His wife was acting like such a harpy, and that made Lily have stronger feelings for Kit. Then, when he came home with only one eye, and Eleanor treated him abominably, it was Lily's tender heart that once again made her want to reach out and give Kit the love he deserved. When she learned he was being held for Eleanor's murder, she'd dropped everything and run back to *Claybourne-on-Colne* to try and help him. When she accomplished what she'd set out to do, before she knew it, he was asking Win if he wanted her to be his Mummy. What in the world could she have said?

But, did she *really* love him? For that matter, did he *really* love her? If she didn't know *him*, he didn't know *her* any better. He thought she was that pretty, young girl who had crept up the hill to his home, practically begging for employment, in 1914. But, that wasn't who she was anymore. She was strong, courageous and very intelligent. She had a lifetime ahead of her to fulfill her dreams - to be the best she could be. Was being the Countess of Gloucester the best she could be? She got back into her bed and lay there thinking?

On the other hand, she knew of many marriages where the husband supported his wife in achieving her goals. John and Gena Garrett were a good example. There was no reason to think that Kit wouldn't be equally supportive. And, certainly, she *did* love him. From the moment she'd met him, there was chemistry that she'd never felt with any other man. It wasn't just his handsome face, or his firm, virile body. Not even his thick, streaked blonde hair that had a tendency to flop onto his forehead. It was his kindness. His gentleness. His sensible maturity. It was hard for Lily to imagine that Kit had ever done anything impulsive or stupid in his life. That simply wasn't who he was. Those thoughts served to calm her, and to ease the racing of her heart, as well as the fear lurking inside of her. Of course she was frightened. Wasn't that usual for girls who were about to walk down the aisle? It was truly a life altering moment. If a girl wasn't a bit concerned, there would be something amiss. Finally, she felt better. She laid her head on the pillow, turned on to her side, and fell into a restless sleep.

When dawn came, she was aware of the sun rising, and the pink sky in the East, but she turned over and went back to sleep - her last morning as a single girl. She knew her Mum would wake her when it was time to start preparations for the wedding. Sure enough, at seven o'clock her Mum rapped on the door, and Lily told her to come in. Lily was propped up in bed, with pillows behind her, looking into a hand mirror, trying to decide if she needed to pluck her eyebrows.

"Good morning, sweet girl. Whatever are you doing?" her mother asked

"What do you think, Mum? Do my eyebrows need shaping a bit with the tweezers?"

"I don't think so Lily. But, you girls have different thoughts from back in my days. If you do that, please just pull out a few hairs from the bottom. You have lovely shaped brows, so don't do anything to ruin them."

Lily put the hand mirror on the bed. "I probably should leave them alone. I'd no doubt regret fooling with them. So, are you here to tell me that breakfast is on the table? she smiled.

"No, it's being brought up here to you. I'm going to treat you posh on your last morning as my girl."

"Mum, you don't need to do that. I'll probably get my fill of that sort of thing at Claybourne Court. I'd like to have breakfast with you and Will."

"All right, dear. Whatever you prefer. I just wanted to spoil you one, last time."

"Mum, you've spoiled me all of my life. I'm so glad I'll still be living close to you. I'd hate to be separated by a wide distance, unable to see you very often."

"Well, you'll be very busy with your new life as a countess. We'll have to make certain to set a regular time to meet for lunch or tea."

"Mum, you're welcome at Claybourne Court anytime you want to come visit. You don't need an invitation or an appointment. I have no intention of letting my life be consumed with too many formal duties. I'm not marrying royalty for goodness sake."

"Now Lily, I know that. But, you must do what your husband expects of you. Good wives put their husband's wants and needs first. If after that, there's time for me, then we'll enjoy it together."

"Oh rubbish, Mum. Of course Kit will have all of the time and attention he needs. But with so many servants, I'll surely have time for my own Mum. Now what is the agenda for the day?" Lily asked.

"Breakfast – I guess in the dining room, with Will and me. Then, a nice, long bath. Then, I'll do your hair. Do you want me to give you a manicure?"

"No, I did that yesterday. Don't you think they look all right? Lily inquired of her Mum.

"Let me see." Lily held out her hands. "Yes, they look lovely. Just simple, plain and buffed. I'm glad you didn't decide to wear any of that new polish some girls are putting on. Your nails are so naturally pretty."

"It's a lot easier this way. I'll put some lotion on my hands at the very end of dressing. So, what comes after doing my hair?

I imagine your bridesmaids will be arriving. They stayed at Claybourne Court didn't they? I assume they'll come in their gowns, or are they putting them on here? Elisabeth asked.

"Neither. They're putting them on at Claybourne Court, and waiting there at the chapel. They didn't want to worry about wrinkles while riding in the car over here. There will be no rides for them, then, since we can walk through the cloisters that separate the house from the chapel to the reception."

"I see. Will it only be you riding in the Claybourne Court chauffeur-driven Rolls Royce, then?"

"Yes. I want to be able to spread my gown out on the seat. I guessed you and Will would drive yourselves. Right?"

"Also, David and Melinda. Since Jane will be with the bridesmaids, we'll take them," answered her Mum.

"And then we'll all meet up at the chapel. What about the flowers, Mum? When do they arrive, and where?"

"At the chapel. There's a special room where the photographer can take photos, and you girls can re-do lip rouge and tidy hair if need be."

"What about any gifts that are brought to the church"? Lilly asked.

"Will and I will gather them and take them to Claybourne Court. You aren't expected to open them at the reception. You can open them when you return from London."

"Whew. What a lot to think about. You've really done a splendid job of organizing everything, Mum. I'm so appreciative. If it weren't for you, I wouldn't be having such a lovely wedding."

"Well, let's give Lady Cynthia a lot of credit. After all, she and Kit are picking up the majority of expenses, and Lady Cynthia helped with the entire thing. I wouldn't have been certain about what was and wasn't proper," Elisabeth answered.

"I know she's been wonderful, and I do appreciate everything she's done. Well, I suppose it's time to get on with breakfast, so the day can get started," Lily said, as she got out of bed, and put on her dressing gown.

"Just one more thing, Lily. This is probably the last time we'll have to speak alone. Is there anything at all that you want to know, or that you're frightened about?"

"No. Thank you, Mum I think I understand what's expected of me. I've packed the lovely nightwear that you and Lady Cynthia bought me. I think I'll look like the quintessential bride, rather innocent, but also beguiling in satin and lace. I'm counting on Kit from there on."

"That's the thing to do, dear. Don't worry if you don't enjoy anything too much that first night. That's very common. Even if it hurts, just bear it and smile. Things will improve with time."

"Yes, Mum, That's what I've been told from others, too. Don't worry about me. Thousands of girls get married every day, and they all seem to get through their first night perfectly fine. Kit is very kind and I know he'll be understanding."

"So do I, dear. Just remember, you're giving him a gift."

Lily stood in her magnificent lace wedding gown, with all of her friends crowded around her in their charming pastel, print frocks. The man from the flower shop filled the maid's baskets with a perfect arrangement of colors, and then handed Lily her own exquisite bouquet. The girls put on their broad-brimmed hats, and Lily's mother pinned her gorgeous headpiece into place. The organdie band was wide, and one side ended in an enormous bow. There were white rose buds adorning the organdie. She wore a string of perfectly matched pearls, which had been Kit's gift to her, along with matching pearl earrings.

"You are absolutely the most beautiful bride I've ever seen," her mother exclaimed.

"Oh, thank you so much, Mum. I do look quite posh, don't I?" She laughed.

Her beautiful face was glowing. Her cheeks needed no artificial color, as they were a lovely shade of pink, and looked like porcelain china. Her luscious lips had just a touch of pink that she had added and her brows and lashes had been darkened a bit. Her splendid, green eyes sparkled happily. There was simply nothing that might have been improved upon.

All of the bridesmaids looked equally charming. It was truly a perfect wedding party. Lily couldn't believe that the day had finally arrived. She wondered how Kit was feeling. Knowing him, he was undoubtedly not the least bit ruffled. He was always so relaxed and calm about life. The only time she had ever seen him angry was when he'd tried to deal with Eleanor. She didn't want to think about Eleanor today. This was her day – hers and Kit's.

She laughed to herself. How silly she'd been to think that she would have a small, country wedding. That didn't seem remotely possible when one was marrying an Earl.

Will Morris came into the room, which was off to the right of the entrance to the chapel. He looked at her and said "Lily, Love, if I'd had my own daughter I'd have hoped she'd be as beautiful as you. Of course, David's Jane is a beauty as well, so I have two gorgeous women in the family besides your Mum – and of course David and Jane's Melinda. Wait until Kit sees you start down the aisle. He'll probably be lightheaded by the time you reach the altar."

Lily laughed. "Well, as long as he's standing and can repeat the vows. I'll prop him up if I have to. I'm the one more likely to faint."

"Don't you go fainting on me. This is my big moment. I feel like I'm escorting a movie star into those American Academy Awards."

"You'll do wonderfully, Will. I have to try to remember to smile. Poke me in the ribs if I look too solemn."

"I'll give you a big, old jab," he teased. All of the girls were fussing with their hair and making last minute touch-ups to lip rouge. Lily heard music begin to play, and saw her mother get in line to be escorted down the aisle by Tom Holiday. She was dressed in a shell pink, ankle length gown, of silk taffeta with an organdie overlay. She wore a new cameo brooch at her neck that Will had bought her. The sleeves on her dress were long, and the cuffs were covered with white embroidery. The neckline copied the cuffs, high on her throat. She wore a pink and white orchid corsage. As she started down the aisle, she took the edge of her dress in her right hand, and swung it out as she took the first step. It was a very elegant motion, rather like a high fashion model might do in a Paris show. Lily was very proud of her Mum who still looked nearly as young as Lily.

Lady Cynthia looked incredibly posh, also in pale pink. Her dress had a short jacket, trimmed with white ribbon, and a narrow, tiered skirt. She wore a very stylish hat, swathed in white gauze and covered with real pink and white roses. She was the image of what a Dowager Countess was expected to look like.

Suddenly, it was time for Lily to begin her walk. The bridesmaids were slowly taking steps down the center of the chapel, holding their heads high and smiling. Lily could see Kit at the altar dressed in a grey morning suit. Next to him stood his ushers, with John as the best man, nearest to him. As Lily and Will waited at the top of the aisle, all of the guests stood up to see her begin her graceful walk toward her husband-to-be. Lily saw Kit, and he smiled at her. A warm, loving smile. She returned his happiness with a large smile of her own, and there was no need to remind her to keep that beautiful expression for the rest of her stroll toward her fiancé.

She and Will reached the altar, the Vicar asked "Who gives this woman in marriage to this man?" and Kit reached out his hand to grasp Lily's.

Will answered, "Her mother and I do." Then he stepped back, and sat down in the pew, next to Elisabeth.

Then Lily and Kit moved up one step, and knelt. Jane spread her train all the way out, and it reached a long way behind her. Lily handed her bouquet to Jane, and the ceremony began. It was the traditional, Anglican ceremony. Lily listened carefully to each word. She had no intention of being one of those brides who really had no idea what she had promised. She'd convinced Kit that she did not want the word 'obey' included in the vows. More girls were making such a request, and Kit didn't have any difficulty with the omission. They exchanged rings and the Vicar pronounced that they were man and wife. There was no veil covering her face, so Kit didn't have to lift it. Instead he just leaned toward her, and putting one hand to the back of her head, pulled her close and gave her a lovely, proper kiss. Then they turned, and the Vicar presented them as Lord and Lady Claybourne, the Earl and Countess of Gloucester. It sounded so foreign to Lily's ears. Just a moment before, she'd been just plain Lily Barton and now she was the Countess of Gloucester. She felt like Cinderella. What would happen at midnight?

The photographer kept the bridal party and family's behind after the ceremony so that he could take some formal pictures. Lily was glad of that, as she hoped for a lovely photo from which she could have a portrait made to hang on the wall at Claybourne Court. Following the photo session, they all hurried over to the elegant wedding reception awaiting them in the ballroom at Claybourne Court. Lily had only been in that room a couple of times when they were discussing plans for the wedding. When she'd seen it before it was a very large room that ran from one end of the house to the other. It was on the third floor of Claybourne Court, and she had worried that the steps might prove difficult for some of the guests. The chapel had been over-flowing with guests, and some were definitely older. To Lily's immense surprise, during the period of wedding planning, Kit had installed a lovely new elevator that took guests up and down from the third floor. She was stunned. Kit laughed and said that he thought she would like it.

"Oh Kit, that was so thoughtful. I've been concerned, as you know, especially about elderly people, and even David, because of his artificial leg. I know he wouldn't have said anything, but still. . ."

"Yes. There were likely to be many who could benefit from not having to struggle up and down the stairways – starting with our own servants. I also had dumb waiters installed, so the food can be sent straight up from the kitchen. Imagine – when my mother and father married, the servants would have had to carry large, silver trays from the kitchens up to the ballroom. It was time to do this."

Lily was so glad that he'd noticed her concern and acted upon it. Obviously, he hadn't minded that she'd made a suggestion that would modernize Claybourne Court. So she wasn't always to be told 'That's how it's always been done.'

The room was banked with flowers. In one section, where Lily, Kit and both of their mothers were to receive guests, there were large potted plants and enormous urns spilling English roses, lilies, and nosegays of white violets. Others overflowed with delightful spring flowers, like daffodils, hyacinth, Lily of the Valley, Iris and Paperwhite's. The scent in the room was so lovely. Tables sat around the edge of the dance floor, draped with white linen cloths, with pink organdie overlays. Each was set with white Havilland china, and the finest crystal glasses, as well as beautiful sterling silver with the Claybourne Crest on the handles. The first hour of the reception was taken up with cocktails and champagne. The waiters circled about the room with drinks on a tray, or took orders for individual drinks from the guests. Then, a sit-down dinner was served in five courses. It began with a chef's appetizer and progressed to one of six starters; then to a refresher course of mango sorbet, and on to the main course of either Rib Eye Beef, Salmon Filet, Baked Chicken, Tenderloin of Pork, or Supreme of Duck. Sumptuous desserts followed with choices of Praline, Peach and Champagne Torte, or

Bailey's Crème Brulee. The dinner ended with a cheeseboard, coffee and petit fours.

After the dinner, a wonderful band began to play lovely dance tunes. The first dance was a waltz, which Lily began with her step-father Will, and ended with Kit, after he cut-in, symbolizing the handing off of Lily from her step-father to her husband. The band was marvelous, playing everything from memorable old songs to the new songs sweeping the country, which allowed for the more daring of the guests to demonstrate the Charleston and Black Bottom. Of course Maddie was a star at that moment.

About three hours after the reception began, Lily disappeared to the second level. She went to the room adjoining Kit's. There, she changed into her going-away frock. It was mint green, sleeveless and scoop necked, with a low sash on her hips, and a matching coat of linen. She wore a small hat in the same shade of green, encircled with tiny white rosebuds. Of course, her shoes were mint green as well. A quick trip to the adjoining bathroom to check her hair and lip rouge, and she was ready to go. While she'd been getting ready, Kit had been changing into a dark suit, white shirt and tie. They met in the hallway and made their way back up to the ballroom. Lilly carried her bouquet. When they reached the place where they'd received, they stopped. Everyone gathered round, and the piano began to play a pretty tune. All of the single girls present, and those of the bridesmaids who were still unmarried, gathered in front of the bride and groom. Lily gave a big toss, and the bouquet landed in Maddie's hands. Everyone cheered and laughed, and Maddie blushed. With that, Kit and Lily ran down the stairs, hoping to reach the car before the groomsmen and bridesmaids, as they descended on the elevator. Everyone arrived at just about the same time, and the newlyweds were caught in a shower of rice and rose petals. Lily's parents were by then in the Great Hall as was Lady Cynthia. They all hugged one another goodbye. Lily and Kit picked up Win, and gave him a giant cuddle. Then, they ran to the Rolls Royce, and slipped into the backseat. Edward started the engine and off they went on their trip to London.

5

Lily threw her head back on the leather seat and heaved a sigh of relief. It had been a perfect wedding, and everything had gone according to plan. Kit pulled her over to him, kissing her.

"Lady Claybourne, you looked good enough to eat. You still do. My God, but I'm a lucky man. I love you so much, Lily. Are you happy, darling?"

"I'd be the biggest fool alive if I weren't happy. Of course I'm happy. Wasn't everything perfect? Your mother did a beautiful job with the flowers, the menu, and – well – everything. She looked gorgeous, too."

"So did your mother. You look so much like her."

"Yes, people have always said that," smiled Lily. You don't really look like your mother. I don't remember your father. Do you look like him?"

Kit thought for a minute. "Yes, I think so, when he was younger. But, he got round and lost his hair. Don't let that happen to me," Kit laughed.

"I can't stop the hair problem, but I'll watch your weight. You don't seem prone to gaining though."

"Are you excited about seeing London," he asked.

"Oh yes, I really am. It's truly amazing that I've lived in England all my life, and never traveled to London. Shall we be able to see all of the famous spots?"

"Such as . . .?" Kit asked her.

"Well – you know. Buckingham Palace, London Bridge, The Tower, Big Ben, The Houses of Parliament, the Changing of the Guard, Westminster Abbey . . . I could go on and on."

"The problem is that you're now a Countess, Lily. And, we were just married, which means there will have been an enormous photo in the *Times*. People will recognize us. Well, they'll recognize me, and of course, since we're together they'll know who you are. The new Countess. I think it would be very uncomfortable. Besides, my dear wife, Earl's and their wives shouldn't be spotted sight-seeing in London, with a *Baedeker's* tour book in their hand. It isn't the 'done thing'. I'm sorry to disappoint you."

"No, that's all right. I didn't think of those things. Perhaps sometime I can sneak back and wear a wig, or something, so people won't know me. I did so want to see all of the historic sites in London."

"I'm truly sorry, Lily. I should have made that clear to you. We can go to the theater at night, and dine out. I'll have the driver take us past Buckingham and Westminster. So you can see some things."

"Well, yes, but it will be at night. I won't see much. But, if that's the way it is, then I'll just have to accept it. The important thing is that I have you."

"That's the way I feel too, Lily." He kissed her again. Lily was having trouble not showing her disappointment. Why were they even on their way to London if they weren't going to see anything? Couldn't members of the gentry ever go touring and see famous places? She didn't understand the reasoning behind such a silly tradition. If they weren't to tour, what would they do all day long? Finally, she mustered up her courage, and asked that very question.

"We'll have lovely, long days to just relax. I know you love to read, and I'll enjoy catching up on that too. If you like you can go to the hair salon and let yourself be pampered. That's a specialty of Countess's." He laughed. "There are shops in the hotel. You can buy clothing to your heart's delight."

"I see," she murmured. "Perhaps I could have Edward drive me around to some of the major attractions while you stay back at the hotel. No one would recognize me," she suggested.

"No, Lily. Absolutely not. We're on our wedding trip. That means one of us doesn't run off all day without the other. Now, I really *am* sorry, but you'll just have to accept that neither of us is going to be a tourist. I don't mean to sound harsh. This is just one of the many things you'll have to learn as you grow into this new role in your life. You understand, don't you?"

"I suppose so," Lily answered, although she really didn't. It all seemed so terribly foolish.

Kit laid his head back, and closed his eyes. She looked over at him. He was clearly exhausted, and so was she. They both needed to recuperate from what had been a splendid, but arduous day. This wasn't the time to discuss sightseeing. After they drove along in silence for a few more miles, Lily asked Kit another question that had been bothering her.

"Kit why aren't we staying at our own house in London? I'm just dying to see it. Especially since it's been totally re-built. It seems like we could have had total privacy, and enjoyed the surroundings more than a hotel."

"Lily, you aren't thinking straight at all. What do you suppose we'd eat? Who would build the fires in the fireplaces? Who would change the bedding? We can't stay at the townhouse until we can bring servants from Claybourne Court."

"Oh. Well, I'm really a wonderful cook, Kit. I'd love to show off some of my recipes. And, goodness, do you think I haven't changed beds thousands of times? Don't tell me you've never built a fire? I think it would be very cozy to be alone and to do for ourselves. At Claybourne Court we're waited on hand and foot, and we're never really alone. Wouldn't you like a change?"

"Darling, are you daft?" He leaned over and kissed her cheek. I know that sounds romantic to you, but I assure you it wouldn't be. I'm not having my new Countess rattling around in the kitchen. Goodness, Lily. I don't think my mother knows how to brew a cup of tea."

"What? You said she didn't come from aristocracy. You told me that her father owned a shop in London. Surely she didn't have servants on the order of Claybourne Court?"

"Well, the shop he owned wasn't a tiny shop. It was rather the size of *Selfridge's*. It was known as *Swanson's*. They closed some years ago. Have you heard of it?"

"*Swanson's Department Store*? Of course I've heard of it. Kit, she had to come from one of the wealthiest families in the land. Technically, her father was in trade, but he wasn't exactly selling frocks to the ladies himself."

"No. He was the Chairman of the Board. My mother's maiden name was Swanson. But, the point is, she didn't come from the peerage, or landed gentry. She was considered a tradesman's daughter."

"Oh for heaven's sake, Kit. That's a far cry from my father, who operated his medical practice out of our small cottage. Mum didn't even have a kitchen helper, or a cleaner."

"Now, Lily, don't raise your voice. Goodness, you sound angry. The point I was trying to make to you was that neither you nor my mother come from titled backgrounds."

"That may well be, but I'd be surprised if she didn't have a debut and a bow to the King."

"Well yes, she did, but what difference does that make?"

Lily sighed. If you don't know, my trying to explain won't do any good. Anyway, I'm sorry I brought up the idea of staying in our townhouse. It was silly of me. I guess I do have a lot to learn, Kit."

"That's alright. I don't expect you to learn everything overnight. You can ask me if you're ever wondering about something, just like sightseeing and not staying at our own home. We'll stay there, I promise. The next time we plan a trip to London, we'll bring some help along."

"That's fine, Kit. I'm sure that would be more appropriate," Lily answered.

He patted her hand. "There, you see, once something is explained, it makes perfect sense doesn't it?"

Lily wanted to scream at the top of her lungs. It made no sense whatsoever. But, if she did scream, she would end up sounding like Eleanor. Oh Eleanor. Perhaps these were some of the brick walls she ran into? But, this was Kit's world and Lily had known it. These things were not terribly important, and she certainly had no intention of having a row on her wedding day. She had promised in her wedding vows, that she would love and honor Kit. It was his world. She would learn to adjust.

Edward pulled the car up in front of the Savoy Hotel. Lily took a deep breath, and was overwhelmed at how lovely it was. It stood on the Strand, looking over the Thames and the Thames embankment. She knew from having read about it, that the hotel was considered the most palatial in all of London. It was the first to have electrical lighting and air-conditioning throughout, as well as many other unheard of accoutrements, such as a bath for every room. Many, many famous people had stayed there. The gorgeous River Room restaurant had wonderful food, and also allowed dancing to a lovely string quartet. Edward took their luggage from the boot of the Rolls, and carried it in to the front desk, followed by Lily and Kit. Lily was so thankful that she had stayed at the Plaza Athenee during the war, when she'd traveled to Paris with her group of chums from the *Aubigney* Causality Clearing Station in 1917. She had learned what it was like to stay in such elaborate surroundings, so she felt much more comfortable when they checked into the Savoy.

Edward took the keys to the Rolls, and departed, telling Kit where he could be reached if they needed him during their two week stay. Then, a bellman escorted them to the elevator, and took them up to the bridal suite on the top floor. He opened the door, and Lily was knocked for six. The suite she'd had at the Plaza Athenee had been magnificent, but this was like nothing she had ever envisioned. Thick white carpeting covered the floors, and silk wallpaper decorated the walls. It was soft pink and white ribbon stripes. The furnishings was all French antique, right down to bibelot cabinets filled with priceless collections of porcelain, and crystal chandeliers adorning the ceilings. Lily was enchanted. She followed the bellman into the bedroom, which had a mammoth, French bed, finished in antique white and gold gilt. It was covered with an exquisite down comforter, also in pink and white stripe. There were heaps and heaps of fancy pillows piled three deep – organdie, silk, satin, and velvet. Ribbons were woven in and out of them. The night tables had magnificent Capidimonte lamps, with tiny flowers in pink scattered across the white base. Each flower had been artfully attached by hand. As she walked into the adjoining bath, she almost lost her breath. It was all done in marble, from the lavish tub, to a double shower area, and marble counters surrounding oval sinks, with hand painted rose buds on the china bowls. It truly was unimaginable. Kit didn't make any comments as he gave the bellman a tip, and told him he would call the desk if they needed anything. Lily knew he was used to such opulence, and had undoubtedly stayed at the Savoy many times, but to her it was like something out of the cinema. Even lovelier. She wished her mother could see it. She got busy putting away her clothing in the built-in drawers in the bath, and hanging frocks in the large ornate cupboard. Then she set about putting her toiletries upon the shelf above one sink in the bath.

Kit wandered in and put his arms around her from the back. She was facing the mirror, and could see how terribly handsome he was. He bent down and kissed her neck. "Lily, the hotel's ladies' maid will take care of unpacking us. I thought we might have a lie-down before a bath and dinner. Would you like that?"

Lily was a little embarrassed. She hadn't known that a maid would unpack their luggage. A shiver went down her spine. This was the moment she'd anticipated. She only knew that she should follow Kit's lead, and that's what she did. She turned, facing him, and put her arms around his neck. Snuggling her head into his chest she murmured "I think a lie-down would be just wonderful."

"Would you like to change into a night dress, "he asked sweetly.

"Yes, I believe I would, if you don't mind. I'll only be a tick," she smiled again, as she took a white satin, slip-like gown, trimmed with delicate lace and pink ribbons from the drawer. She quickly undressed, and slipped it over her head. Then, she tidied her hair, put on a bit of perfume and re-entered the bedroom. Kit was sitting up in bed, with the covers to his waist. His chest was bare, and she couldn't tell if he was clothed at all. He reached over and turned on the wireless by the bed. He found a station playing lovely romantic tunes. Then, he flicked off the light, and said, "Come here, my darling Lily." He patted the bed next to him. She quickly crawled in next to him, and pulled the sheets up high. They were cool, smooth linen. Turning to Kit, she put her arms about him, and fell into a deep embrace. Soon, he was kissing her tenderly, and murmuring how much he loved her. She began to feel a tingling sensation in the lower portion of her body – a feeling she'd never had before. Kit stopped kissing her, and laid her down on her back. Then, he ran his hand over her cheek, and told her again how beautiful she was, and how deeply in love he was. Slowly, he slipped the straps of the nightgown off her shoulders. Moving it down, he kissed above her breasts, working his way toward them.

"Let's take this lovely bit of silk off you," he whispered.

Lily reached down, and pulled the gown over her head. Kit, was as naked as she, and she could feel what so many friends had described to her – his stiff, hard maleness touching her thigh. She'd seen men's private parts many, many times while performing medical work in the French hospital, but never when a man was aroused. Lily began to wish he would put his hand between her legs and stroke her, but she was frightened to ask him to do so. What if he thought she wasn't acting ladylike or proper? It was better to wait for him. Next he kissed her breasts, which brought a whole new sensation. He kept kissing her, and murmuring that he had never wanted someone so much in all of his life. Surely, she thought, he will touch me down there next. But, he didn't. Instead, he seemed to grow harder and more erect. Then, in a flash, he threw himself on top and entered her. With no preparation, and no foreplay, she was not ready for him, but it didn't seem to faze him. He started pushing and pumping up and down, making strange grunting noises.

"Just relax, Lily. It will be over in a minute, "he breathed rapidly.

She didn't want it to be over in a minute. It seemed like she hadn't even begun to have any feeling before his body had thrust into hers. She clung to the side of the bed then, with curled up fists, because it hurt, and she didn't know what to do. Suddenly, she felt that he had thrust very deeply, and something broke or tore. She felt a very sharp pain. He was in his own world and was practically yelling quite disgusting things like 'Give it to me baby' and 'Ohhh, Lily, you are so tight and small."

The motion of his pumping speeded up, and then he called out her name and said "Ah, Lily, you're magnificent –I'm coming darling, I'm coming." He fell onto her chest, exhausted. Lily lay there for what seemed forever. Was that all there was to it? Why in the world had Gena said that she couldn't imagine going through life pretending she didn't like making love to her husband? Was that what making love was all about? And, why did he speak so obscenely to her? She waited for him to speak, but he didn't. After a time, he simply rolled off of her, and went to sleep lying on his side. Lily quietly crept out of the bed and tip-toed into the bath. She pulled a sheet of tissue and examined herself. Sure enough, there was blood. She hurt quite a lot. No one had told her it would hurt so badly. She suspected that if he had initiated some foreplay, her body would have been more ready to accept him. She used the bidet in the toilet area, with the door closed, and the warm water felt soothing. She felt like crying. Was this the kind, elegant, gentleman she had married? Using such foul language, and acting like he had no consideration at all for her feelings? Were all men like this? Surely not, or someone would have told her. How frequently was she going to have to go through this?

She stood up, and took her satin dressing gown from the gold hook on the door. She had to decide what she was going to say to him, before he woke. What if he wanted to do it again? That was absolutely out of the question. She decided to run a bath and soak in it. If he heard her bathing, he would leave her alone. She poured scented bath oil into the tub, unwrapped a new bar of soap, took off her dressing gown, and gently slid into the warm water. It felt heavenly. She laid her head back, and just let herself soak. Her body felt bruised. How could this be her wedding day? And it *was* still only daytime. That meant he probably would want to do it again before they went to sleep, after dinner. Well, she would just have to tell him that it was out of the question.

The door opened slowly, and Kit entered the bath. He had a hotel robe on, for which Lily was thankful.

"Are you alright, Lily?" he asked.

"I don't really know, Kit. I'm terribly, terribly sore, and bleeding. Is that normal?"

"Yes, it's normal. You're very, very tiny, and it was your first time. But, now that's over. It won't hurt as badly next time."

"Kit, there cannot be a next time, until I have begun to heal from this time. I think it would kill me."

"No, Lily. It won't kill you. Actually, the more often we do it, the easier it will become for you. You won't be so tight."

"Kit, you don't understand. I'm not just a little bit sore. I'm really hurting. I felt something tear inside of me, and I wonder if I shouldn't have a physician look at me."

"Lily, what tore was perfectly normal. I'm sure you've been educated about the fact that when you have intercourse for the first time, a thin membrane inside of you breaks."

"I know all of that, of course, Kit. But, I'm telling you, this isn't normal. I want to have a physician."

"Lily, that's totally uncalled for, and would be highly embarrassing for me. If a woman had to call a physician on her wedding day, the doctor would think that she's experienced terribly rough sex, or even rape, although that isn't possible when I'm your husband. I'm not having a physician."

Lily slumped her head down, and opened the drain in the tub. Then, she reached for her dressing gown, and stood up. She slipped it on. "Kit could you please leave while I dry off. Then, I'll come into the bedroom, and we can have a chat."

Kit turned and left the bath. Lily washed her face and smoothed back her hair. She didn't want to act like a spoiled little girl – like Eleanor. But, she wasn't going to subject herself to more pain, and she wanted to know if she'd been physically harmed in any way. She was a nurse. She knew enough medically, to understand that such an injury could bring about infection, scar tissue, or even prevention of conception later in life. She dried herself, and put the dressing gown back on. Then, she re-entered the bedroom. Kit was back in bed with a scowl on his face.

"Kit, we need to chat" she began.

"All right, Lily. What do you want to chat about?"

What did she want to chat about? She couldn't believe he was asking such an inane question. She scarcely felt that this was the Kit she knew and loved.

"Well, I guess, first and foremost, I don't understand how it is that you can go from being such a lovely, kind, dear gentleman to practically a rabid animal in a matter of minutes. Kit, I didn't even feel as though I knew you. You weren't at all considerate of what I was feeling. I don't even think you would have stopped if I'd shouted for you to."

"Well, no, I doubt that I would have. I knew it would be painful for you Lily, but it needed to be done. There would have been no sense in stopping. You would only have had to go through it again. As to why I seemed to change from the passive man you generally know —well-that's the nature of men. The needs of men are such that when making love to a women, especially one he adores, he lets down all of his guard and sometimes says things that under other circumstances would be inappropriate. I'm sorry if I offended you. I certainly didn't mean to frighten you."

But, Kit, I've talked this subject over with many of my female friends. Most say that woman enjoy this act as much as a man does. I have to be honest when I say that I found nothing enjoyable about this. I'm terribly naïve about the entire subject, but aren't you supposed to enter into some sort of foreplay with me prior to the act, so that my body will be more ready to accept yours?"

"Lilly, I don't believe in foreplay. That would be akin to my operating on the assumption that you're as anxious for the act as I am. A lady shouldn't be anxious for sex. It's a gift that she gives to her husband – pure and simple. The only kind of women who throw themselves into it, and allow a man to perform really quite abhorrent acts upon them, are ones who are loose. A lady expects the man to satisfy himself, while she lays still, and of course, enjoys being shown how much she's loved. You like to be kissed, I know that."

"Of course I like to be kissed. But, don't you think if you had gone beyond kissing me, and stroked me, showing some concern for my enjoyment too, I would have been more ready for you when you entered me, and it might not have hurt so badly?"

"Perhaps. But, that isn't the way I make love. That's the manner in which lower class people make love. Do you think a woman thrashes round, moaning and crying out? Surely you don't think that a woman reaches a . . . a . . . orgasm, do you?"

"I have no idea Kit. I don't really even know what that is. I guess it's something akin to a man reaching a climax. What's wrong about a woman getting to that point?"

"Oh Lily, no, no, no. Men who have sexual relations with those sort of women are involving themselves in unclean pleasures. Sex should not be pleasurable for a woman, Lily. How can I make it any plainer? God gave women the ability to please a man, and of course the primary reason for the act to begin with is procreation. Have you ever read anywhere in the Bible where Eve actually enjoyed her experience with Adam? She gave herself to him as a symbol of how greatly she loved him. Men have different needs from women. It's just the way we're made. Lily, there are things I could ask you to do to me that would excite me very much, and make the act even more pleasurable for me, but I would never ask them of you, because I would never expect a lady to do anything indecent. Do you understand? In that regard I'm most definitely thinking of you."

"Who taught you about this subject, Kit?"

Primarily, my father. Of course, the boys at *Oxford* and *Sandhurst* all discussed it. But, their experiences were most always with loose girls. That's the way it is with men when they're young, before they fall in love and marry. They don't care whether a lady is proper and decent when they're just boys. Not one of us at *Sandhurst* would ever have married any of the girls we fooled with at that time. That's the way it's always been with men. My father taught me that. He's the one who explained to me that decent, well brought up ladies don't allow their bodies to become overly fevered by the sex act. They understand their duty, and they perform it. In return, a man loves and protects his wife, and shares everything he has with her. Do you understand now Lily?

There was quite a lengthy silence, for she didn't really understand at all. She understood that this was Kit's way of believing. And she understood that probably nothing would change his mind. Worst of all, she understood that this was the way she would live for the rest of her life. She wished she could talk to Gena – or even to John. From things Gena had said, that wasn't what John expected from her. Yet, he was at *Sandhurst* with Kit. Where did John's beliefs come from? Kit sat looking at her, with a kind but puzzled look on his face.

"I love you, Lily. So much. I want you to be happy. But, don't ask me to go against my principals and beliefs. I think, in time, you'll come to enjoy the closeness of our making love, and be thrilled to know that you're giving me something that no other women could to make me joyful." He put his arms around her, and pressed her to his chest. She was still hurting fiercely, and didn't want to start something again. She pulled away from him.

"Kit, I love you too. Very much. Of course I want you to be happy. I totally understand what you're telling me, and I'll try to readjust my thinking. I wish we'd spoken of this before we married, but I suppose that wouldn't have been proper either."

"No dear, it wouldn't have," Kit answered.

"Will you give me a bit of time to adjust to this change in my life? I'm a bit frightened of more hurt," Lily asked.

"Of course. Let's get dressed and dine in the River Room. Afterwards, we'll have a couple of after-dinner drinks, which will calm you. Then, we'll try again when we go to bed. I think you'll feel much better."

Feel much better! Lily was terrified. When she'd asked for more time, she meant at least a few days. Well — she'd simply have to tough it out. Perhaps he was right. Perhaps it wouldn't be so painful a second time. She remembered that Gena had given her a small tube of lubricant, and had told her to use it, so that she wouldn't be dry. She certainly intended to try that.

6

It was no better the second time. The tube of ointment Gena had given her, did help a bit. But, in spite of the ointment, once Kit reached the area where there was already severe pain, it became much worse. He wasn't gentle, and just pushed through, with little if any concern for the discomfort she felt. It was just a repeat of before, except that he toned down his language a bit. Lily made up her mind that she would endure this throughout their wedding weeks, and then would immediately visit John Garrett upon her return to Claybourne Court, and ask him to examine her. He would be able to tell her if everything was normal.

Thus, unfortunately, the wedding trip did not begin on the note she had hoped it would. She had pictured long, lazy mornings, lying in bed, making love and chatting about the future. Now, she got up very early – before Kit- and was completely dressed by the time he rose. If he thought it odd, he said nothing. He was always cheerful in the mornings, and Lily grew to like that time of day best, for he would cuddle her, and murmur little endearments in her ear, but it wouldn't go further. They always ordered their breakfast and hung it on the doorknob at night, writing down the time they wanted it to be delivered. They usually put down nine o'clock, and it was always delivered piping hot, right on time. A waiter would roll a small table into the room, topped with heated chafing dishes. The table could be set up with two leafs that came up from the sides, providing an intimate place where they could dine. There were plates, silverware, napkins, and glasses already set, so then the food was served. They ate wonderful, large English breakfasts, consisting of fruit, eggs, sausages, grilled tomatoes, fried toast, white pudding, and a rasher of bacon. Of course there was also tea. Because they ate such large and late breakfasts, they didn't find themselves hungry again at noon. Some days they wandered down to the hotel dining room, and had a bite to eat there at about two o'clock. Then they had a magnificent tea in the lobby at four o'clock. They would eat their fill of finger sandwiches, homemade scones, fancy cakes and assorted pastries. Thus, they usually didn't dine until quite late. Dinner was usually taken in either the River Room at the Savoy, or in one of the other posh hotel dining rooms. When they decided to dine elsewhere, Edward picked them up and drove them.

They saw 'The Maid of The Mountains', a wildly popular play in the West End, 'Napoleon' at the Queen's Theatre, and 'The Merchant of Venice' at The Royal Court Theater. Lily fell in love with London Theater and would have attended a production every night. Kit also made an appointment for Lily to visit one of the less well-known, but spectacular fashion design houses, Florrie Westwood, who produced elegant, high end, conservative fashions. They were breathtaking and Lily was thrilled. She ordered three incredible frocks with high waists, which anticipated the androgynous look of the 1920's, with the linear, straight silhouettes. The first was of mauve taffeta and ninon, with insertion of ivory lace. It had a sash of mauve ribbon to match the dress, and was ankle length. Lily's second choice was a simple evening frock of powder blue satin and shell pink tulle. The broad sash was pansy black ribbon with bright applique of lavender flowers. The third was a frock of ivory crepe georgette with two deep bands in the skirt of peach colored, self-material. The insertion was very fine lace. In addition, Kit bought her an extravagant sable wrap. Lily had never owned a fur in her life, and the wrap sent her over the moon. She'd never dreamed of having something so luxurious. Aside from not being able to see the historic destinations she had longed to visit, and the difficult nights she spent gritting her teeth and waiting for Kit's satisfaction, Lily wasn't unhappy. Kit was very kind to her and obviously generous.

There were tiny things that bothered her, like the fact that he wouldn't give her any money of her own, and expected that she ask him for anything that she needed. It was just another of his beliefs that the husband should have complete responsibility for the care of his wife. However, Lily felt that it wasn't worth a fight, and she had nowhere to spend her own money, anyway.

She spent her days reading a marvelous new bestselling book – The Four Horsemen of the Apocalypse by V. Blasco Ibanez. Kit was not as settled. He'd brought along his attaché case, which had papers from his estate agent regarding Claybourne Court. His agent's name was Henry Henson, and Lily did not know him well. They had met on just one occasion. Henson had responsibility for Claybourne Court's accounts. Plus, all of the details of the property were left to him, such as making certain that the tenant farmers paid their tithes on time, making out cheques to the employees, hiring extra laborers at harvest time, keeping the tenant's houses in good repair and making certain that any difficulties that the tenant farmers or their families were facing were dealt with properly. Claybourne Court was a small estate, by English standards, particularly in comparison with some of the country houses which owned five thousand or more acres. But, there were about one fifty tenants on Claybourne property, which definitely required the assistance of the land manager. The entire estate comprised at least 3000 acres. These tenant's had what could rightly be called their own small town, with even a church to serve their needs. Kit had the power over who would fill the position of Vicar at said church, and Superintendent at their school. The residents in the village of *Claybourne-on-Colne* didn't really have much contact with the tenant farmers, because their children were sent to different schools. Lord Claybourne provided the housing for the tenant farmers, in return for tithes. Kit had discussed his thoughts for expansion with Henson, and the papers he'd brought with him to London contained notes on research conducted in advance of these new ideas taking hold. Henson indicated that many of the tenant homes needed refurbishing, due to disabilities suffered by many of the tenants, such as wider doorways to accommodate rolling chairs, and better equipped bathing facilities. Most didn't have bathrooms at all, and still relied on use of outer buildings and tin tubs. Henson had shown a list of the estimated costs for the updating of the farm houses, and Kit was staggered at the final number. There was no way he was going to see his way clear to accommodate the agent's suggestions. He'd go over them with his mother, but he knew that Lady Cynthia would not be in favor of such an enormous outlay of money.

On the last day of their wedding trip, both Kit and Lily spent a lot of time packing for the return trip. Lily finally took advantage of Kit's offer to visit the Savoy Beauty Salon for female guests. She had her hair trimmed, and a manicure and pedicure. Kit gave her money to tip the employees in the salon, and the rest was put on the hotel bill. She kept her hair in the mid-length style she had been wearing, with pretty, soft waves around her cheeks, but decided to have the stylist cut wispy bangs, which Lily was told would bring out the beauty of her eyes.

When she returned to their room, Kit took one look at her, and was fit to be tied. He loathed the way her hair had been trimmed. He said that she looked like a little girl, and not at all like one expected a Countess to present herself. Taking her by the hand, he walked her back to the salon, where he demanded that the stylist manage to make her hair look like it had before she cut the bangs into it. Lily was mortified, and she blushed bright red. The lovely girl who had styled her hair was very understanding, and looked rather sadly at Lily. She sat Lily down in her chair, and began to work on her hair. Kit sat in a separate chair, which he pulled up right next to hers, watching every movement. Because the bangs had been cut quite long, it wasn't an enormous problem to sweep them to the side and blend them into the hair above her ear. She used a special sort of cream which held it nicely in place. Lily heaved a sigh of relief and smiled at Kit.

"There, you see. It wasn't a catastrophe after all," she murmured.

"It certainly looked like it was going to be. I would have hated taking you back to Claybourne Court looking so unsophisticated."

The stylist sent her a sympathetic look and Lily rolled her eyes. Kit paid the bill, and they returned to their room. When the door closed, Lily turned on him with a vengeance.

"Let me make something clear, Kit. Don't you ever, ever treat me like that again in front of a stranger. I won't stand for it. I was utterly humiliated. If that's the way you spoke to Eleanor in public, then no wonder she was so unhappy. I'm sorry I'm so angry, but no one has ever treated me like that.

I've listened and followed all of your instructions on this trip. I gave up my plans to see places I'd dreamed of seeing all of my life; I tolerated your treating me like a child when I simply asked for my own pound note; I let you hurt me unbearably, while supposedly making love to me, although I cannot see what is loving about causing pain to someone you supposedly care for; and you embarrassed me in front of the salon stylist."

Her voice had reached a fever pitch. "Lily, Lily. Calm down. You're being terribly unfair. Now, we've discussed each of these subjects in depth, and I've explained to you the rationale behind every one of my decisions. You're going to have to learn that I'm your husband, and it's my responsibility to make certain you follow the proper decorum for any Countess. Would you rather I said nothing about your hair, and then let you arrive at Claybourne Court looking unseemly? Surely not."

Lily sat down in a French velvet chair and burst into tears. Every time she tried to talk to Kit about her feelings, he rationally explained his reasoning in a calm voice and confused her miserably. She truly didn't know if she was right or wrong. She'd never been a Countess before. The rules seemed so different.

"I apologize, Kit. I'm just on edge. It isn't easy to go from one class in life to another, especially when the rules are so very different."

He put his arms around her. "I love you Lily. The only reason I sometimes suggest that something be done differently is because I want you to become the loveliest, most revered Countess in the land. It would be so easy to make mistakes at this juncture. It's important to me that I have a wife I can be proud of. I know it is to you too. That's why I'm making certain that nothing gives the impression that you aren't just prefect in every way. The upper classes can be so unforgiving. Wouldn't you rather be a tiny bit embarrassed by me, then treated like a parvenu by some Duke's wife?

Lilly continued to weep. "I suppose so. But, Kit, this is our honeymoon. I feel like I've been sent away to school."

"Now, Lily, think about it. We've had a wonderful, special trip. Yes, there have been some slip-ups, but over-all we've had a lot of fun. You adored the theater and ordering your lovely new frocks. Not to mention your new sable wrap. You told me yourself that the hotel was beyond your wildest dreams. Now, I want you to have a bit of a lie-down, while I run to the lobby, settle the bill and buy some newspapers for the drive home. Remember, you're near your monthly curse, and I know that can cause women to become quite emotional. He kissed her sweetly, and told her he would return shortly. Lily did as he asked, and lay down upon the lovely bed. Perhaps he was right. Perhaps she just needed to relax, and remember that change doesn't always come easily.

She woke when the door opened, and Kit breezed through, holding the *London Times* and a couple of foreign newspapers. He threw them on the bureau, and produced a very prettily wrapped box. He handed it to her and told her to open it. Sitting up, Lily brushed her hair out of her eyes, and looked at her husband questioningly.

"What in the world is this, Kit?" she asked.

"Just open it and see," he replied, smiling.

She unwrapped the package, and saw that it was from the jewelers in the Savoy lobby. Lifting off the top, she caught her breath when she saw a magnificent diamond necklace, with lovely, large stones. "Oh my Gosh! Kit, you didn't need to do this. I'm overwhelmed. I 've never seen anything like this."

"Here, let me put it on you. I wanted you to have a keepsake from our wedding trip. This will help you to always remember how much I love you. If I've made you sad, I'm sorry. I have things to learn too, Lily. There – it looks lovely on you. The diamonds sparkle so prettily. The jeweler said the diamonds are all of the very finest grade. Not a flaw in any of them."

Lily put her arms out, and Kit entered them. "I love you my darling husband. I too am sorry if I hurt you. I didn't mean to. Marrying a member of the gentry is a nerve-wracking ordeal. But, I'll continue making progress. I promise," she smiled, before she kissed him with deep passion."

"You're perfect as far as I'm concerned. It's just the rest of society I sometimes have to worry about. Don't ever, for one moment, think that I'm not proud of you Lily. You're the most beautiful lady in all of England." They kissed again.

"Well, I'm afraid our lovely trip has come to an end. Edward is ready to pack the car. Do we have everything?" Kit asked.

"Yes. But, Kit. Shouldn't we have purchased something to bring back for Win? I can't believe we overlooked that. After all, we married on his birthday, and I know that was a gift to him, but little boys want more than weddings on their fourth birthday." Lily laughed, but looked concerned.

"Don't worry Lily, I remembered him too, as I was buying the necklace for you. I found some items in the shop designed for children. I bought him a gold signet ring, on the order of the one I wear, only of course, quite small. When he turns eighteen, I'll buy him one with the Claybourne crest. But, I think he'll love this for now."

"Oh, I'm so relieved. I would have felt dreadful to have forgotten about him."

"Also, I purchased gold bracelets with the Claybourne 'C' on a charm, and pairs of gold cufflinks, also with the letter 'C'. I felt that we should mark the occasion with gifts for the entire staff. Don't you think so?"

"Absolutely. What a lovely thought. They'll all be thrilled. Naturally, they'll be excited about the jewelry itself, but also because we thought of them. That was very good of you, Kit."

"Yes, well then, everything seems to be in order. Check the drawers one more time, and the cupboard, and then we'll be off. "

Lily did as he asked, and they left the room, taking the elevator to the lobby. Lily wasn't certain yet how she felt about being married. She was glad to be going home, where she could sort everything out and talk to Gena and John.

Before Edward took the road that led to Claybourne-on-Colne, Kit gave instructions for him to drive to Dower Road in Kensington. He turned to Lily, and told her that he was taking her to see their London townhouse. She was so thrilled. Before a very long ride, the car stopped in front of a magnificent English house. It was three stories high, and painted white. It also had round columns in the front of the shiny, black doorway.

"Oh, Kit, can we go in and look around? I just love it. It's much more than I'd dreamed."

"Yes, of course, Edward parked the car in the space allotted on the property and Lily and Kit walked up the few steps to the front door.

As they entered, Kit began explaining about the home's history. He said it had been built in 1845 at one end of a very wealthy family's estate. Of course, it had been completely re-done after the Zeppelin raid during the war. Everything was totally new. As they strolled through, Lily was amazed.

There were eight bedrooms, eight bathrooms, and four reception rooms. In addition, there was a substantial ground floor drawing room. The main dining room, the library and a guest bedroom suite were also located on this level. The master suite, located on the first level, comprised the bedroom, en suite bathroom, dressing room and also access to the adjoining roof terrace. There was one more bedroom suite on that level, and the second floor had three additional bedroom suites. At lower ground floor level were two additional bedroom suites. A large kitchen/breakfast room and a good-sized family room had direct access to the large West facing garden to the rear. The back lawn was almost perfectly oval.

"Kit, I thought the house would just be a tiny cottage," Lily laughed.

"Oh no. It's large enough to accommodate many people, as you can see. I had it re-built almost exactly as the old plans showed it. The only addition was the family room, so there's a place that's less formal. But, Lily, in years past, during the Season, Mother would have twelve or more guests here. All of the rooms were used."

"Oh, I can't wait to come and stay here someday. There's so much room. What a grand home to use as a London base."

"I thought you'd like it Lilly. Now do you see why it would have been quite difficult for us to stay here alone?"

Lily didn't see that at all, but she didn't argue.

They'd only been back at Claybourne Court one day when Lily paid a visit to John Garrett's office. Of course she rang first and made certain that he was free to see her. Gena answered the telephone. She was still assisting in her husband's practice. She was happy to hear from Lily, and delighted that she was going to come for a visit. Then, Lily explained that besides wanting to see them both, she actually wanted an appointment with John, because she needed an examination. Gena didn't question her, but only said that he was free all afternoon, so it would be fine to drop by anytime. Lily told her she would be at the office right after lunch, at about two o'clock. She knew that Kit was meeting with Henson right after the midday meal, so there would be no reason for an explanation about where she was going.

They ate with Win in the dining room, and he chattered non-stop about all that had happened while they'd been gone. He adored his new ring, and wore it proudly. That fall, Win would be starting his schooling at *Beaudesert Park* in *Minchhaven*. Edward would be driving him to and from, so he wouldn't be leaving Claybourne Court overnight. School would be another watershed moment for Win, and neither of them wanted it to be traumatic. He was starting to call Lily 'Mummy', which thrilled her, and Lily certainly didn't want him to go away before she was firmly established in that role. He was going to begin riding lessons with Howard, and Kit told him he could have his first riding habit. Lily looked forward to all three of them taking long rides through the wooded trails together, as a family. One thing she wanted to speak to John about was the possibility of a pregnancy, and when he thought it would be appropriate to consider adding another child to the nursery, without fear of upsetting Win. Lunch time ended, and Kit left to keep his appointment with Henson. As soon as he departed, she rang for Edward to bring the car around and asked him to take her to Dr. Garrett's cottage.

In no time at all, they were pulling up in front of Lily's old home. It seemed strange to think of it that way, and stranger still to think that John had replaced her father in those old, familiar office's at the back of the building. She asked Edward to wait for her, and entered by the front doorway. Gena was sitting at a reception desk, and she jumped up, running around to the front area when she saw Lily.

"Oh gracious! You're home. You look splendid. I want to hear every word about your holiday. Was it wonderful? Are you happy? How do you feel about being a Countess? Gosh. Just think, you really are Lily Claybourne, Countess of Gloucester. Who would have believed that, when we were back at *Aubigney?*

"Whoa. Slow down Gena. I have tons to tell you, and to ask you, but I haven't time now. Let's make plans for lunch. As soon as you're available. I can do it anytime. Right now, my main concern is seeing John. I'm sorry to be so abrupt, but it's important to me."

"That fine, Love. Let's have lunch tomorrow. Come here at noon, and we'll walk to the village. You aren't feeling ill, are you? I only ask because of your rush to see John?"

"No, not really ill. I just need him to examine me, and I have some important questions for him. I'll share everything with you tomorrow, and we aren't going to walk to the village. Edward will take us, silly girl. Can I see John now?"

Gena laughed. "Absolutely. Just follow me. We've changed things around a bit. John's examining room is where your father's office used to be." Lily followed Gena down the short hallway, and through a door on her right. She asked her to remove her dress, put a cotton robe on, and John would be with her in a moment. Then, Gena kissed her on the cheek, and left the room. Lily did as instructed, and then sat herself upon the examining table. Soon there was a soft knock, and John peeked his head in.

"All set, Countess Lily?" he smiled.

"Hello, John. It's lovely to see you. Please come in. I'm so glad I was able to see you so quickly after my return."

"When exactly did you get back?" he asked.

"Just yesterday. We were pretty tired out. I'm glad to be back."

"Well, tell me what it is you wanted to see me about? You aren't feeling ill, are you?"

"No – no – not really. But, well, John, I'm confused about a lot. First of all, let me explain about our wedding night. Actually, it was our wedding day – right after we checked into the Savoy. It was the first time we made love. I assume you know that I was a virgin, so this was all a new experience to me. I'd talked to all sorts of people, from my Mum to Gena, and got a lot of different responses. Primarily, I was led to believe that I should leave things up to Kit -that he would be gentle, and would know how to proceed."

"I agree with that advice," he nodded.

"Well . . . "Sorry, but it turned out to be rotten advice. Kit didn't seem to have any concern for me at all. There was no – no –foreplay. Do you know what I mean?"

"Yes, of course," answered John.

Lily went on to explain about the pain she'd experienced, and about how Kit's solution was that things would improve as they made love more frequently. John proceeded to examine her, and afterwards, she dressed and they resumed their discussion.

"Well, Lily, I see why you've had pain. You have an extremely abraded area. It will heal up just fine, but I want no sexual activity of any sort. I don't think Kit realized how serious the pain was. He probably assumed it was simply because you'd never been active sexually. In the event, I am going to give you something called 'Vaseline', and I want you to treat it every day. After you resume love making, you're to always use it. You're very small, and therein lies the problem."

"All right, John. I think that's what Gena gave me before we left, and I did use it the second time. It helped. But, are Kit's actions, or I should say 'non-actions' normal?

"Lily, I don't know that there is such a thing as 'normal' when it comes to this subject. I'd suggest that you let it go along for a bit, and if you're still concerned, I'll talk with him."

"Oh – I would hate that. Then he would know that I'd complained to you. I don't want that."

"Then, wait and see how things progress. The first few months of marriage aren't easy. If you're not going to tell him about your visit to me, how are you going to explain my prohibition on making love?"

"Well – I'll tell him I visited you, about the pain, and that you gave me the ointment. Then I'll also tell him that you prescribed a period of inactivity. I just don't want him to think that I ran to you with complaints about him."

"That's fine, Lily. Actually, you should feel able to talk with Kit about your worries, without me having to intervene. He's your husband and he loves you. All couples have to adjust to one another."

"I understand. And, I agree. I'll wait a bit. I shall talk to him if I feel the need." Lily thanked him, and he shook her hand.

"You'll be fine, Lily. Just always try to be open and honest with your husband. That's the best advice I can give you."

"I shall, John. Thanks so much. Gena and I are having lunch tomorrow, so I'll fill her in on everything we did in London then."

"Good show. I'm sure she'll tell it all to me. Have a good day now, and give Kit my regards."

Lily left John's office, feeling better. Primarily, her concern about the pain was gone. She didn't look forward to telling Kit about her doctor's visit, but she knew she must. Surely he would understand? Perhaps she should have told him before she went? He seemed to become upset over such trivial things. If she didn't tell him every little thing, she wasn't being a good wife. It was all foolishness. Surely a woman could visit a doctor without first reporting to her husband?

Edward was waiting in the car, and he drove her back to Claybourne Court. Upon arrival, Kit was sitting in his library. She immediately went to him. He was working on some papers, and he looked up at her, with a frown on his face. "Where did you go in the car? I didn't know you had any plans?" he remarked.

"I just went down to John's office. I thought I should have him take a look at me, since I'm still having that pain I told you about."

"You went and had John examine you? Does that mean what I think it means?" Kit answered.

"I suppose it does. There's only one place I'm having pain. In order for him to know what's causing it, he needed to examine the area."

"Lily. I really don't like that at all. If you needed an examination, you should have mentioned it to me. I would have taken you to a doctor in London, or even in one of the other villages. John is a friend. Do you mean to say you didn't feel uncomfortable having him perform such an intimate examination? I don't see how in the world we can see them socially again."

"Oh, Kit. That's silly. I didn't feel any more uncomfortable with John than I would any doctor. I know he's good, and I can speak honestly to him. I know he cares about me – and you, too. Please remember that I asked you to take me to a doctor in London, and you wouldn't do it."

"Oh, yes, I do remember, but that was right after we'd made love, and it seemed foolish to me. But, I don't like the idea that John has peered around at my wife's private parts."

"Kit. You didn't have any problem with the doctor examining Eleanor when she was pregnant. What's the difference?"

"The difference is that that doctor wasn't one of my best friends, and someone you worked with for two years in France. I don't normally even associate socially with my family physician. In this case, John happens to be the only physician in the village, and a good friend. so certainly I'd expect to see him for certain things. But, not for things of an intimate nature."

"Aren't you even interested in what he told me?" Lily asked.

"All right, then. What did he tell you?"

"He said that I have a very badly abraded area. I don't need to spell out what that's from. He has ordered a complete halt to all sexual activity, until I'm completely healed, and he gave me an ointment that I'm to use once that activity resumes."

Kit's face turned red. "My God, Lily. You discussed our lovemaking with John? I'm dumbfounded. I thought you had more sense than that. I suppose he thinks I have no concern for you, and that I caused harm to you purposely."

"Of course he doesn't. He said nothing of the sort. In fact, he indicated that I'm abnormally small, and that if anything, you wouldn't have realized there was anything different."

"I told you that. Damnit, Lily, I told you that myself, when we were in London. Why did you have to run off and have John say it again?"

"Because you assumed that it would get better with time, without giving me a restful period for healing."

"You astound me sometimes. I never know what to expect from you. I thought Eleanor was independent, but you take the cake."

"Kit, that's awfully unkind. John suggested that we talk to one another about things that concern us. You seem to be doing quite a good job of that. I haven't complained about anything. I didn't even want you to know that I was still having pain, for fear of worrying you. That's why I didn't tell you that I was going to John's office. The last thing I dreamed was that you'd be upset because it was John that I chose to see. I'm going to overlook your nasty comment about Eleanor, but I'll tell you this. I don't want to hear myself compared to her again. And I shall go to whichever doctor I wish. I expect that you'll do the same. I'm going up to see Win," she said calmly, as she turned and left the library.

7

Not another word was spoken about Lily's visit to John Garrett. When they readied themselves for bed that night, Kit asked her if she'd prefer that he sleep in his own room. She told him she wanted him to do whatever he wished, but that she certainly always loved to have him near her. Thus, he acquiesced, and slid beneath the covers in her room. He didn't go against the doctor's orders, and both were asleep very quickly.

The next morning, over breakfast, she told him that she was having lunch with Gena. She sensed that Kit wanted to say something negative, but he didn't do it. He simply nodded his head, as if giving his assent. He told her that he was going to ride across the property and make some decisions about where he was going to plant new crops. She answered by telling him that she was very interested in his new projects, and hoped he would take her to see what the plans were when they were in order. Lady Cynthia was at the table with them.

"Oh no, dear. That wouldn't be the 'done thing' at all. Earl's wives don't involve themselves with issues concerning the property. You are to make decisions that have to do with social matters, and household concerns. Like most women, including me, you wouldn't understand the inner workings of a large estate anyway. I never bothered myself with such things."

Lily thought about remaining silent, but she decided that she was not going to start her marriage being submissive, and pretending to agree with things she was in opposition to. "Mother Claybourne" – as she now referred to Lady Cynthia –"times are changing. I want to be a full partner to Kit. I'm aware that I don't know anything about the mechanics of running a large estate. But I can learn, just as I learned about nursing. It seems to me that it would be very good for our marriage if I were able to discuss the concerns he has. Perhaps I might even be able to make suggestions to him. To me, that's what a partnership means. What would have happened if you hadn't been able to make decisions about the estate while Kit was fighting in the war?"

"Oh, Lily. I didn't make decisions about the estate. The land agent, Henson, made all of the decisions. Certainly, he talked things over with me. But, I didn't disagree. I always left the final word up to Henson."

Lily closed her mouth. There was no point in arguing. It was two against one. Kit would surely agree with his mother. The truth was that the longer she knew the two of them, the more she began to realize that Kit had been born under an iron gloved mother. No matter how kind she was, or how dearly she loved her son, she was exceedingly strong and he bent to her will. Lily wondered if the former Earl had been the same way. She hated the way these first few weeks of her marriage were unfolding. She loved Kit, and she knew that he loved her. In spite of her statement about not wanting to be compared to Eleanor, she couldn't help but think of some of the things she and Eleanor had discussed. In particular, she remembered Eleanor telling her that she felt Kit wanted to mold her into someone she wasn't. Wasn't that the way Lily now felt? Kit had been so loving – so uncritical – so understanding, before their marriage. Now it seemed that she couldn't do anything right. Obviously, the difference was that she was now a Countess, when before she had only been a ladies' maid or nanny. Different behavior was expected in each role. She needed to discuss her feelings with Kit, and made up her mind to do so that night, when they were not within hearing of 'Mother Claybourne'.

But, now she was looking forward to lunch and a good chat with her best friend, Gena. She thought long and hard about how much she should share with Gena. Finally, she decided that in order for anything positive to come from their talk, Gena needed all of the facts. They had always shared everything, from the day they'd met. Lily needed a friend who would understand her concerns and give her sound, solid advice. Gena thought Kit was wonderful, so she wasn't about to say anything negative about him. After breakfast, Lily kissed Kit goodbye and went back to her room to change into something appropriate to wear for lunch in the village. She chose a simple day frock and a pretty hat. Then, she went into the nursery, and spent some time playing with Win. At four years old, he was becoming a typical little boy. He loved to build blocks into a high pile, and then crash them down. He also had a small, metal car and he loved to run into things, and made crashing noises. He would clap his hands and laugh uproariously. Lily played those sorts of games with him for a while, and then read him a short book. Soon, it was time for her to leave. She gave him a big cuddle and a kiss. She told him she would see him very soon. Mrs. Briggs came upstairs to take him down to the kitchen area, where the other staff would spoil him.

Lily arrived at John's cottage at exactly noon. Gena was waiting for her outside, dressed in a pretty, yellow frock, with short sleeves and a low waistline. She jumped into the backseat with Lily, and Edward drove them into the village. There was a small teashop which they both liked to visit. Lily told Edward she would ring him when she needed to be collected. Then, she and Gena went into the shop, and found themselves a table for two in a private area, where they could talk without being overheard.

After they settled themselves, and spoke a few comments about how nice it was to be together, Gena inquired about how things were going. It was Lily's opening. She started with the ride on the way to London and ended with breakfast that very morning. Gena didn't say a word during the entire recitation. When Lily was finished, she leaned back in her chair and put her hands on the table.

"So now you have it. Gena, I'm in a conundrum. Kit seems to have changed so much. I want your opinion."

"Well, it *is* a perplexing situation," Gena started. Lily, I'm going to be very honest with you. I was afraid that some of these things you're telling me might happen. I don't think that Kit understands how much France changed you – how much you grew. I know you've had some of those thoughts yourself. He thought you were the same, little compliant person who applied for a position at Claybourne Court. Well, you aren't. On the other hand, I think you believed that Kit was a knight in shining armor – the perfect man. Of course he is terribly good looking, not to mention being very gallant, kind, steady and decent. But, along with those traits, Kit is a traditionalist in the strongest sense of the word. He was brought up following the old adage that 'this is the way things have always been done'. He holds to that tradition."

"But, Gena, there are some situations when I've seen and heard Kit take viewpoints that I think are quite modern. I remember before he went off to war, he made mention of the fact that he thought it very silly that he was to bring his valet to France with him. He said England was going to have to change."

"Yes, well, quite. I'm not saying Kit is some relic out of a past era. I also noticed that he's willing to make changes to Claybourne Court, in terms of crop additions, raising sheep and the like .Also decorating. But, when it comes to women, I think Kit sees his mother as the quintessential Mistress of the Manor. He was raised to think that way. My belief is that it will take him quite some time to see that the world has changed. His ridiculous notion that a lady shouldn't enjoy lovemaking is a perfect example. Really, Lily. That comes straight out of his mother's era. I'm only conjecturing, but I suspect Eleanor was quite a wild one in bed. He must have had very mixed feelings about that. He probably enjoyed it, but in the final analysis, Lady Cynthia's thinking prevailed. Eleanor was *not* a lady. You are. At least, that's what he thinks."

Lily laughed. "So, I'm *not* really a lady?"

"Of course you are, Lily. You know that. But, unless you like lying stiffly in bed while he pumps away, then in Kit's mind, you aren't a lady."

"How do I know what I like? I've never had any other experience. I know I don't like things the way they are now."

"Then, from as much as I know, you aren't going to enjoy it. You're going to have to talk to Kit. He's made it very clear that he isn't about to want to hear from John about improving your sex life. My guess is that he would be mortified to think you'd spoken to John about it."

Lily put her head in her hands. "Oh Lord. I can just imagine such a conversation now. What do I say when he tells me that my wishing for more – more lovemaking – foreplay-whatever you call it, is not proper? "

"You tell him it *is* proper. That the world has changed. Tell him that you spoke with many women while in France – nice girls from nice families - and you know much more than you used to."

"Oh Gena, that sort of conversation is horrible to contemplate. But, I think you're right. If I don't say anything, I'm going to spend my life in the same awful state I'm in now. But, what about Kit's other attitudes? Gena, I don't want to be relegated to the pretty, little Countess, whom he loves to show off, in fancy frocks and dainty slippers. I want to be a full partner to Kit. To be a helpmate in decision-making. I also don't want to be told that if I want to enrich my life experience by seeing interesting, historic sights, I'm not acting appropriately. Lord, Gena, according to him, I'm not ever to think about cooking a meal again, or making up a bed."

"I really don't know what to say about the latter two. It's true that you're a countess now. I don't think you would find many who enjoy cooking and housework," Gena giggled.

"I understand that. And I'm not suggesting that those things be a part of my regular routine. Of course not. But, I think it would be sort-of fun to stay in our house in London and act like normal people once in a while."

"The problem there, Lily, is that Kit doesn't think his way of thinking is abnormal. He's never seen anyone in his life cook a meal, or make-up a bed, except a servant. He cannot imagine such a thing."

"Well, all right. I can live without those additions to my life. That isn't the end of the world. But, it's the entire, general attitude that concerns me. I can't imagine spending my life planning menus with Mrs., Briggs, organizing dinner parties, and penning thank you notes. Gena, it's important to me that I live my life in a way that has meaning. Even though France was a horror, I felt so useful. I loved helping people. That's why I wanted to be a doctor. It's obvious to me now that any thoughts I may have entertained about eventually picking up my studies, and going on to medical school were insane. Kit would never, ever hear of it. I think he only *acted* like he thought it was an admirable ambition for me to have, but then, when faced with the actual possibility of such, he was horrified. I suppose I knew that such a goal was unattainable if I married Kit. But, I did hope that my deep need to do for others would be fulfilled in some other way. I honestly thought that when one is given the power of an Earl's wife, that power could be used to do good for others."

"It could be, Lily. But, once again, that isn't the way Kit sees the role of a countess. The problem you're faced with is that neither you nor Kit is a bad person. But, Kit is firmly entrenched in one mindset, and you either have to acquiesce to his way of thinking, or rebel against it. Frankly, I don't know if your make-up is such that you can live the rest of your life acquiescing to his age-old beliefs. Yet, if you rebel against them, there's going to be a rocky road ahead."

"Gena, how in the world could this have happened? I love Kit. I really do. I don't want to fight with him. I don't like confrontation. You know that. But, I have a very strong need for self-fulfillment. I don't mean in a selfish way. I mean that I want to be the best I can be. I believe I was put on the earth for a purpose, and I don't believe that purpose is to look my part as a beautiful and angelically pure young Countess, whose only duties consist of bestowing my sweet presence on entertainment for the tenantry, and prize giving at the annual agricultural fair. What that amounts to is for me to be a loving and adoring looker-on. Is that all life should be Gena?"

"No. Not in my opinion, and obviously not in yours. Perhaps there are some women to whom such a role would appeal. Interestingly, I would have thought Eleanor was one of those, but apparently even she felt like a caged bird, according to you. I wonder who the perfect wife would be," Gena pondered.

"His mother," Lily replied. "Plain and simple. I don't know why I didn't realize it before, but Kit grew up under the iron rod of a mother who, during his minority, managed his life. She still does to a large degree. When I think back upon things, I remember that it was almost always his mother who confronted Eleanor and made decisions. He took his cues from her. Do you think I should attempt a conversation with her?" Lily asked.

"You could try. She doesn't sound like an unreasonable lady. You two have seemed to get along well. Perhaps you could approach her with some of your concerns. Not the sexual part, but your feelings about wanting to contribute more. After all, she's a woman too. I should think she could understand your feelings."

"I don't know. But, I think I should start with her. To tell the truth, I feel that if I try to have a conversation with Kit about my feelings, he'll simply go to her with everything I've said, anyway. So, I might as well make my first attempt at bringing the Claybourne's into the Twentieth Century by trying to reason with Lady Cynthia."

"It's surely worth a try," Gena replied. "Now, let me see your lovely smile. The world hasn't come to an end, yet. Marriage can be difficult in the beginning. I'm fortunate that I married a doctor, who shares my interests and wants me to be a helpmate. But, as I said, Kit is decent, and good, and I think he can be brought round."

"Oh, Gena, I hope so," Lily answered.

She finally smiled.

Lily returned to Claybourne Court in the early afternoon. Kit was not yet back from his ride through the property. She had a headache, and didn't feel up to par. Perhaps it was from the rather heavy conversation she'd had with Gena. She decided to go to her room, and have a lie-down until Kit returned. She took off her frock and put on a dressing gown. Then, she picked up a book and lay down on the chaise lounge. Her eyes were burning, so she gave up trying to read, and put her head down. Before she knew it, she was fast asleep.

When she woke, Kit was sitting in the chair in her bedchamber. He smiled when she lifted her head, and said "I didn't want to wake you. It looked like you needed the rest. You're so beautiful when you sleep. Your eyelashes touch your cheeks."

"Thank you, Kit. That's a sweet thing to say. How was your ride? Did you accomplish what you set out to do?"

"For the most part. I'm going to go over my thoughts with Henson, and probably with Mother."

"Mother?" thought Lily. Lady Cynthia had just that morning said that she never involved herself in affairs that had to do with the property. But, Lily didn't feel particularly well, so she let his comment pass.

"Kit, dear, would you do me a favor?" she asked.

"Of course, Lily. What do you need?" he replied.

"Would you ring Gena for me? I don't feel terribly well. I don't want to bother John, but Gena is a nurse, and I'd like her to check me over. It's probably nothing. Maybe a little cold coming on."

Kit frowned a bit, but didn't argue. He went to the telephone, and rang Gena's number at John's office. After he told her what Lily had requested, she said she'd be at Claybourne Court in a tick. He hung up and told Lily what Gena had said. Lily stayed on the chaise lounge, and asked Kit if he would bring her a glass of water. Kit rang for one of the servants, and a glass of water was directly delivered. By the time the water arrived, so had Gena. She was sent directly to Lily's bedchamber. Lily greeted her, and told her she wasn't feeling well. She asked her friend to feel her forehead to see if she thought Lily had a fever. Gena did so, and said that "yes" she did think so. Lily's face was flushed, and she said that she had not been feeling well since her return from their luncheon. Gena asked her what kind of symptoms she had, and Lily told her – a headache, body aches, a sore throat, and that she felt like she was getting a cough. Gena got up and walked over to her, and looked at her friend carefully. Lily's eyes were also bloodshot. Gena knew immediately what it was, and Lily had a pretty good idea herself.

The Spanish Flu. That frightening, deadly flu that had led to panic across the world. Both girls had known soldiers toward the end of the war who had come down with it, and there were people all over the globe stricken. It seemed to hit young people, in their twenties, and most especially pregnant women. The pandemic had seemed to wane in the past months, and most people were less frightened than they had been. In the larger cities, like London, almost everyone wore masks over their faces for quite some time. Because Lily was a nurse, she'd been extremely careful with hygiene, making certain that hands were washed frequently, and that the downstairs servants took extra care with sterilizing kitchen utensils. No one they had known in the village had come down with it. But, the symptoms Lily was having were almost certainly a bad forecast for what was to come.

Gena helped her put on a nightdress and got her into bed, while Kit sat helplessly watching. Then, she got the thermometer, which Lily told her was in the dressing table drawer, and took her friend's temperature. It was 104 degrees. That fit the profile of flu symptoms perfectly. There was almost always a very high fever. Gena took the glass of cold water, and gave Lily some pain reliever. Then, she told her that she would be back in a tick, and ran to ring John, who she wanted to examine Lily. Kit didn't argue. After Gena was out of Lily's hearing, on her way down the stairway to ring John from another room, Kit stopped her.

"Gena. What's the matter with Lily? She doesn't look well."

"I'm not a hundred percent Kit, but I'm fearful that she's come down with the Spanish Flu. I'm going to ring John and have him look at her. If it's the flu, it's very serious. I'm sure you know that."

"Oh my God. What can be done for it?" he asked.

"Not a lot. There's no treatment. It's killing people world-wide. That's why I want John to make a firm diagnosis, and then we'll proceed with the best care possible."

Gena turned and continued down the stairs, going to the drawing room immediately and using the telephone in there to ring John. Thankfully, he wasn't busy with a patient, and he answered on the first ring. Gena told him what was happening and he told her he would leave that instant. She went back up to Lily and checked on her. Kit was back in the room too, and he'd had a fire built, as Lily was complaining of feeling cold. She lay wrapped up in the blankets, suddenly feeling chilled to the bone. Lily knew what it probably was, and she was afraid. She'd read recently that this second wave of the flu was more ravaging than the first had been. And there was no treatment for it. No one knew its cause. All anyone could do was treat the symptoms and pray the patient would make it through.

Gena rang for the housekeeper. She met Mrs. Briggs outside of Lily's room. "Mrs. Briggs," Gena exclaimed. "I'm afraid we've got trouble here. Lily isn't feeling at all well, and from her symptoms, I can almost say with certainty that she's come down with the ghastly Spanish Flu."

"Oh my goodness. My niece in Wiltshire died of that last fall. It's ghastly.

"Yes, I know. I've rung my husband, John. You know he's a physician. He's on his way over. This new strain of the flu is even worse than that which struck your niece. I need you to alert the other staff members, but don't put them into a panic. My primary concern is that everyone wash their hands thoroughly several times a day. If anyone coughs or sneezes, they should be certain to cover their mouths and noses, and again wash their hands. John will probably suggest cotton face masks, which he can distribute to everyone. Win needs particular attention. This flu strikes young people. The older you are, the less danger. Thank God, Lily isn't pregnant. Pregnant women are one of the highest risk groups. Make certain that whomever looks after Win keeps the nursery absolutely spotless and sterile. I'd like him to be given a good bath right away."

"Of course, Miss Gena. I'll go and make preparations immediately. Can I do anything for the Countess?"

"No, not right now. Just send my husband up as soon as he arrives." Gena returned to Lily's bedside. Kit remained in the room as well. Neither of them spoke, and Kit sat smoothing his wife's forehead with his hand.

8

It was the flu. John analyzed all of the symptoms, confirmed the diagnosis and set about doing everything possible to save Lily's life. He expected the high fever to last about three days. That was a critical period, because if the fever couldn't' be controlled, pneumonia could be the next stage. Lily's pulse rate was unusually slow, another classic symptom of this deadly killer. In addition, she had an unproductive cough, and she began to hemorrhage from her nose. John did not want her transferred to a hospital. He felt it was best to let her recuperate in her own surroundings, with one-on-one care. He used hot blanket packs, to ease the pain in her back and legs. Cold compresses were used for headaches, and for her very high fever. A cold compress was used immediately after a short blanket pack. She was encouraged to eat three or four small meals each day, with bran added to each. She was also urged to drink three or four quarts of water, or fruit juice a day, every half hour when awake.

The entire household went into a solemn, medical watch. Word was spread from Lily's room, to Mrs., Briggs and found its way to the other staff. In spite of Gena's warning not to let the staff become hysterical, each time anyone sneezed or coughed there was immense concern. Everyone wore a surgical mask. Win was watched with eagle eyes by everyone on the premises. Day and night, everyone prayed. For the first day and night, there seemed to be no improvement at all. John and Gena stayed at Claybourne Court twenty-four hours a day. While John slept a few hours, Gena kept watch at the bedside. When Gena slept, John was there. Kit scarcely left her side, except to check on his son. At several points, hope faded. Lily's heart rate speeded up, and an ice pack was placed over her chest. Whether that was the reason or not, the heart rate returned to near normal.

In desperation, John put the word out in the immediate area surrounding *Claybourne-on-Colne* to determine if there was anyone who had survived the flu living in the vicinity. He discovered a soldier over at the *Minchhampton Aerodrome*. He quickly sent Gena to collect a blood sample from this survivor and injected it into Lily's body. John had read numerous articles that discussed the immune system in relation to treatment of the widespread epidemic. Some researchers believed that giving a severely ill patient some blood from a recovered victim, might help to develop antibodies. It appeared to work. Within twenty-four hours of trying the injection, Lily's temperature came down, and she showed signs of improvement. No one ever really knew what saved her, but there was no question that John and Gena were given the credit by everyone at Claybourne Court. Kit broke down and wept when he realized that his wife was going to live, and he vowed that they would never speak an unkind word to one another again. Even Lady Cynthia was terribly emotional, and took her turn at the bedside with the rest of the caregivers.

After ten days, Lily was able to sit up in bed and have her meals on a tray. Her aches and pains were gone, along with the dreadful headache and sore throat. She was very weak – "like a baby kitten"- cried Mrs. Briggs, but the important thing was that she had come through it. John would not allow her to be out of her bed for another week, but finally she could sit by the window and enjoy the fresh, summer breezes. The windows had been open the entire time, as it was deemed that clean, refreshing air was good for patients. At long last, Lily was able to spend a few hours alone every day, reading and simply enjoying being alive.

She used that time to think. She came to the conclusion that when one comes so close to dying, it does something to the soul. She thought about what she wanted the rest of her life to be like. She thought about why her life had been spared when so many millions of other people had succumbed. She thought about how fortunate she was. If her two years in France had changed her outlook on life, nearly coming to the end of her days on earth, due to the Spanish Flu, had substantially altered her entire attitude about everything. She had a new need to know the meaning of life – to understand her purpose in being here. She made a firm decision to discuss these feelings with her husband.

Later one day, when Kit came into the room and sat down in the chair, she brought up the multitude of things she'd been thinking during all of the days and nights of her illness. Kit listened, and seemed to understand.

"Lily. I had similar feelings when I returned from France. Knowing that I'd survived when so many others hadn't. I felt the need to do something more with my life. I too have had a hard time understanding why I was spared. So, I know what you're going through –at least to some degree. In my case, I didn't have a lot of choice about what to do with my life. It was all planned out from birth. But, I knew that I wanted do it as well as I possibly could. However, I was so overcome with the difficulties that faced me with my marriage that I wasn't able to do much with regard to pursuing the bettering of Claybourne Court, and the tasks that were laid out for me. You're rather in the same situation, if you think about it. Not in terms of our marriage, I would hope, but with regard to having your life quite well-mapped out. You're a countess. That closes many doors, of which I know you're aware. But, it also opens others. For instance, you know that our family has set up the Foundation which will provide the means for a hospital to be built in the village. That's going to be an enormous contribution to the welfare of the residents of *Claybourne-on-Colne*. You and I haven't spoken much about this undertaking. Frankly, I didn't really consider you for any role in it. But, listening to you now, I wonder if I shouldn't have. You have medical knowledge and interests, and I don't know anyone who cares more about helping others. Of course, there will be a Board set-up to oversee this endeavor. I'd intended for my mother to be on the Board. To be honest, I haven't the knowledge, nor the time. I want to put my new thoughts regarding crop additions and raising sheep into action. Eventually, I'm considering building a Mill, to utilize the wool we'll derive from sheep herding. The Claybourne name will be associated with business enterprise for the first time. Now, I think that *you* would make an excellent addition to the hospital Board. What would you say to that?"

"I'd have to think about it, Kit. But, I think I'd like it. My concerns are twofold. Am I to be treated as nothing more than a figurehead, because I have a title, and bear the name 'Claybourne'? And, how much of my life would be dedicated to this venture? If it's only a day a month, or something on that order, that doesn't sound terribly fulfilling to me. I appreciate your offer, and it *is* a beginning. But, Kit, I want to really make a difference in the world. I'm not certain how I can best accomplish that, and it's going to take a lot more than one conversation to answer the questions that I have. For now, I need to know that I'll have your support and understanding as I begin to seek out a new path to take in life."

"Lily, of course you'll have my support and understanding. The only thing I must remind you of is that there are undoubtedly some paths which are blocked because of your position in the aristocracy."

"Which paths would those be?" Lily asked.

"Lily, I think you're fairly well aware of the responsibilities a countess can and cannot undertake. For instance, at one time in your life, you considered becoming a physician. Needless to say, that's out of the question for someone of your status. Nor could you consider such a thing as social work, or working with the poor in any capacity, other than lending your name to a charity, helping to plan fund-raising balls, or donating funds to worthy causes."

"That rules out a lot of things, Kit."

"Yes. I suppose it does. I've never given it much thought, but then I was raised to know what was and wasn't acceptable. You know I'm not what is commonly referred to as a toff. Good Lord, Lily, I had Tom Holiday as one of the attendants in our wedding. He scarcely comes from the peerage. But, he's a fine chap, and he saved my life. I don't look down on people less fortunate than we are, but I do have to remember my own position in the aristocracy. The 'Claybourne' name is old and revered. It was drilled into me from the time I was a child that our heritage is meaningful, and no one in the family should ever do anything to sully or taint the family reputation. I've always tried to uphold that commitment. Now, you're my wife, and the same sort of commitment pertains to you."

"Can you explain to me what in the world would be considered disgraceful about practicing medicine, or hands-on helping others?" Lily asked, with a slight frown.

"Lily, those things wouldn't necessarily be disgraceful, but people in our position simply don't do them," Kit answered.

"In other words, they aren't the 'done' thing?" she retorted.

"Well, no Lily, they aren't. I couldn't name you one countess in the land who has ever undertaken those sorts of roles. It wouldn't be considered decent. True ladies don't involve themselves in such tasks."

"Oh Kit, how foolish. I'm sorry, but I don't see the sense in what you're saying. Just because things have always been done a certain way, is that a reason why they can't be changed? On the basis of what you're saying, there would never be any advancement in society. We would still be living in the dark ages. As it is, you're defending living in the Victorian era."

"Change is wonderful in certain arenas. Medical research, new and better ways to grow foodstuffs, automobiles, manufacturing methods. All of those things make society better. And, yes, certainly bettering living conditions for the poor is a positive change. But Lily, you can't be the one to initiate such transformations. You're considered a model for women who aspire to become ladies. "

"Exactly, Kit. And what better model in the world than to break with tradition and pave the way for women to make their way in fields that were once considered unfit for females?"

"What are you saying, Lily? Surely you aren't reviving your old, foolish ideas about studying to become a doctor?"

"Kit, those ideas aren't foolish. There have been women physicians since the 1880's. I wouldn't even be breaking new ground."

"There are no female physicians who are countesses, Lily. Please, can we drop this subject? I've said that I'm willing to be supportive, and to try very hard to understand your needs. But, you need to understand my viewpoint as well. I can only be what society tells me I can be. The same is true of you."

Lily sat quietly for a few moments. She didn't want to drop the subject, and he had convinced her of nothing. But, she also didn't want to argue. It was obvious that she wasn't going to change Kit's mind. Apparently, she had married into the only perfect family in the world, where no one had ever done anything that led to unrest in their social realm.

Kit got up from the chair and walked over to the chaise lounge where Lily reclined.

"There now, Lily. I think we've had a good conversation, and I'm very happy that you shared your feelings with me. I spoke with John early this morning, and he told me that he's going to allow you to become more mobile again. I should have told you that when I first came into the room." He leaned down and kissed her. "If you like, you can do some horseback riding again. I think the fresh air and exercise would be good for you, in moderation of course. John agrees. So, if the weather is good tomorrow, you can take Taffeta out for a nice ride through the trails. Would that cheer you?" Kit asked.

"Oh, yes, Kit. It would. It seems a lifetime since I did anything so normal. I'd love to see Howard, and to enjoy the out-of-doors from Taffeta's gentle back. I'll look forward to that very much."

Kit smiled at her, and gave her another kiss. "I love you very much Lily. I'm so glad that you're well again, and shall do everything in my power to see that you're happy and fulfilled. Now, I really must see to some paperwork. Would you like to have dinner downstairs tonight? I think you're ready to rejoin the world."

"Indeed, I would, Kit. Tell Halsey to have the table set for the entire family," she smiled.

The next morning, Lily woke with the birds. It had been so long since she'd had anything to look forward to. She dressed in her riding habit, and met Kit in the dining room at the usual time for breakfast. Everyone was cheered by her presence. The previous night had brought a sense of calm to the house. The traditional routine could now be re-established. The entire staff was pleased that their lovely countess was once again gracing the table with her presence. There was no question that Win had been over-the- moon. The poor little chap had been confused by the mood of the house, and the obvious concern on the faces of those he knew and loved. While he was too young to understand the gravity of Lily's condition, he sensed that something was surely amiss. Now, his new Mummy was back where she belonged, and everybody seemed to be much happier. Lily made a great fuss over him, and gave him lots of cuddles.

After breakfast, she told Kit that she was going to slowly stroll down to the stables, and ask Howard to saddle up Taffeta. Kit asked if she wanted him to accompany her, but she declined, and said that she rather thought she might enjoy just a quiet ride by herself. Kit kissed her goodbye, and told her to enjoy herself. He said that he would see her at the noon hour.

Lily was delighted to see Howard, and he was very pleased to see her. They exchanged a few words, and then he saddled Taffeta, and she took her round the ring a few times. After feeling comfortable again in the saddle, she went for a long ride on the wooded trails. It was a lovely day, and she so enjoyed being out of doors again. Tree boughs fell over the trail, and dainty wildflowers poked their heads through the woodland floor. For a while she just sat still, and let Taffeta graze on some delicious clover she'd spied. Of course, Lily's thoughts were seldom still, and as usual, in that quiet place, her mind continued to mull over the conversation she'd had with Kit that morning. More and more she'd begun to realize that they seemed to be on different wave lengths. It wasn't that he was wrong, and she was right. It wasn't as simple as that. There *was* no right and wrong. They were both good people, and each wanted to live according to what they considered to be the best path for them. But, it was hard. She totally understood that Kit had been brought up in a certain manner, with strong convictions about keeping to tradition. Lily, on the other hand, was used to much more freedom to explore her world, and the various options it presented to her. She made up her mind to find a way to live within his world, and keep to tradition, but to find a way to use the power that came from being an Earl's wife to do good for others. She loved Kit, and didn't want to have difficulties in their marriage. She came to a forked path in the woods, and decided to take a different route than she usually did. As she rode, she found that the path led her past the tenant's houses on the estate. It was a place she'd never seen. She was astounded at the conditions she saw, and humiliated that people who lived on their land were in such poverty. She slowed Taffeta, and noticed a woman hanging clothing on an outdoor line. The woman gazed at her, and nodded her head, subserviently. Lily stopped, and spoke.

"Good morning. I'm Lily Claybourne. May I ask you name?"

The woman performed a small curtsy. "I'm Mrs. Gunderson," she replied.

"It's a lovely day, isn't it?" Lily continued.

"Yes, Milady, it is. I see you're enjoying it. We heard you was quite sick for a spell."

"Yes, Mrs. Gunderson, I was, but I'm feeling much better now. I'm happy to have a chance to meet you. I'd like to meet more of the people who farm our land. We're very grateful to you for your hard work."

Mrs. Gunderson looked amazed. "We ain't used to folks from the big house telling us thanks," she said.

"Well – you should be. And we should know you better. After all, you're our neighbors. Someday, perhaps I can return and we can sit and have a chat. I'd like to know more about your life."

"Milady, I don't think that would be proper. Me husband wouldn't like it."

"That seems silly, doesn't it?" answered Lily.

"I don't know. Seems silly to me you wanting to chat with me."

"We're both women, and wives. I should say we have a lot in common," Lily continued.

"I'm not thinking so, Milady. But, I thank you for saying so. I need to get back to me washing now. Good day, Milady."

Lily said "Good day, and rode on down the path. The poor women had seemed astounded that someone from Claybourne Court would speak to her. Lilly hated it when people felt like that – intimidated by others. Somehow, she intended to change that attitude. But, she wouldn't tell Kit about this incident. It would only start another row. She returned to the stable, and then meandered her way back to the great house, and went to change into a suitable frock for lunch.

It was now July, and the days were growing quite warm. She slipped on a lightweight voile dress, with cap sleeves and a skirt that fell mid-length. It was amazing how quickly fashions had changed since the war. The fact that women were now in the work force had necessitated clothing that was less likely to cause accidents such as tripping over long skirts or sleeves getting caught in factory machinery. Lily liked the change. It was much less cumbersome than having to dress in layers and layers of crinolines, not to mention corsets. Waistlines were still dropped, and most frocks had sashes at the hipline. Since Lily was very slender, the style looked attractive on her. She brushed her shorter hair, and went back down the stairs to join Kit for lunch. He had just entered the dining room, and Win was already in his youth's chair. Kit pulled the chair out for his wife, and they settled comfortably.

"How was your ride, Lily?" Kit asked.

"Just splendid. It's such a lovely day. I can't tell you how good it felt to enjoy the out-of-doors again."

"Mummy, can I learn to ride a horse?" Win asked.

Lily looked over at Kit. She wasn't certain what her answer should be. Was he too young for such a thing? Kit nodded his head in a positive direction. She smiled, and looked back at Win. "Yes, sweetheart, if you would like to do so," she answered.

"Daddy will have to buy you a little pony of your very own, Win. Would you like that?" Kit asked.

"Oh, Daddy, yes. Can we do it soon?"

"Yes. I'll look into it immediately. I'll talk to a chap I know who raises Shetlands. We'll find you a nice, gentle, little pony. Then you can ride in the ring. Eden will teach you all of the things you need to know." Kit always referred to Howard by his surname.

Win was terribly excited, and Lily was glad that Kit had agreed with his wishes.

9

That night Lily and Kit made love again, for the first time since their honeymoon. She had asked John, who said that enough time had passed, and she should be quite well healed. He reminded her to use the ointment he had given her. Lily wasn't looking terribly forward to it, but she knew it had been quite some time, and that her husband needed love and affection. When they were upstairs, preparing themselves for bed, Lily asked Kit to spend the night in her room.

"I'm quite well now, Kit. I miss having you beside me at night. Don't you think it's time you resumed your marital privileges?"

Kit looked at her with a rather startled look on his face. Apparently he hadn't expected such frankness from his wife. But, he didn't seem put off. He walked to her and put his arms around her. Kissing her longingly, he whispered, "Oh Lily, I've missed being close to you. If you're certain it's alright, of course I want to be with you."

She kissed him back passionately. She tried to put her entire being into the kiss, to let him know that she truly wanted him. He gently removed her nightdress, and took off his robe. They were still standing, and she could see that he was terribly aroused. She had used the Vaseline ointment that John had given her, so she wasn't frightened of being harmed. In addition, she hoped that he would show more consideration for her and take a bit more time showing her how much he loved her. They came together in another embrace, both unclothed, and Lily was surprised at how much her body responded to his. She truly wanted him to make love to her. She wanted him to touch her, and kiss her breasts, fully enjoying the act and allow her to explore his body. They fell back onto the bed while kissing and the pace of their breathing increased. He was running his hand through her hair and telling her how much he loved her. She responded by doing the same. Then, she ran her hand across his chest, and down his abdomen, following the line of hair that grew in an almost straight line toward his groin. It was clear that such a motion pleased him, for she could feel him grow more aroused. He put his hand on her breasts, and kneaded them. Everything was progressing nicely, and Lily believed that she would finally be satisfied and would come to know what everyone talked about when they said that this act was enjoyable. Suddenly, he leaped on top of her. This time there was no discomfort, because of the ointment, but there was no pleasure either. It was too soon. A few moments more, and some stroking and kissing, would have made all of the difference. She kept her arms around him, but otherwise lay still. Once again, there was the up and down plunging motion, like a water pump on an old-fashioned sink. After less than a minute, he collapsed on to her chest, breathing rapidly. "Oh Lily, that was so gratifying. Thank you darling. It was a marvelous release for me." He stayed in that position for a few minutes, while she absent mindedly stroked his hair. Then, with a satisfied sigh, he rolled off and went to sleep.

Lily turned onto her side, put her head on the pillow and tried not to cry. She was utterly confused. It was clear that Kit had normal, sexual desires. It was clear that he enjoyed the act itself, and felt satisfied when it was finished. He didn't ask her not to touch him on any part of his body. But, he had what appeared to be almost a distaste, or at least no desire, to touch her. That didn't seem the way it was supposed to be. Should she talk with him about it? Would he understand what she was trying to get across to him? Would it matter to him? She thought it would. He wanted her to be happy. He had said so, over and over again. However, she knew what the problem was, and that was the rub. If she brought up her lack of satisfaction, he was certain to tell her that no lady would want those kinds of inappropriate things done to her. Or that he didn't feel comfortable demeaning her in such a way. How did she get across to him that she wouldn't feel demeaned? That there was nothing wrong about a woman wishing for her own satisfaction? She didn't know the answer to that. And she was loathe to bring the subject up. She sighed heavily. Perhaps things would improve. After all, this time had been a slight improvement over the last time. If she just continued to try taking it a bit further each time, perhaps he would get the urge to reciprocate. She fell restlessly asleep.

The next morning, Kit acted particularly loving. He gave the impression that he was quite happy with the ways things had progressed the previous night. In fact, he even spoke with her about the possibility of a baby.

"Lily, we're getting along so well now. After our long chat following your flu scare, I feel we've crossed over any difficulties we had. Last night was heaven to me, darling. I'm wondering if there could be any chance that you might fall pregnant as a result of such a splendid night of love-making."

"Oh, Kit, I hadn't thought about that. I'd have to count back and see whether it was a promising time. You've never mentioned children to me before. Of course, I want a baby, but I thought you wanted to wait to make certain that Kit wouldn't feel left behind with a new baby in the nursery. Do you think he's ready for such a big change in his life? It would mean learning to share, and he's not had any experience with that. He's never even had much exposure to playing with other small children."

"I know that, but he'll be off to school in the fall, and he'll meet other children there. His days will be filled with the need to share. When he comes home, he might like a little brother or sister waiting for him."

"Well, if you think it's time, I really have no problem with the idea of a pregnancy," she answered. "I wonder if my body has fully recovered from its terrible ordeal and is ready to go through the demands that having a baby would put on it?"

"Why don't you consult a physician?" Kit suggested.

"Do you mind if it's John?" Lily asked.

"No, Lily. Not if that's what you prefer. I was wrong to tell you that you shouldn't see John if you have a question or problem. After all, he saved your life. How could I possibly refuse to have him as our physician?"

"Thank you, Kit. I do appreciate that attitude. I'll ring for an appointment, and get his approval for a pregnancy." Lily stepped over and kissed him, as he was about to go to his own rooms and call for Michael to shave him.

He smiled at her and left the room, leaving Lily a bit confused. She wasn't one hundred percent certain that she was ready for a baby. It hadn't been foremost in her mind. But, she did love children, and had indeed hoped that she and Kit would have them. Perhaps, a baby was exactly what she needed to do away with the feelings she'd been experiencing since her illness. A baby would be a tiny being to which she could devote a lot of attention and love. The more she considered Kit's suggestion, the more enticing it became. She intended to ring John as soon as she finished dressing, and she did just that. She was able to make an appointment in two days. Lily joined Kit at the breakfast table and shared the news with him. He smiled broadly and was obviously pleased.

"Lily, there's another subject that I've been wanting to bring up to you, but so much has happened that it's been hard to find the proper time. Now that you're well, and we're considering a baby, I think we're in need of two new hires."

"Really, Kit? What do you have in mind?" Lily asked.

"I feel strongly that you should have a ladies' maid, and I've begun to think that a nanny would be wise now."

"A nanny?" But, you were always so opposed to that. Why now?"

"Because, you'll be busy with other projects, such as the new hospital, and it would be selfish of me to expect you to devote all of your time and attention to another woman's child. In addition, if another baby is added to the nursery, you would absolutely have to have help."

"Kit, I'm not opposed to a nanny. In fact I think it's probably a good idea. With Win being able to run anywhere he wants in the house, Lord only knows what sort of mischief he could find himself in. But, please don't ever again refer to him as another woman's child. I have known Win since birth. I was the first person, besides the doctor, to hold him in my arms. I love him just as much as I could ever love a child I gave birth to. I am his Mummy, and that's all there is to that."

"I apologize, Lily. That was a foolish thing for me to say. You've been the most wonderful mother in the world to Win. I know that. Forgive me. I don't even know why I said it."

"That's fine, Kit. I'm not angry, but it surprised me. Anyway, to go back to your suggestion, yes, I'm completely in favor of both a ladies' maid and a nanny. I do want to make certain you understand that I want to have a say in who the people we hire will be."

"Well – that's a bit out of the ordinary. But, if that's your wish, I don't see any reason why I can't grant it. After all, it will be your ladies' maid, and I think you probably will have a better sense of who'll be the proper nanny." Lily heaved a sigh of relief. Things were going more smoothly than before. She had expected Kit to balk at her wanting to have a say in who was hired. He did seem to have altered his views on some of the positions he'd been so doggedly firm about before. She remembered that she had one other thing on her mind, and it needed to be discussed.

"Kit, remember back before we were married, when you said that Eleanor's parents were going to plan a trip to England this summer? It's already July, and I wonder if you've heard anything from them? Otherwise, should I, or you, be writing to them?"

"Oh, God, Lily. Yes, I did have a letter from her father. I'm so sorry. I completely forgot in all of the worry and anxiety there's been of late. I should have told you. Mr. Evans wrote quite a decent sort of letter, which came right when you fell ill. It was a very cordial piece of writing. His name is Chad Evans. I believe 'Chad' is the name they use for men who are named Charles in America. Or one of them. Anyway, the letter said that Chad and his wife, Dorothy, would be coming to England in August. They'll be visiting friends in London, and plan on getting in touch then. Of course, their primary interest is meeting Win. I suppose it's only proper that we invite them to stay at Claybourne Court, though it doesn't please me. From what I recall, they're very nice people – how they ever raised Eleanor is another question. Although now that I think of it, I think she was spoiled rotten. In the event, I have no real difficulty with their pending visit. I just hope that they don't have ideas about trying to negotiate some sort of agreement whereby Win would spend some part of the year in America."

"Oh, Kit, he's far too young for that. I absolutely refuse to consider putting him on a ship and sending him abroad. Even if he were accompanied by a nanny, I don't like the idea at all. When he's older – say in his teens - he can decide for himself. Otherwise, I feel strongly that if they want to be a part of his life, they'll have to make trips to England for the next many years. My goodness. He doesn't even know them, Kit. And if he does meet them, and like them, that's one thing, but to send him that far away from home with virtual strangers is quite another. Please don't let them coerce you into any such arrangement," Lily implored.

"No Lily, I agree wholeheartedly. I can't imagine that they wouldn't understand our thinking. They have other children. I'll put it to them whether or not *they* would let a four year old travel across the pond to people he didn't really know well. No good parent would allow such a thing. But, sweetheart, we're probably getting ahead of ourselves. We have no idea that they'll request any sort of arrangement. Once they meet Win, and realize that he has very little memory of Eleanor, that should do it."

"Don't be too sure of that, Kit. His not remembering Eleanor could have a reverse effect. They may be very upset that their grandson doesn't even remember his biological mother. That could give them more impetus to want him to know about her – to know where she grew up, and so forth. They might think that if he could spend a summer with them, or some such thing, he would grow to love her memory. Of course, it wouldn't be the real Eleanor, but that isn't an issue to be discussed with them."

"Lily, when you put it that way, I can almost guarantee you're correct. So, what's the answer? Do we begin to remind Win of Eleanor?"

"No. I don't want that, Kit. It would only confuse him. I think we should just let things take their natural course. When they arrive, we'll allow Win to get to know them, as we should. After all, he is their grandson. But it's a far leap from that to agreeing that he be allowed to travel abroad."

There was silence for a moment, and then Lily spoke again. "Kit, I have a thought. Of course, Win is enrolled already at *Beaudesert Park School* for the autumn, but it's the summers I'm concerned about. That's when the Evans' might be likely to want him to visit them in America. Since Win is showing interest in horseback riding, I think we should definitely encourage that activity. Then, let's look into what schools or camps are available for children who have a love of horses. That way, if the subject is broached, there will be the answer that Win is already committed to an activity during the summer months."

That's brilliant, Lily. I'm going to look into buying a pony today, and we'll absolutely encourage his riding. He should be a fine horseman anyway, since as the heir to Claybourne Court, it will be expected of him. I'll also speak with Eden at the stables, and make certain he's keenly aware of our wishes."

"All right, Kit. That's a plan. Goodness, we have so many things happening all at once. I need to make certain I pace myself, as I don't want any relapse."

"Lily, if you don't think you're fit to have guests, I shall by happy to tell the Evans the truth. I can meet them for lunch or dinner in London and have done with it."

"Oh, no Kit. I think that would be terribly unkind. Obviously, they're coming all of this way to meet their grandson. Even if you took Win along for a dinner or lunch, that isn't what they're hoping for. They deserve to spend a bit of time with him. After all, it isn't their fault that your marriage to Eleanor was a failure and that she ended up meeting such a ghastly end. Also, they'll want to visit her grave. They must be allowed to visit Claybourne Court."

"You're right," as usual, He smiled. I wonder how long they plan on visiting."

"I would assume at least a week, and it could be up to a month." Lily shuddered. "Kit, you don't think we need plan a formal dinner party in their honor, do you?"

"I can't imagine that they would have a whit of interest in meeting any of our friends. But, I can write and ask if that's something that might interest them."

"All Right. Well, dear, I have some notes to write, and if you're going to look into that pony, you'd best be at it," Lily smiled. They kissed one another goodbye and she retreated to her sitting room.

10

When Lily visited John's office the following day, he gave her a complete physical examination. He could find nothing amiss, and pronounced that there were no ill effects from her dreadful flu attack. He could not tell her whether or not she was pregnant, which she had expected. He told her he could see no reason why she shouldn't get pregnant, although ideally, he would like to see her wait just a while longer. Her body had suffered an awful trauma, and he wanted to see her completely back to full strength. He said that if she happened to be pregnant, he wasn't concerned, but if she wasn't, not to purposely try to make it happen.

"I always prefer to see these things happen naturally, anyway. When a couple starts 'working' at it, sometimes the stress interferes. Just, relax, and when your body is ready, you'll conceive."

Lily was happy to take his advice, and rather hoped that she would have a few more months before she had to worry about being confined with a pregnancy.

Kit had an adorable Shetland pony delivered four days later. It was dark brown, with a white mane and was the perfect size for a boy of Win's age. He immediately named his pony 'Bean', which no one could make head nor tail of, but he liked it. After a bit, she became 'Beanie." Every day, he raced down to the stables, and Howard put him on his pony. Kit bought him a riding habit, and he began to learn to ride like a proper English boy. Lily adored the way he looked in his hard hat, jodhpurs, and high, leather boots. It was obvious that he felt very grown-up. Kit began to put aside time to ride with him at least a few times a week. At that early stage, he was still limited to the riding ring inside of the paddock. Eventually, Howard wanted to teach him to jump, but he wasn't rushing it. Lily made a point to ride with him in the ring quite often. Howard said he showed signs of becoming a fine horseman, which made both Lily and Kit proud.

August was upon them before they realized it. Another letter arrived from the United States, telling Kit and Lily that the Evans would be arriving on the twelfth. Lily went into action, making certain that Mrs. Briggs had a guestroom ready for them and planning meals that she thought would appeal to Americans. She had no idea how sophisticated these people were. Kit said that they weren't exactly country bumpkins, but that they weren't exactly polished gentry either. So, Lily took her cue from what Kit knew. Kit asked via post if they were at all interested in letting the Claybourne's host a lovely formal dinner for them while they visited in *Claybourne -on-Colne*. In the next letter, Chad Evans said that he didn't think they were interested in such a fuss. He made it clear that they were coming to visit because they wanted to get to know their grandson, and because they wanted to visit Eleanor's grave. Lily was pleased that they were only interested in a quiet visit. She had never overseen a large, formal dinner, and knew that the time would come, but she didn't necessarily want it to be when Eleanor's parents were visiting. Kit and Lily tried to prepare Win for meeting his grandparents. They explained to him that they were very nice people, who were traveling all the way from America to meet him. They also told him that they were Eleanor's Mummy and Daddy. He said he didn't remember Eleanor. So they sat him down for a chat.

"Win, don't you remember that before Lily became your Mummy, there was another lady, with very pretty long, light hair, who was your Mummy?" Lily asked.

"Oh, yes. She pinched me. And I think she kicked me too."

Oh gracious, what if he popped out with such a remark in front of his grandparents?

"Win, your first Mummy, Eleanor, didn't mean to hurt you. She just didn't know very much about raising a little boy. She did love you, Win, in her own special way."

"I didn't like her special way. I didn't like her."

"Win, son, you didn't really know her very well. That's when Lily was still taking care of you in the nursery. She was your nanny, and your Mummy was gone from home a lot."

"I always loved my now Mummy better," he replied.

"Thank you, Win. And I've always loved you so much. But, you need to understand that as much as I would have liked it, I didn't actually give birth to you. Do you know what that means?" Lily asked.

"Yes. It means a baby comes out of a Mummy's tummy. The baby grows there."

"Yes, that's absolutely correct. Well, you didn't grow in my tummy. You grew in Eleanor's, tummy."

"So, Daddy got married to the other Mummy, and then she had me put in her tummy, and then 'Ba' took care of me before she got to be my real Mummy?"

"That's pretty much the way it went, Son." Kit smiled. "Do you remember that Eleanor was killed?"

"Sort-of. Someone hurt her. Someone hated her, and I don't blame them. I did too."

"Win, little chap, one should never hate anyone. Eleanor, your other Mummy had some pretty bad problems. She didn't seem very nice at times, but she never meant to hurt you," Kit tried to explain. "You need to try to forgive her."

"Okay, I'll try, but I'm not sure I can."

"Well, just try your hardest," Lily replied. The important thing for you to understand is that she had you in her tummy and gave you life. That's a pretty important thing for anybody. If it weren't for Eleanor, you might not even be here."

"Why do we have to talk about all of this?" Win asked.

"Because Eleanor's Mummy and Daddy are coming here to Claybourne Court for a visit. They want to meet you."

"What if I don't want to meet them? Will they give me cuddles like Granmummy Morris and Grandpa Will?

I think it would be a big surprise if they didn't.," Lily replied.

" I love them. I love Grandmother Cynthia too. They all give me cuddles."

"It will be exciting to meet them, don't you think?" asked Kit.

"I guess. If I like them. They better not pinch me."

"No – no more pinching. Let's try to forget about the pinching, Win," Kit implored.

"I'll try. But, you try being pinched all the time, and see if you forget it."

Kit and Lily had to try hard to keep from smiling. "It's really not very polite to talk about pinching in front of visitors, Win, so let's try to keep that a subject you only speak of to us," Lily suggested.

"Okay, I'll try," he mumbled.

With that conversation behind them, they waited rather impatiently for the arrival of the Evans. Lily scarcely knew what to expect. She considered leaving it all to Kit, and disappearing from the scene. A sleep-over at her Mum's for a week, or even a trip to London, perhaps with Gena. But, Kit wouldn't hear of her leaving her own home because his former wife's parents were paying a visit. If they weren't happy with the fact that he had married a little over a year after Eleanor's murder, they would have to learn to deal with it. Kit was fully prepared to tell them the truth about what had transpired during his marriage to Eleanor. He hoped it didn't come to that, as he had no desire to hurt them, nor to become embroiled in an argument.

On August the twelfth, a large Rolls Royce, driven by a chauffeur, pulled into the Claybourne Court graveled drive. Kit and Lily walked out to the front of the house to greet them. Of course it was Eleanor's parents. Kit had met them previously, so naturally Lily let him take the lead. Inside of the house, they had Win dressed in his Eton suit ready to meet his grandparents.

When the Evans' stepped out of the car, Chad, Eleanor's father, immediately reached out and shook Kit's hand. He was a good looking man, in an unpolished, but virile sort of way. Large but not fat, he had a thick head of silver hair, a rather prominent nose and a friendly smile. He was dressed in what Lily would have termed 'American Western Apparel," which included brown slacks, a giant belt with what looked like some sort of crest on it, an

American sport jacket, and strange-looking boots. They weren't like anything Lily had seen before. They certainly weren't like English leather riding boots, nor did they resemble the boots the men in the war had worn, which had strings that laced up and tied. These had pointed toes, and a scrolled design on the leather, with scallops at the top. His shirt was white, but it had snaps instead of buttons, and his tie looked like those that the Quakers wore in the 1800's. Still, she liked him immediately. After shaking hands with Kit, he immediately walked to Lily and engulfed her in a huge embrace.

"Well, aren't you just the prettiest little thing," he bellowed, in the same, drawling accent that had marked Eleanor's speech. Lily was a bit undone. He turned round and introduced his wife, and Lily immediately knew where Eleanor had inherited her beauty. Dorothy Evans was an older version of her daughter. She had the same blonde hair, worn a tad too long for a woman her age, and she wore a very youthful dress, with a tiny waistline. Having borne several children didn't seem to have caused her to lose her lovely silhouette. She was equally as friendly as Chad, although Lily sensed the same thing she had in Eleanor - a lack of sincerity and a personality overflowing with self-esteem. In short, she loved herself.

One of the first things she said to Lily was "I'm sure you didn't expect me to look so young. Everyone is always surprised when they meet me. I still menstruate, which is probably why I look so youthful." How did one respond to such a statement? Lily certainly didn't know. She tried to smile pleasantly and let the comment pass.

"We're very glad to see you here at Claybourne Court. Did you have a pleasant trip from London?" Kit asked.

Chad threw his arm over Kit's shoulder, and they strolled toward the house. Lily lagged behind with Dorothy. All she could think about was what a long visit it was going to be. The Evans' had been fitted out with the Rolls Royce and chauffeur by their friends in London. Kit suggested that the driver take the car around to the carriage house, and that he would ring for Edward to take care of it. Then, Ian, the Evans' chauffeur would be shown to the servant's wing.

"I think we have everything, then," Kit remarked, as he led the way to the Great House.

"Oh, my. There's just nothin' I love more than a man who has every thin'," Dorothy drawled, as she flitted up the steps to the house.

Lily winced. The moment the foursome entered the door, Win was waiting for them, and Dorothy went bonkers.

"Oh my Lord Almighty. Is this my precious Eleanor's little angel? Your name is Win, isn't it? You look just like your Mama. I'm your Meme. That's what you're to call me, you adorable, little boy. I look too young to be a grandmother, so I would like you to call me Meme. Now come here, and let me give you a giant hug."

Win shied back and went to Lily. He stood behind her skirt and held on to it.

"I'm sorry Mrs. Evans. Win is a bit shy. He's not used to strangers. You'll have to excuse him. I'm sure he'll warm up to you soon."

"Oh, that's quite all right. I understand children. He so reminds me of Eleanor. Of course I look just like her, so he may think he's seein' a ghost." She went to him and bent down. "Win, I'm not your Mama. She died, darlin' boy. But, I'm her mother, and I'll just bet that I look a lot like her, don't I?" Lily and Kit both silently shuddered.

"I don't 'member," answered Win.

"Do you mean to tell me that you don't remember your own beautiful Mama?"

"Mrs. Evans, I don't believe Win understands what the word 'Mama' means. We don't use that much in England. Here we use 'Mummy'," said Lily.

"Oh, please call me Dorothy, Lady Claybourne." She pronounced it Dar-a-thee. "All right, Win, don't you remember your beautiful Mummy, Eleanor?"

"Win looked at the ground. "Un uh," he shook his head sideways.

Then he glanced up at Kit and Lily. They were both silent, fearing what might come next. Kit tried changing the subject, by asking them if they would like a cocktail.

Chad said "You betcha," and the two men walked over to the bar cart.

Dorothy Evans continued to pound away at Win's lack of memory. "Well, my sweet darlin', there just can't be any way in the world that you've forgotten my dear Eleanor. I'll bet she held you and rocked you, and gave you lots of kisses."

"Un uh," Kit repeated. There was silence again, while he continued to hide behind Lily, and then he finally spoke. "She pinched me. That's all I 'member. She didn't like me."

Dorothy Evans' face turned bright red. "What in the world is this boy sayin'? She pinched him? Why, that's the silliest thing I've ever heard in my life. That's a naughty thing for you to say about your own, sweet Mummy," she scolded Win.

Apparently he picked up on her tone of voice, and before Lily could intervene, he began to cry and shout.

"She did so pinch me. Ask my Daddy. She pinched me all over, all the time. Daddy made her go away from here, cause she was hurting me. She kicked me too, and told me I was a brat."

Lily was amazed that he remembered so much detail. None of it had ever been spoken about in front of him.

"I am so sorry Mrs. Evans'. We had hoped that Win had forgotten those incidents. Apparently he hasn't. I wasn't here at the time, so perhaps you should speak with my husband about them. But, I *can* tell you that Win is telling the truth. I would prefer, however, that this subject not be spoken of in front of our son," Lily stated.

"*Your* son? Well, no wonder he doesn't remember Eleanor. You've tried to take her place in his little, bitty heart."

"No, no. On the contrary, I've only continued to love him as much as I have from the day he was born. I was the one into whose arms the doctor placed him when Eleanor gave birth. Please excuse me, but I'm going to have Mrs. Briggs, our housekeeper, take Win to the nursery. He's upset, and I don't want to add to it." Win was crying even harder.

'Ba' is my Mummy now. She's never been mean to me. Not ever. My first Mummy was bad. I hated her," he screamed. Win broke away, and ran up the stairs to the nursery. Lily excused herself and said that she had to make certain that he was all right. She followed after him. That left Kit to deal with the Evans'.

"I'm terribly sorry that your first introduction to Win didn't go well, "Kit began. "He's known Lily from birth. She was his nanny, and he scarcely knew Eleanor. I feel I have to be totally honest with both of you, but please understand that I'm telling you the truth, and I have no desire whatever to hurt you. But, if you're to have a relationship with your grandson, then I think you have to face reality."

"What reality," Chad asked, as he moved to place his arm around his wife's waist.

"Why don't we all sit down here in the drawing room and make ourselves comfortable. Dorothy, would you care for a drink before I explain everything?"

"I think I'd better. I'd like a bourbon and branch."

"What"? Asked Kit.

"Darlin', I don't think they know what 'branch water' is over here. How about just bourbon on the rocks?"

"Oh, Chad. These fools in England don't use ice in their drinks," she said loudly.

"Dorothy, we're well equipped with ice. If you'd like a glass of bourbon with ice in it, I can fix that up in a tick."

"That will be fine," she answered, sulkily. Chad was drinking a single malt scotch, neat.

"All right, so what's all of this nonsense about Eleanor pinching and kicking her boy," Chad asked.

"Let me try to explain, "Kit began. I'm afraid Eleanor never really wanted to have Win. She said she didn't care for babies. She told me after he was born that she didn't want to be tied down to him, and that perhaps when he was old enough to carry on an intelligent conversation, she would take more interest in him. As a result, she really just rather gave him off to Lily, when she was the nanny. Eleanor had it out with the physician because she refused to nurse, saying that it would ruin her breasts."

"Of course she said that. I taught her that myself. I've never nursed one of my children. It does completely ruin the shape of a woman's breasts. My babies always had a wet nurse at *Cloverhill.*"

"But, you see, Dorothy, there was a war on in England. Milk was in short supply. We don't have wet nurses, at least not in this part of England. The baby needed nourishment from his mother. She finally did give in, and nursed him for a bit, but it was a very short time. As soon as should could, she weaned him and put him on a bottle."

"He looks healthy enough to me. It doesn't seem to have harmed him."

"Probably not, Dorothy, probably not. At any rate, what I'm trying to get across to you is that Eleanor just didn't have any love for Win. I never heard her say she loved him. She never rocked him, or cuddled him. All of that was left to Lily."

"Were you there every minute of every day? I thought you were off fightin in the war when he was born. She may have done all of those motherly things – you just never saw her."

"No, I'm sorry Dorothy, but that just isn't the case. Lily told me, and so did our housekeeper. Actually, Eleanor told me herself. The truth is, I should never have married her, and I take full responsibility for having done so. She was a lovely girl, and I temporarily went head over heels for her. But, the moment we arrived in England everything changed. She hated it here. She refused to adhere to any of the standards the English aristocracy are expected to uphold. My mother tried to teach her our way of doing things, but it was all for naught. I *did* discover that Eleanor had been punishing Win by pinching him. Not once, and not in one place. She pinched him regularly, and I discovered black and blue marks all over his tiny body. My mother will vouch for me on this. There are also several friends of ours who saw those dreadful wounds. In addition, the same people can describe the time she purposely dropped him and then kicked him in the ribs, when he was only a tot. I could go on and on, but I should think you would understand why Win doesn't have happy memories of Eleanor."

Both of the Evans' sat with their mouths open. There was little they could argue. Dorothy tried a couple of times, to no avail.

Finally, Chad spoke up. "I suppose we have to admit that Eleanor was just spoiled to beat the band. Both of us doted on her. I was worried when she wanted to marry you, and move to England. I thought you'd make a great husband, but I knew she was very willful, and I also had heard that English people have a lot of strict rules they have to follow. I don't think the English like Americans anyway," he stated.

"If I'd had any negative feelings toward Americans, I would never have married Eleanor. I'm afraid it was rather a lark for her – marrying an English

Earl and all of that rot. I thought she would make a splendid Countess for Claybourne Court, but I was mistaken. She wasn't ready for such responsibilities."

"Would you eventually have divorced?" Dorothy asked.

"I'm afraid that's where it was heading. I really wanted our marriage to work, but when I returned from the war, with my eye missing, Eleanor showed her true colors. She called me a freak, and a monster, and said she didn't want me near her."

"'Wail' said Dorothy, which is the way she pronounced 'Well', she *was* very young to have to face something so frightening."

Kit was gritting his teeth, but he said nothing.

"Under the circumstances, I don't believe we should be putting down any stakes here at your home," interrupted Chad. "To tell the truth I don't know what to do. We have a grandchild to think about here. He has our blood in his veins. We'd hoped to grow to know him, so that in time he would come to love us."

"I understand perfectly, Chad and agree that you should get to know your grandchild. But, I think it's important that you understand why he has the feelings he does toward Eleanor. Neither Lily, nor I, wants you to leave. We, too, have been hoping that Kit would develop a bond with you. I still think he can and will. But, if you say things about Eleanor that he knows aren't true, at least from his experience, he isn't going to trust you. I think the best route to take is to try to ignore any negative comments he makes about her and let him get to know you – just you."

"Wail, I'm sorry, but I do believe that your present wife hasn't done anything to place positive memories into his baby head."

"Lily is a dear, wonderful woman. She has never said an unkind word about Eleanor. She isn't like that. If you're implying that Lily put these notions into Win's head, you're dead wrong. You're misplacing the blame here. Win's memories are solely his. He remembers what his mother did to him. That's not something that a child forgets easily, unfortunately. My hope would be that as Win grows, and has more understanding of how everything came about, he'll find it in his heart to forgive her, or at least see two sides to the story. He just turned four years in April. Give him time. In the meantime, show him love," Kit begged of them.

There was more silence, and finally, Dorothy said that she agreed. "I think it best if we stay off the subject of Eleanor. All of us. We each have our memories, and they differ greatly. But, I want to know my little grandson. So, yes, I think we should stay and try to make this work."

"Oh Dorothy, I'm most happy to hear you say that. Lily will be too. Let's have another drink, and I'll go and check on Lily and Win. I'm not going to force him, but perhaps I can coax him downstairs again."

"If it will help at all, tell the boy that his Paw Paw, which what I want to be called, and his Meme have some lovely presents for him."

"That just might do the trick, "Kit smiled. Let's see what I can manage. Help yourselves to another drink, or ring for Halsey, the butler. The buzzer is there on the wall."

11

Things settled down. Win was coaxed into coming back downstairs, and he sat for a while on Lily's lap. Dorothy stopped fawning over him, and finally the subject of presents was brought up. Win's eyes lit up, like any normal four year old boy's would.

Kit rang the carriage house, and Edward replied, asking what was needed. Kit explained that there was luggage and also some wrapped gifts in the boot of the car, and that he wished to have them brought inside. Only a few moments later, the luggage had been taken to the Evans' room, and the packages were spread out on the drawing room floor. There was also a bottle of quite excellent wine for Kit, and a large box of Pralines for Lily. She opened the box, and passed them about the room. They were delicious. The wine was a red cabernet sauvignon and Kit uncorked it, pouring each of them a glass. It was superb. Win kept eying the boxes on the floor, and then he pulled Lily's head down to his level and whispered in her ear. "Of course, you can," she replied. It was obvious that he had asked if he could open the boxes. "Pick out which one you would like to open first, and bring it over here," Lily instructed.

Win hopped down from her lap, and meandered about the packages, with his finger between his teeth, trying to make up his mind. Finally, he settled on a quite large box, wrapped with blue paper and a white ribbon. He brought it back to Lily, and she helped him unwrap it. When they took the lid off, Win had a puzzled look on his face, and then he grinned.

"It's like the American cowboys wear," he exclaimed.

His eyes were shining. Inside of the box lay a complete outfit in Win's size, including what were known as 'chaps', spurs, a shirt like his 'Paw Paw was wearing and a similar black tie. There was also a big cowboy hat. Win put on the hat, and he looked adorable. He had read stories about American cowboys and had even gone to the cinema to see some western movies. This was something not one of his little friends would own. Lily reminded him to thank the Evans and he did so, very politely. The next box he selected was smaller, but heavy. Again he brought it to Lily, and when he opened it, he discovered a pair of Western cowboy boots. Win was over-the-moon. He liked his English boots and his riding habit, but these were so very different. The third box contained a holster with artificial guns. Lily was not terribly pleased with the guns, but didn't say anything. Of course, as with most little boys, Win thought they were just wonderful. In the next box he found a twenty pound note, for him to use in purchasing a new puppy- one that could be all his own. Again, Lily wished they had asked her and Kit about the wisdom of such a gift, but when she thought about it, she really couldn't see any harm. She adored dogs and loved Ginny, their little St. Charles Spaniel. They also had two outdoor cats. 'Mousers' Kit called them. Adding another animal to the menagerie wouldn't be a problem. His grandparents promised to go with him to help pick out a fine dog. He said he wanted a Golden Retriever, which was fine with both Kit and Lily. Lastly, they'd purchased a new, Western saddle for his pony. That way, he could ride in either one of his outfits. Kit and Lily knew that this certainly meant a set-back for his English horsemanship, but there was no harm done. The gifts had managed to break the ice considerably between Win and the Evans. He even approached Chad and let him put the guns and holster on him. Lily had to warn him not to play with the guns in the house. She could just imagine Mrs. Briggs coming round a corner and seeing Win standing there with a gun. They were also going to have to explain to him the dangers of real guns, and that English people were generally not in favor of that sort of weapon. They used guns only for shooting while hunting. Those were always rifles.

Finally, Win approached Dorothy, whom he'd seemed to be more frightened of – probably because she reminded him of Eleanor. She set the cowboy hat at the proper angle on his head and told him what beautiful hair he had. He immediately said that he got it from his daddy. Dorothy's mouth formed a straight line for a moment, but then she let it pass. Win set about putting on the entire outfit, while everyone helped and watched. Then, Chad made a remark that sent Kit reeling.

"Well, young Win, did you know that your Paw Paw has a great, big, horse ranch in America? I have twenty-three thoroughbred horses, of all sizes and colors. Our house is named '*Cloverhill*', and it's one of the biggest stables in the United States. We go horseback riding every day. Sometimes, we even go on overnight camping trips with the horses. We sleep outside, under the stars, and eat food we prepare out of doors. It's just a good, ole time."

Win looked amazed. "Twenty-three horses? Gosh. I never knew people had so many," he said. "I sure wish I could go on a camp-out overnight."

"Wail, perhaps someday you can, sweet boy. Maybe your parents would let you come over to America and stay with us on our ranch?" Dorothy said, coaxingly.

"Oh, Dorothy, what a lovely idea. But, Win's much too young for anything like that. He couldn't board a ship and cross the Atlantic Ocean," Lily remarked.

"Wail, I don't really see why not. Doesn't he have a nanny?"

"No, not yet. In fact, we're just in the process of hiring one. But, what difference would that make?" Lily asked.

"Wail, my dear. Couldn't his nanny accompany him on a transatlantic trip? It's done all of the time by Americans."

"Oh, my, well, I think that's something we would have to think about long and hard. I'd be worried sick about him, to tell you the truth."

"Why would you be worried about him? Surely you could trust his nanny to watch over him. We would be happy to pay his fare."

"Well, we have one difficulty, where that sort of thing is concerned. We already have Kit enrolled in a summer program for horseback riding, in the hope that he will someday become a great English horseman," Kit spoke up.

"Where could he better get experience with horses?" Chad asked. "I realize you want to concentrate on English riding. Well, we can provide that too. We've had horses of ours run in the Kentucky Derby. Our trainer and our jockeys could see that he develops wonderful skills."

Kit and Lily were dumbfounded. Their plan had backfired in an enormous way. Why hadn't they remembered about the Evans ranch, and their reputation with horses? It appeared that they had run out of excuses. Lily tried one, last thing.

"I think Win would be frightened to be so far from home, with strangers, or practically strangers. He would be completely out of his element. Things are done differently in America. What if he were to become desperately homesick?"

"We would deal with it. If it became a true problem, wail, we'd send him on home," exclaimed Dorothy. She turned her attention to Win. "Sweet boy, would you rather spend your summers in America on our ranch, with lots of other children to play with, who are your cousins, and meet your aunts and uncles, than to spend it at some silly riding camp in England?" It was obvious what Win's response would be.

"In America. Going on camping trips and sleep-outs. Oh, Daddy and Mummy, could I do that?" he asked, practically whining.

"We'll have to think about that, Win. Daddy isn't certain that he wants you to be so far away from him for so long," Kit replied.

He wished these damned people would shut their mouths. It was beginning to look like he and Lily were stuck. Finally, Mrs. Briggs showed the Evans to their rooms- a lovely bedchamber and a nice-sized sitting room, with an adjoining bath. Mrs. Briggs had taken it upon herself to unpack their luggage, and to hang everything appropriately. She had folded and put other items away in drawers. Lily had made certain that there were fresh flowers in their rooms. By the time they all retired, Win was feeling much friendlier and even allowed a cuddle and a goodnight kiss from each of them.

When Kit and Lily got to their own room, they sat on the side of the bed and simply stared at one another. Things had not gone the way they'd hoped. Not at all. Of course, they wanted Win to develop warm feelings for his grandparents, but the idea of giving him up for entire summers was overwhelming. He would be going away to school when he was thirteen – to

Eton – and both of his parents wanted to share as much of his life as they could. These years were so important, and changes took place so rapidly. Neither wanted to miss out on milestones in their son's life. At least they didn't have to make a decision about such a journey until the following spring. It was only August now. Perhaps the trip would fade from his mind as the months rolled by.

The Evans only stayed a week, but it seemed longer to Lily and Kit. They did not mesh with Lady Cynthia at all. She'd insisted from the beginning that Win call her 'Grand'Mere," which was quite a far way from Meme and Paw Paw. Cynthia was not *really* a full-fledged snob, but she came close. She'd lived her entire life in England, and had never cared for Americans. She thought they were all savages. When Chad Evans embraced her upon their meeting, everyone held their breath that Cynthia wouldn't faint. Actually, she handled it quite well, considering her innate feelings. But, there would never be any love lost between the grandparents on the mother's side, and the Grand'Mere on the father's. It wasn't a horrendous visit. Just one of those sort that one is glad to have ended. The only real problem was the influence that they had on Win. Both Lily and Kit worried about what being around them for a two or three month period would do to him. They talked it over at length, and decided to let it rest until nearer the time that such a probability became reality. Win would be starting school in one month, and a good gauge would-be how he handled being away from home all day long.

When it came time for the Evans to leave, Kit and Lily promised to give their suggestion serious thought, and told them that they would keep in touch. Before they could even contemplate something like sending Win abroad for a summer at such a young age, they needed to hire a nanny and see how he took to her. Dorothy and Chad were in agreement and said that they would write to Win often. They didn't want him to forget them and would also keep Win and Lily abreast of things. They also promised to send photos of their ranch and their horses. When the door closed, and the big, chauffeur-driven Rolls Royce departed, Lily and Kit looked at one another with utter relief. By the time they left, Win had become a doting grandchild, following them wherever they went. After the departure, he spoke of them every day. It was difficult to believe that he would ever forget his great desire to go to America to visit them. His parents discussed it from every angle, after he was in his bed at night. Part of the time, they thought that it would be all right for him to undertake such a journey. The other part of the time, they were dead set against it. It would be easier when the Evans were back on their side of the pond, and Lily and Kit were on theirs.

September arrived and Win had his first day of school at *Beaudesert*. Lily accompanied him, while Edward drove. It was milestone event. Lily was certain that her little boy would want her to come into the school with him, but that wasn't to be. When they arrived, Win just crawled out of the back seat, and said "Goodbye, Mummy and Edward. I'll see you this afternoon. Don't forget to collect me," and off he trudged into the building. *Beaudesert Park's* main building was set into thirty acres of lovely land in the Cotswold Hill region. It was built as a private home in the late 1800's for a wealthy London widow, and was in the traditional English style, with half timbers, and beautiful oak interior. Lily could see other little boys playing out-of-doors, and while utterly thrilled that Win had taken his first big leap from home so nonchalantly, her heart ached at the casualness with which he waved goodbye.

Returning to Claybourne Court, she changed clothing, and went for a horseback ride. It seemed very lonely in the house without her little boy. Later in the day, she would be interviewing a candidate for a ladies' maid and another for a nanny. Halsey and Mrs. Briggs had spoken to both previously and felt strongly that these two women were perfect for the openings at Claybourne Court. The ladies' maid had moved to Claybourne Court after the war, when her parents had decided upon a move to the country. They were simple people, who farmed the land. The young lady's name was Ruth Nelson, and she had already served in the position of Ladies' Maid at another Country House for two years. She brought an excellent letter of recommendation.

The prospect for the position of nanny sounded perfect. Her name was Emma Church. She came from a wealthy family in Essex, and had attended a school for nannies in London. Her ultimate goal was to open her own private school for young children. Mrs. Briggs and Halsey had a very high opinion of her and believed that Lily would as well. It turned out they were correct on both counts. The moment Lily met each, she felt that they were meant to find positions with the Claybourne's. Even better, both were available immediately, so Lily set a starting date for the following Monday, which allowed some time for any preparation that was called for. They were introduced to the other staff members, and everyone agreed that they were excellent choices who would fit in well. Kit was a bit put out that Lily had not at least given him the last word on hiring. But, Lily made it clear that these two ladies would be within her sphere at Claybourne Court – one attending to her own personal needs – and the other in the nursery, where Lily still spent a good deal of time. Kit finally acquiesced, and no more was said about it. Win returned from his school at about half after three in the afternoon filled with chatter about the other boys and his teacher, Mrs. Fraser. He already loved *Beaudesert*, and was over-the-moon that they had stables and a riding instructor. He changed his clothing, and immediately ran to the stables to see his pony, Bean.

For the next few weeks things went smoothly at Claybourne Court. Of course there were worries about the usual things that people ruminate over in every household, but nothing terribly upsetting. Both the new ladies' maid, Ruth, and the nanny, Emma, fit in beautifully, and there was no question that they were a great addition to the household. They got along very well with the others on staff, and performed their tasks to perfection. Win liked Emma a lot, primarily because she wasn't terribly strict with him, and liked to play the games he liked. Win began receiving letters from Meme and Paw Paw in Virginia, and he eagerly awaited them. He loved to come home from school to find one waiting. Lily would read the letter aloud, and it would excite him greatly. He continued to talk about the fact that he was going to America in the summer. Lily and Kit continued to be vague with their replies. Lily helped him write letters back to them, and all were filled with excitement about coming to see them. They explained the situation to Emma, so she would know not to overly encourage his dream of an ocean voyage, and kept hoping that after school continued, he would meet other little boys with whom he would rather spend time during the summer months.

Lily and Kit's lovemaking did not improve, but Lily reached the point where she just accepted it for what it was. She'd never known any different sort of love, and it didn't seem worth rocking the boat. She didn't even discuss it with Gena, as she was somewhat embarrassed and knew that her best friend would recommend that she speak up and demand that Kit learn better techniques. Lily couldn't imagine doing so. Gena and John had a very different marriage, and it wouldn't have been at all awkward for her to have gone to her husband about something so intimate. Lily envied her in that regard.

She *was* growing to know her husband better. Kit opened up to her more about his school days and his boyhood. Apparently, he'd had quite a wild spell while at Oxford his first year. Not unlike many boys that age, he'd done his share of drinking and party-going and had also taken a six week tour of Italy. He always seemed reticent to speak about that trip, and Lily couldn't understand why, because she'd always longed to visit that lovely, historical country, and was fascinated to hear about his experiences there. But on that subject, Kit was rather tight-lipped. She sensed that perhaps he hadn't enjoyed himself very much, or had experienced some unpleasant incident. Lily dropped the subject. It wasn't that important, and Kit was entitled to his privacy. After all, she still had never told him about her trip to Paris with the other doctors and nurses on furlough during the war. Not that there was much to tell – certainly Lily wasn't involved with any man- but, she knew her husband's strict moral code, and knew that he would never have approved of a 'lady' traveling to Paris with a group of other unmarried people of both genders.

Lily attended her first hospital Board meeting, and honestly enjoyed it. The others present listened to her thoughts, and she didn't feel that they were simply being polite because her last name was Claybourne. The proposed hospital was going to be an incredible addition to *Claybourne-on-Colne*. It was important to her that it be planned with the utmost care and consideration for patient's comfort and care. It would be a seventy-five bed facility, which was considered large for a village the size of *Claybourne-on-Colne*. Each room would be private. Lily involved herself in every aspect of the planning, from the actual structure and its layout, to how many nurses and doctors would be needed, and the type of food facility that should be considered. She suggested a special floor for maternity patients, and all thought it a splendid idea. They went a step further, and made one entire wing a gynecological addition, which she knew women would particularly favor. In her heart, there were times when she wished she could be practicing at the new facility, but of course, that was out of the question. She and Kit had already had that conversation. Always upper most in her mind was that she never consider doing anything to besmirch the family name. Kit was proud of what she was accomplishing with the Hospital Planning Board, and praised her often. So did 'Mother Claybourne'.

Lily made certain that she kept in touch with her own mother and step-father and frequently invited them to dinner. They were very happy together, and Lily was so relieved that her Mum had found such a wonderful man. Will was obviously madly in love with Elisabeth, and it was so good to have worries about her Mum off Lily's mind. Of course, there were frequent questions from her mother about when she could expect a grandchild, and Lily did admit that they were not doing anything that would prevent her becoming pregnant, but it just didn't seem to happen. Her Mum always patted her hand and said "God acts in his own time." Lily believed that too, and was not upset that she hadn't fallen with child yet. It seemed that there had been so much to accustom herself to during that first year of marriage that she was almost happy she didn't have to worry about a baby too. The latest addition to the family had been a beautiful Golden Retriever puppy named 'Chelsea', since that is where they bought her, from an excellent breeder. It was a lot of fun having a puppy, and Ginny, the St. Charles Spaniel welcomed her sister with no difficulty. Win explained, in a very grown-up fashion, that dogs were pack animals and that they always needed one of their own kind as companions. Kit and Lily smiled at each other, as Win was busy waxing eloquently upon the needs of canines, while petting Chelsea.

All of that summer, Lily continued her rides to the area on the estate where the tenant farmers dwelled. She didn't say anything about her visits to Kit, because she knew he wouldn't approve. She simply couldn't help herself. Now that she knew where these people lived, she was almost obsessed with wanting to help them in some way. At first, they all seem wary of her, but in time, one by one, the women warmed to her. Finally, Mrs. Gunderson, whom she had met on that first day, when she'd discovered the tenant houses, gathered together a group of other wives and introduced them to Lily. From then on, when she went to visit, they all met and enjoyed tea together. They discovered that Lilly was, indeed, just like them in a lot of ways. In turn, Lily learned a lot about their lives. Most couldn't read or write, so she took along books and began teaching them. She made notes about which home had special needs, and what she could do to improve their living conditions. One interesting thing that came out of her visits was Lily's learning that the women in the tenant homes didn't tell their husbands that she visited, as they knew the men wouldn't approve of their wives mixing with the gentry. Lily told them that she had the same problem, in reverse. They had a good laugh about it.

After a lovely summer and autumn, everything in the Claybourne's world changed. It might as well have been an earthquake, for it altered their placid existence in the blink of an eye, and nothing was ever the same again.

12

Lily was relaxing in her bedchamber, reading a new book. She'd had little time for such pleasures of late, what with Win's school, the Hospital Planning Board, the hiring and training of Ruth and Emma, and her secret forays to the tenant farms. It was a chilly November day, and there was a lovely fire roaring in her fireplace. She was interrupted when Halsey knocked on her door, and entered.

"Sorry to disturb you Milady, but we have a visitor. I'm not certain about how to properly handle this."

"What on Earth, Halsey . . .?"

"Well, you see, it's a young lady – quite young. About fifteen or so. She says she walked here from the station. She isn't dressed for this weather at all – a light frock, what there is of it," he said, in a rather disapproving tone. "She has no coat or hat on. Just a white scarf covering her head. She rather resembles a gypsy, Milady."

"Whatever does she want at Claybourne Court?" Lily asked.

"That's the difficulty, Milady. She won't tell me. She assured me that there is a valid reason for her to speak to the Lord or Lady, and that she simply cannot, and will not, leave until she has seen one or the other of you.

She seems foreign, in that she speaks English, but with an accent. I can't make out what she says half of the time."

Lily placed her book face down on the chaise, and stood up.

"Don't bother with it, Halsey. I'll handle it. She's probably a poor beggar girl, perhaps seeking employment. I'll see her in Kit's library."

Lily proceeded down the stairway, and made her way to the paneled room, where she sat down behind Kit's desk. A few moments later, Halsey showed a young, underweight waif into the room. She was dressed in a very short frock. Lily supposed it was an attempt to look current, as it was styled in a 'flapper' design, cheaply made and very dirty. Her hair was quite long, and very dark. Nearly black, and she had very dark eyes, the color of black olives. Her skin was lovely, with Mediterranean coloring, and she had a pretty mouth, with full lips. Her hair didn't look like it had been washed in weeks, and she was much too thin.

Halsey made the introduction. "Lady Claybourne, this is Miss Pia Lorenza. Miss Lorenza, this is the Countess of Gloucester, Lady Claybourne." Halsey left the room. Lily smiled, as the girl stood stock still, looking around.

"Miss Lorenza, would you like to sit down?" Lily asked.

The girl glanced at Lily, and then took a seat across from the desk. She kept her hands folded in her lap. Lily couldn't help but feel sorry for her. She was really just a child.

"Would you care for some tea, or perhaps something to eat with it?" Lily asked.

"Si – yes. Something to eat will be good."

Lily rang for Mrs. Briggs, and gave instructions to bring the girl some tea, and a luncheon plate. Then she turned back to Pia. "Why have you come to Claybourne Court, Pia? Can you explain slowly to me where you are from, and what brings you here to our home?"

"Si -yes. I am Pia Lorenza. My mama is big star in Italia. But she die. She tell me if she die to come here. Lord Claybourne is – how do you say? – my *not legal* Papa."

Lily's heart plunged. Could this girl be telling the truth? Pia unfolded a grimy piece of paper from her pocket and handed it to Lily. "Here. This will tell everyting," she said.

Just then, Polly, from the kitchen, brought a large tray, with a lovely meal of roast beef stew, homemade bread, salad and tea. Lily had her put it on the round table in the library and told Pia to go right ahead and eat, while she read the piece of paper. Pia almost jumped from the chair onto one next to the table, where she tucked into the food like a starving animal. Lily observed her and told Molly to bring another serving of everything. Then she settled back and read the unkempt piece of paper, which had obviously been handled often.

It was written in quite a nice hand, with few errors. It was dated June, 1919, five months previously. It said:

"My Dear Lord Claybourne,

I am sorry for the need to be contacting you again. I know that our agreement was that I would never contact you, and I have kept to that promise. But, now everything is changed. You know how grateful I was so long ago when your father paid me such a large amount of money, to have my baby delivered by a good midwife and to raise her properly. Pia has grown into a fine girl. I am very proud of her. Unfortunately, I am a stupid woman. I should have put the money away for Pia's future, but we needed it to live. During the war, I was not able to do any acting performing's. Before that, I was very busy. I met an American man who said he wanted to marry me. This was during the war. He loved Pia, and we would have a good life. I rented a nice apartamento, so that my American friend could live with us while he was in Roma. I spent a lot of lire, to dress nice for him, and to furnish the apartamento. Well, I am broke, and now sick, and my American has gone back across the Ocean. I have a very bad disease, and am going to die. There is no money for Pia after I am gone. I have told her that you are her Papa. There was no other way. I do not want Pia wandering streets, when she has a Papa who can look after her. If I die, then you will be reading this. Pia will come to you. I pray to God and the Holy Mother that you will treat her kindly. None of what happened was Pia's fault. I beg you to care for her, and give her a start in life.

Your Humble Servant,

Maria"

Lily couldn't help but gasp. Of all of the things that had been going through her mind, this had never crossed it. My God! Kit had gotten an

Italian girl pregnant, probably when he was in Italy during that long ago break from Oxford, when he was a mere boy. The result of that foolish act now sat eating like a mad dog in their library. Lily wanted to cry, primarily for the pitiful, young girl. If she were cleaned up, and dressed properly, she would be a lovely young lady. There was no question about what they had to do. The girl's mother was right. What happened to her daughter was not Pia's fault. Damn Kit. Damn him. So there had never been a stain on the Claybourne family name? Lily wanted to laugh. Ah, what money could conceal. Kit was out riding on the property, and she didn't know when to expect him. But, she wasn't going to wait for him, and she didn't care what his thoughts were about the decision she was about to make. He was this child's father, as much as he was Win's, and Pia would be given a home, with love and all of the attention that her brother now received. Lily sat back in her chair, pretending to be re-reading the letter, in order to give Pia the chance to finish eating without feeling as though she were being stared at.

When she was finished, and the dishes had been collected, Lily asked her to come back over to the chair that was nearest the desk.

"Pia. Do you understand English quite well, or shall I attempt to speak Italian?" Lily asked.

"No, no. Speak English. I understand. I need to learn to speak better."

"All right. Let me explain what is going to happen to you. My husband and I – your Papa-are going to bring you into our family, and you will be treated as his daughter, which is how you should always have been treated. We shall give you your own bedchamber, new clothing and lots of good food, because you are too thin. I shall make an appointment with our physician so that we make certain that you are healthy. You have a little brother named 'Win', who is four years old. He will be happy to have another person in the house. A sister. We have stables, and Win has a pony. We shall make certain that you are given a pony or horse too. When you are older, you will be trained for a proper career. For now, I shall research and find a good school for you to attend – a school where you can live here at home, and you will be driven back and forth each day."

Pia sat with her mouth open, not able to take in all that Lily was telling her.

"I went to good school in Roma until Mama get sick. A Catholic school. Records can be sent by post."

"That's good, Pia. We'll ring the school and have them sent. Do you have any questions for me? I'm so sorry that you have had to go through this ordeal. I did not know about you, or I would have made certain you were all right. I'm glad you came to us. How did you come so far?" Lily asked.

"I walk, Milady."

"You walked all of the way from Rome? When did your Mama die?"

"In June. It take me five months. I sleep on farms, and under trees. I had enough money for ferry ride and train to your town."

Lily was so angry, she wished she could shake her husband. But, there were other considerations at the moment. "Pia, you needn't call me 'Milady'. My Christian name is Lily. You may feel free to use that. Our son calls me 'Mummy', but I know you loved your mother, and I don't expect that. So, will 'Lily' do for you?"

"Yes – Lily. Grazia. It is pretty name. Thank you for everyting. I will try hard not to be bother. I am good student, and make my Papa proud."

"I have no doubt of that. Now, let me take you upstairs and show you where your room will be. I shall loan you some of my clothing, and tomorrow we shall go shopping. Right now I think you need a nice bath and a good rest."

Pia smiled for the first time, and followed Lily as they climbed to the second floor. Lily walked down the hallway, and pointed out what each room was as she went along. She already knew which room she was going to give to Pia. It was Lily's old bedchamber – the one she'd had when she first came to Claybourne Court. The room was only three doors from Lily and Kit's, and very near the nursery and Win. Pia began to cry when Lily opened the door. She had never seen anything so grand. The room had a fireplace and a big four poster bed. It was still decorated in pink florals – perfect for a young girl. In addition, it had the adjoining bath, so Pia could have privacy, which Lily knew young girls needed. She showed Pia how to operate the tub and where the towels were kept. Tears kept rolling down her face. Lily stopped, and put her arms around the frail girl.

"Everything will be fine, Pia. I'm so glad you are here. I wish I had known about you sooner. We would have come to fetch you in Rome. But, you *are* here now, and you won't have to be frightened or go without anything ever again. Now get undressed and run the tub water. I'm going to dash across the hallway and find you some clothing. I won't be a tick."

Pia smiled, and hugged Lily, thanking her repeatedly. Lily could hear the water running as she thumbed through her wardrobe. Pia was much too thin, but Lily thought she was about her height. Lily's dresses were all small, so they would do until she could buy Pia her own clothing. She gathered up blouses, skirts, and several frocks, along with shoes, stockings, and underthings. She also threw in two pretty nightgowns and a robe. The poor girl didn't appear to have anything except the clothes on her back, so Lily also put toiletries, a brush, comb and toothbrush into a basket for her. She brought them all back to Pia's room, and found her standing by the tub, wrapped in a towel, waiting for Lily. Lily helped rub her dry and slipped one of the nightdresses over her head. Then, she turned down the bed covers and told Pia to slip under them. She showed her how to ring for the maid, and told her not to be frightened to knock on Lily's door if she needed her. Then, Lily bent down and kissed her and told her to sleep as long as she wished.

Lily went back to her own room and Ruth was in there, putting back some frocks she had mended. Ruth was just wonderful about keeping on top of things. She and Lily had already become quite good friends. Lily sat down and explained everything, from start to finish. She even read Ruth the letter. When she was finished, Ruth looked astonished.

"Oh my Goodness. Well, isn't this a fine kettle of fish? This just knocks the socks off me. All of these years, and that poor girl never knew her own daddy. Oh, Lady Lily. That's truly pathetic."

"Of course it is. And, I suspect that my husband's mother may have known all about this. I'm not saying that he should have married the child's mother. He was much too young for that. But, the child should have been a part of the family. She is his own flesh and blood. Just as much as Win is. Just because she was conceived on the wrong side of the blanket doesn't mean she should have had to pay the price."

"I agree, Milady. I think what you've done is very fine. I'll make certain that all of the servants know that she's to be treated as a daughter of the house. Poor thing. Well, her life will change now."

"Yes, indeed it will. I have an inkling that Kit is going to be furious with me for making all of these decisions without his input, and I don't care a whit. I don't like the decision that was made when the girl was born. And if his father made it for him, certainly Kit has grown up and has been old enough for a long time to rectify this mess."

Ruth nodded her head in agreement. "Unfortunately, Milady, I don't believe either your husband or your mother-in-law will agree with you. I know it really isn't any of my business, but I surely hope you stand your ground. Don't say I said that, please, but I'll be cheering for you."

The nice thing about having a ladies' maid was that a woman could unburden herself, and know that whatever she said would be treated with complete confidence.

"Don't you worry, Ruth. I'm in control of this situation. Now, will you please ring the Dower House, and tell Mother Claybourne that I should like to pay her a visit immediately."

Ruth did as she was asked, and Lady Cynthia said she would be delighted to have Lily visit. Lily rolled her eyes, and said "She may not be when I leave."

Ruth smiled.

Lady Cynthia opened the door to the lovely Dower House, which sat near the front gates. Lily liked it rather almost as much as she did Claybourne Court itself. It was smaller and cozier. It was not small, but manageable, with mullioned windows and a French Mansard roof. Lady Cynthia had her own household staff – not as large as at the big house. Lily was surprised that the butler didn't greet her, but was glad to see her mother-in-law alone.

"Come in, dear. What a lovely surprise. I didn't expect to see you today. To what do I owe such a pleasure?" she asked.

"May we sit down, Mother Claybourne? I have a rather disturbing bit of news," answered Lily.

Lady Cynthia looked puzzled. "Why of course, dear. I hope it's nothing serious." She led the way to the pretty drawing room, done up in shades of blue, with white accents. Lily made her way to the sofa. Lady Cynthia rang for some tea and sat down in a chair across from her daughter-in-law. "Now, what is the problem, Lily?"

"The problem, 'Mother Claybourne', is that Kit has a lovely Italian daughter, who just this morning arrived on our doorstep after spending *five* months walking from Rome. I'm appalled. The poor girl's mother, with whom Kit obviously had an affair while at Oxford, has died, and she hasn't a farthing. The mother, Maria, wrote a very nice letter, apologizing for having to *bother* Kit, but she was dying and concerned about her child. The girl's name, by the way, since you're her grandmother, is Pia Lorenza. However, it will become Pia Claybourne. I gather her mother was some sort of actress. She made it clear in the letter that your husband paid this pitiful woman a large sum of money if she would agree to stay out of Kit's life and raise the baby as a bastard. I've come here to ask if you knew anything of this."

"Well – yes, of course I did. It was a very long time ago, Lily. Kit was just a boy himself. We did what we thought was proper."

"Proper?" Lily nearly screamed. "Proper? You believe it was proper to let your own flesh and blood be raised in God knows what sort of environment, with no father, and none of the things that should have been hers by right of birth?"

"She had no right to anything. She was not Kit's legitimate daughter."

"She has as much Claybourne blood as Win does. I cannot believe that this was done."

"What do you think should have been done, Lily? Should Kit have married the girl? He was only eighteen years of age. He hadn't even completed one year at Oxford. He was on a six week break from school."

"No, I'm not suggesting that he should have married her. But, there were two other options that I can see. First, you and the late Earl might have taken the child and raised her as your own, if the mother had been willing to let that happen. Or, at the very least, Kit should have paid regular visits to the child. And, sent her regular bits of money that *he* had earned. She never had the love of a father. It wouldn't have been right to have had the child visit Claybourne Court, as I think it would have been cruel to let her see what she might have had, if only her father had married her mother. But, Kit has certainly been to Rome many times since then. Has he ever made any attempt to contact her?"

"No, of course not. That wasn't part of the arrangement."

"No, Lady Cynthia. It wasn't the 'done thing.' Isn't that the truth?"

"Yes. Of course. It would have been highly inappropriate. It was never considered."

"Well, consider this. I have brought her into our family. She is already fast asleep in what will be her bedchamber. She has bathed, and I have thrown out her only dress. I have given her some of my clothing until we can go shopping and buy her an entire wardrobe. I have told her to call Kit Papa, and me Lily, or in time, Mummy. Furthermore, she will be given everything that Win now has. A pony, education at a fine school, and the Claybourne name. I hope to see her presented at Court when she comes of age. Kit will, of course, adopt her."

"You have what?" shouted Lady Cynthia. "You had no right to make such decisions, without discussing this with Kit. That is not at all what he will want."

"Lady Cynthia. This is his child. His daughter. I don't give a fig what he wants. He will learn to love her, and to show her that love, just as he does his son."

"Well, I think you've overstepped the bounds. I'm sure, under the circumstances, Kit would agree to send her away to a fine boarding school, but to have her live in his home, as a member of the family? It's too much."

"Rubbish, Lady Cynthia. Either that is the way things will be, or I shall take this poor girl to London and live there in our townhouse with her. She is not going to go through any more pain in life at the hands of this family. If you don't want to act like a loving grandmother, I would suggest you not come to dinner with us tonight." Lily got up, and walked out of the front door, slamming it behind her.

She marched back to the house, and immediately went to her own bedchamber. She paced back and forth in front of the fireplace, stopping every few moments to look out of the window, which gave a perfect view of the back of the grounds. She would definitely see Kit when he arrived back home. It wasn't too long before that happened. However, his mother had apparently been watching for him too, and she caught him before Lily did. She saw Lady Cynthia run to Kit, and he bent his head to listen to what she was telling him. Lily could see his color rise, which clearly meant he was infuriated. Kit put his arm around his mother's shoulders and they walked together the rest of the way to the house. Lady Cynthia's mouth was working the entire time, with only brief pauses, while Kit was evidently asking questions. Finally, she patted him on the back and kissed him, as if to say that they were in agreement, and all would be well. Lily heard his footsteps as he entered the Great Hall. She came down the stairway and met him.

"Well, I understand we've had a visitor," he said in a sarcastic tone, with a sneer on his face.

"Not a visitor Kit. A new member of the family. Your daughter, Pia."

"Yes, so Mother tells me. I already know that you're very upset, Lily. I'm sorry to have caused you so much consternation, but what's done is done. I can't go back and undo it now."

No, but you can start today to make up for it," she answered. "Considering the fact that you have never had to accept any responsibility for bringing another life into this world."

"Lily, what you are proposing is utter foolishness. Do you know how many children there are in England – all over the world for that matter – who are conceived on the wrong side of the blanket? I have never in my lifetime heard of anyone taking the child in and giving him or her the family name, let alone raising the child with all of the benefits she might have had if she'd been legitimate. It simply is not the *done* thing."

"So help me, Kit, if I hear the phrase the "done thing" one more time, I shall leave this house and take Pia with me. I mean it. I have thought this over. I shall not continue to live with a person with so little feeling for his own flesh and blood. I shall take her to London, and raise her with the Claybourne name. I don't care who knows about it. I *want* the truth to come out. You're afraid of a scandal, and I promise you, that's what you'll get. This is beyond the pale. Pia is a lovely girl. My God, Kit, did your mother tell you that she walked all the way from Rome. *Walked*. For *five* months. Anything might have happened to her. She should have known you. She should have been able to contact you, so that we could have fetched her. What is the matter with the morals in this family?"

"Lily, you are completely hysterical and very irrational. Now, I want you to calm down and think about what you're saying. Do you really expect me to believe that you're going to give up everything you have here at

Claybourne Court to go and live in London, in the townhouse, with a young girl who is no relation to you? That you would disrupt our family in such a manner?"

"Damn you, Kit. *You* weren't at all opposed in any way to my living here at Claybourne Court with a young boy who was no relation to me. Why is that different?"

"Don't be ridiculous, Lily. There's all the difference in the world. You've known Win from birth, and he's legitimate."

"You are not the man I thought you were, Kit. I thought you said that nothing had ever happened in all of the generations of Claybourne's to taint or sully the family name. Did you just forget to mention your illegitimate child? Or did you think I'd never find out? I'm not even angry about what you did as a young boy. That's probably not uncommon. But, it's what you didn't do afterwards. The fact that you never told me, clearly shows that you were ashamed. I think perhaps it shows even more than that. You knew the sort of person I am. You knew that if I had knowledge of Pia's existence, I wouldn't have simply shrugged it off. I would have searched for her, and found her, and unless you had done the right thing by recognizing her as your daughter, I would not have married you."

"My God, Lily. Are you daft? No man would tell such a thing to a future wife. Once again, we seem to be at odds about something that has to do with the difference in our places in society. Perhaps, in the middle class, your way of thinking is prevalent. But, in the aristocracy, it certainly is not. Now, I shall be happy to meet this young lady, and I'll also be glad to finance a fine education, so that she'll able to find proper work in an office, or perhaps a staff position in a country house. That's as far as I intend to go."

"A staff position in a country house? An office worker? Is that how a legitimate daughter of yours would be raised? Would she not have the advantage of being presented at Court? Would she not be educated at a fine female college, just as Win will be educated at *Eton* and *Oxford?*"

"Lily, Lily. It isn't the same thing. How many times must I say it?"

"You needn't say anything again. I'm going upstairs to pack. I'll have Edward drive us to London, and I'll engage the help we need there. I'm taking Ruth with me, as you'll have no need for a ladies' maid. We can also shop for a wardrobe for Pia at Harrods. If you like, Kit, I'll file a petition for divorce. I may even have grounds for an annulment, since you lied to me about a very important fact before our marriage." She spun on her heel, and quickly ran up the stairway. Breathing hard, Lily went into her room, and slammed the door. She was very aware that her position was extreme. What she was proposing wasn't usually something that would be done in the middle classes. In that scenario, the child would undoubtedly have been adopted out. But, Lily was a different sort of lady. She couldn't tolerate the sort of thing that had happened to Pia. The poor girl had suffered greatly because of a stupid boy's wish to have a lark on a school holiday. What sense was there in not allowing her to never even know her father? She went to the box room, and dragged a large trunk to her own room.

My God, thought Kit. She means it. She'll leave. Or is she only bluffing to get her way? He put his head in his hands. He could hear her upstairs, pulling open drawers and taking items out of her cupboard. What in the Hell should he do? Perhaps she was right. What difference did it make, really? Was it worth losing Lily? How would he explain to Win? My God, what a scandal there would be. His first wife had been murdered, and now, his second wife was leaving him, because of an illegitimate daughter, whom *she* wished to take in and treat as her own. People would understand if it was *he* who wanted the girl to stay, and his wife who fought it, but that wasn't the way things were. Kit went into the drawing room and rang his mother. Quickly telling her everything that had transpired, he asked her advice. Lady Cynthia told him to accept Lily's terms. She thought that perhaps in time, when things settled down, she would agree to send the girl away to school. Otherwise, there was going to be a terrible scandal. Kit hung up and ran up the stairs. He gently knocked on Lily's door, and she told him to enter.

He approached and put his arms around her. The room was in shambles. Frocks were piled high on the bed, and she had dragged the large trunk from the box room. She stiffened when she felt his arms.

"Lily, I'm sorry. I do see it your way. I needed a moment to think clearly. This all hit me so suddenly. You're right. Now, please, calm down, and put your things back where they belong. Do you want Pia to think that she'd caused a row? I've thought it all over thoroughly. I tried to imagine what I would do if Kit did something like this. Naturally, he would be made to accept responsibility. Now, go into one of the guest rooms and have a lie-down. I'll have one of the maids come up and put this room in order. I'll also tell Mrs. Briggs that we want to dine a bit later than usual, so that Pia might sleep as long as possible. My mother has agreed to come to dinner with us, so she can meet her new granddaughter. Everything is going to be fine Lily."

Lily turned around and looked at him.

"I'll be honest with you, Kit. I don't believe you or your mother have changed your attitudes so abruptly. I think that you're terrified of a scandal. I also don't think you want me to leave you. I shall stay, but I'm warning you. Pia had better be treated with every bit of the respect that she deserves as a member of this family. And, before you ask me what I think we should tell people about her presence in our home, don't bother. We shall tell them the truth. Period. Now, I am going to have a lie-down. Tell them to ring the dinner gong at eight o'clock." She left the room without a backward glance, and Kit wondered where the sweet, compliant little girl whom he had interviewed on that September morning in 1914 had gone.

13

Lily woke a bit after six o'clock p.m. She went to her own room, and everything was neatly in order. She went through her frocks and selected what she would wear for dinner. Laying it on the bed, she selected all of the accessories. Then she left her room and walked down the hall to Pia's room. She knocked very gently at the door. Pia opened it at once.

"Oh, Pia, how long have you been awake? I hope you haven't been sitting up here waiting for someone to come and tell you what time we shall eat dinner."

"No, Milady – um – Lily. I just woke. I had a very nice sleep."

"I'm so pleased," Lily replied. "We are going to be dining in a bit less than two hours. Can you make it that long?" She smiled. "If not, I'll bring you up a plate of biscuits and cheese, if you'd like."

"No, Lily, Grazia – thank you. I am fine. What do I wear for the dinner?" Pia asked.

"Let me look through the clothes I brought you. Your grandmother, your Papa's mother, is coming to dinner too. She very much wants to meet you, and of course, your little brother Win will be there. So, you shall meet your entire family tonight. We'll want you to look very special. Let's see . . ." said Lilly, as she sorted through the clothing in the cupboard. "Ah, I think this is just perfect. It's a dress I bought on my wedding trip to London, and it's a perfect frock for a nice family celebration. Lily brought out the mauve taffeta and ninon frock, with the insertion of ivory lace. It was the one that had the sash of mauve ribbon to match the dress, and was ankle length. Pia smiled broadly, and it was clear that she was delighted. Obviously she had never had such a dress before. It turned out they both wore the same size shoe, so Pia fit into the satin slippers that Lily had bought to go with the frock. She showed her where she had put all of the underthings she would need and asked if she could think of anything she was missing.

"No, Lily. Noting. This so magnifico – I treasure it." Lily noted that in time she would have to teach Pia that words like everything and nothing had an 'H' in them. But, actually, she was amazed at how well the young girl got on in a foreign language, and her accent was truly charming.

"All right then, I'll leave you and go to change my own dress. When you are ready, come knock on my door. You remember, it's the third one down to the right - *al la destra*- smiled Lily. She was actually quite amazed that the Italian she had studied in college was still there.

She went back to her own room. With the help of Ruth, Lily's choice was the simple evening frock of powder blue satin and shell pink tulle, which she had also purchased in London. This was the one with the broad sash of pansy black ribbon with a bright applique of lavender flowers. As she dressed, she thought about things they could discuss at the dinner table, in order to keep conversation flowing. She felt strongly that they all needed to pay a lot of attention to Pia and definitely to ignore any mistakes she might make with regard to etiquette. That could all come later. Lily intended to have a chat with Win before it was time for dinner too, so that he wouldn't blurt out something uncalled for. She dressed quickly, and then went to the nursery, where she found Win looking very spiffy in his Eton suit. Emma was just finishing combing his hair. Lily told him she would like him to come to her room for a chat, since she didn't want Pia to knock and find that no one answered. Win followed her. When they reached Lily's chamber, she told Win that he could go and sit in the chair by the fire. Then, she took a small stool and brought it forward, so that she was seated right in front of him, at eye level.

"Win, I have some very exciting news. I hope it will make you happy, although I know it's going to be a big surprise. But, you're very grown-up now, and I know how much you've learned to share since you've been at school. So I don't think you'll have any problem with what I'm about to tell you," Lily began.

"I'm a good sharer. Mrs. Fraser tells me so all of the time," Win replied.

"I know, and I'm so glad. Now, let me tell you what has happened. A very lovely young girl arrived at Claybourne Court today. She is from the country of Italy. Do you know where that is?"

"Of course, Mummy," he answered, as if speaking with a fool. "I've seen it on a map. Mrs. Fraser has shown us where lots of countries are –Spain, France, Italy, Germany, and Switzerland. Italy is shaped like a boot."

"Well – I *am* impressed, Win. "I didn't know Mrs. Fraser taught you Geography in school."

"Yes, and she teaches about the alphabet too. I have it all in my memory."

"I am just terribly proud. What a smart boy I have," Lily smiled. "Well, the girl who came to our house today is from Italy, She was born and raised there. Her mummy knew your daddy a long time ago, when he was a young man. Your daddy made a baby with the woman he met, and the baby is now sixteen years old, and her name is Pia. Isn't that a pretty name?"

"How did Daddy make a baby with her? I thought I was his only baby. "

"Well, I thought so too, but it turns out that you are his only *son*. Pia is his daughter, and you are her brother. How special is that? To be a brother? This means you have your very own sister." Lily was trying hard to explain.

"But, I don't understand. People just don't get all grown-up sisters like that. They have to start out as babies."

"Win, Pia did start out as a baby, but not in your daddy's home. He was too young to marry her mother, so Pia grew up in Italy, where she was born. But, her Mummy got very sick and died, and she was all alone. Pia is very smart, and she decided to come to us, because she knew that your daddy was also her daddy, and that he would take care of her." *God, she was making a mish-mash of it, she thought to herself.*

"Okay, I understand better now. It's sort of like having Paw Paw and Meme over in America, and not meeting them till after I was more grown up."

"Exactly, Win. You are so smart. And, you know that you still have aunts, uncles and cousins in America who you still haven't met. It's like that too. Tonight you're going to meet Pia."

"At dinner? That's smashing. Does she like horses? I could ride with her."

"I don't know, Win, We'll have to ask her. But, she lived in a big city, so she probably doesn't know a lot about country life. You can teach her. I believe she would like that."

"Yes. I'd be a good teacher. I think having a sister is fine."

"That's wonderful, Win. Now, you know that you will have to share attention with Pia, since she's new here and probably feels a little frightened. I don't want you to feel badly if Daddy and I give her a little extra love. She's never had a daddy before now."

"That's sad. I'll be real nice to her. I hope she likes me."

"I feel pretty certain that she will love you, just like everyone does," Lily laughed. She will be coming here to my room any minute now. So you will get to meet her before we all go downstairs to dinner."

Just as the last word left Lily's lips, there was a knock on the door. Sure enough, it was Pia. She looked absolutely divine in Lily's gown from London. She had twisted her hair up on the top of her head. The young lady was absolutely stunning. Lily couldn't believe the difference that a bath, some rest, and the proper clothing made. She had never in her life seen eyelashes like the ones on Pia's face. They touched the bottoms of her perfectly shaped brows. Everything about her was exquisite, and Lily couldn't imagine Kit being anything but proud of this magical creature.

Lily introduced Win and Pia. Win reached out and shook Pia's dainty hand. "You are *really* pretty," he said, very seriously.

Pia blushed, and the color on her cheeks made her even more radiant. "Thank you, Win. You are a very handsome young man, too," she replied.

"Do you like horses," Win asked.

"I do not know. I have never ridden the horse. But, I have seen on street, pulling carts."

"Why do you talk so funny?" Win blurted out.

Lily intervened. "Win, Pia comes from a different part of the world, remember?" People in her country would think that you talk strangely. She speaks beautiful Italian, which is the language she was born with. But, she is still learning English."

"Okay. I could help you if you want. I can already read some, and I know how to say a lot of words."

"That would be very nice of you," Pia answered, smiling.

"Do you want to be friends?" Kit asked her.

"Oh yes. Very much. Maybe we teach each other things."

"I'd like that," smiled Win. "I think it's going to be posh to have a sister. Mummy, can I tell my chums at school about Pia?"

"Of course you can. Pia is a member of our family, now. I want everyone to know that we have a new daughter and sister," Lily stated. She doubted that Kit would agree about those wishes..

The dinner gong rang, Lily took both Pia and Win by the hand, and the three of them walked down the stairway. Pia had a very regal look about her. She had obviously been taught to hold her head high, and her back straight. There was nothing common about her. Kit and his mother were in the drawing room. Lady Cynthia pasted a phony smile on her face, but at least she was trying. Kit looked like his charming self. Lily could see that he was a bit amazed at how truly gorgeous his daughter had turned out. She walked over to him and curtsied, and then did the same with her grandmother. Lily got tears in her eyes.

"I am so pleased to meet you, Milord,' she said to Kit, and then "How lovely to meet you Milady." Both of them were taken aback.

Kit cleared his throat. "Ah, Pia, you don't have to address us formally. I would feel very comfortable with you calling me 'Father' if that's your wish, and my mother will be happy with Grand'Mere."

"All right, Father. And you will call me 'Pia', of course," she answered.

Kit and his mother seemed dumbfounded. Lily hadn't any idea what they had expected, but she was enjoying the little drama.

"Well, Pia, we're most happy to have you here in our home with us. Of course, it's now your home too," Kit managed to stammer. Lady Cynthia sent a scowl his way. Apparently that was not the 'done thing' either.

"Yes, Father. Thank you so much for everyting."

Lady Cynthia raised her eyebrows. It was obvious that the mispronunciation of 'Everything' grated on her like chalk on a blackboard. Lily wondered if Kit's mother had ever spoken Italian, or any other foreign language for that matter. If so, she should have known how difficult it could be.

The family made its way into the dining room, and Kit held the chair for his mother, Lily, and Pia. Win now sat in his own chair, with a little booster. Lily kept the conversation flowing, asking Pia questions about Italy. She answered intelligently and thoughtfully. Lily also turned to Kit and told him that they needed to do something about getting Pia her own horse, and having Howard give her lessons. Kit swallowed hard, and his color heightened, but he didn't argue.

Win clapped his hands and said "Yes, Pia and I are going to ride together."

Mother Claybourne was unusually silent during the meal, occasionally smiling her pseudo- smile, and murmuring difficult to understand words. It was clear that she was not at all pleased, but she had chosen the best of her options. Lily didn't care a whit. She was very pleased with the way the evening progressed and was proud of how well Pia conducted herself. She didn't make one mistake during the serving of many courses, including which utensil was to be properly used. She sipped wine with the others and actually spoke with more knowledge about wine in general than Lily might have. Apparently, her life hadn't been terribly downtrodden. From what she said, her mother *had* acted on the stage, and they often went to lovely dinners in fine restaurants after her performances. Lily imagined that her mother undoubtedly had many male suitors. Kit was probably only the first of many. But, she had obviously cared for her daughter and tried to raise her properly. Lily planned on beginning to look into schools near *Claybourne-on-Colne*, so that she might be enrolled and start as soon as possible.

When the evening ended and everyone said good night, Lily felt it had been a total success. She accompanied Pia to her room and kissed her goodnight. Then she told her that they would definitely go shopping the next day.

Kit knocked on Lily's door after she'd put on her nightdress. She told him to come in, and he did so, still fully dressed.

"I thought we ought to chat for a moment," he began. "I thought the evening went very well, considering."

"I think it was a splendid evening, Kit. What a shame that you couldn't have enjoyed your lovely daughter years before now," Lily answered.

"Yes, I suppose," he replied. "She does seem like a fine girl. Her Claybourne bloodline certainly shows. She has a certain *élan*."

"Yes, she's quite beautiful. Was her mother lovely?"

"Lily, I don't remember. I was just a boy. I suppose she was. She doesn't seem to have any of my features, so she must resemble her mother."

Lily was sitting on the small tool in front of her vanity. She twirled around, and looked at her husband. "Kit, I think we should have an understanding that there will be no more babies in this house. Not for a good while. You seem to have been rather good at impregnating women. I am not going to take a chance on that, until I know with certainty that you truly feel love for Pia. I'm going to have my hands full anyway, what with Win and Pia. I'm not complaining. You know I love Win, and I'm already very fond of Pia. But, another child would just be too much right now."

"But, Lily, I thought we'd decided we wanted a baby. There will be a nanny. Why should Pia's arrival change anything?"

"It changes everything because to be totally honest with you, I am not one hundred percent certain that this marriage is going to survive. I don't want to see it fail, Kit, but I cannot believe the surprises I have received since my marriage to you. Today's is only the latest, and the most life altering. I need time to see how things develop. I need to see if your mother accepts Pia. If she doesn't, then my relationship with her has ended."

Kit looked astounded. "But, Lily, I have no control over my mother's attitude. I can't tell her how to behave. She's her own person. You know that."

"Yes. And I'm beginning to realize that I'm my own person. Apparently I'm the only adult in this family who has a sense of right and wrong, and damn the 'done thing'. I am not going to compromise my values for this marriage. When I met you, and fell in love with you, I thought you were the most principled man I'd ever known. This episode, today, has shaken that belief dreadfully. I shall never be the sort of woman who puts society's expectations ahead of people's feelings – one who walks through life frightened to be honest, for fear of not living up to a set of foolish restrictions. That isn't who I am."

"Lily, I swear I'll do everyting in my power to make up to you, and to Pia, for what I did wrong. I don't want to lose you. Please believe me."

"I believe you, Kit. It's your mother I worry about. I don't know if you have the strength to stand up to her. I don't think you understand that she has ruled your life with an iron glove. She's very good at it. She almost had me fooled. But, she still thinks of you as a small boy, and she makes the rules. You're a man Kit – a grown man. You know the difference between right and wrong, and you know what century we live in. I expect to see you start acting like the man I thought you were when I met you."

"Lily, I do understand your point of view. It's just that I really believe it's as though we live in two different worlds. Our points of view differ so widely. I realize that I hold very hard to tradition. I believe in continuing with customs as they've always been– at least to a point. You, on the other hand, have very modern views in certain areas. You have no problem with flouting convention, if you believe it fosters good. I admire you for that, but it's very difficult for me."

"Kit, I know that you're a good person. I've never questioned that. But, you're so ingrained with society's conception of what is proper and accepted. I'm certainly not a rebel or a dissident. You know that. But, I strongly believe in doing right by other human beings. I could no more have turned Pia away from our doorstep than fly to the moon. Nor, could I ever send her away to a boarding school, where she would feel different from every other girl and would probably be teased unmercifully. She would only feel abandoned. Of course, I'll agree to send her to a preparatory school, or finishing school, when the time comes, and if it's what she wants, but then she'll be coming from a titled household, with an Earl and Countess for her parents. Other girls will admire her. Surely you understand what I'm saying."

"Yes. I do. And, yes, I understand what you're saying about my mother. She has set the standards for our family, and I've tried to follow them, with one major mistake when I got involved with Pia's mother. When a child knows nothing else, and they respect their mother, they assume her point of view is the correct one. That's what I've done. You're opening my eyes to a new way of thinking, and that's very good. But, give me time, Lily. We haven't been married a year. I can't just throw away everything I was taught overnight."

"I know that, Kit, and I don't want to become a shrew like Eleanor. As long as I know that you're making an effort to change your outmoded and really very priggish views, I'll be here by your side. The best way you can show me that you care about me is to show that you care about Pia."

"I'll do everything I can. She is, indeed, a lovely girl. I couldn't have asked for a prettier daughter, and she seems beautiful on the inside as well."

"Yes. I think so too. Also, Win has taken to her. I think we could be a very nice little family." For the first time, Lily smiled. Now, let's put all of this aside for tonight, and think about ourselves. Would you like to spend the night in my room?" she asked.

"Lily, my dear wife, you know that I would. I think that might be just what the doctor ordered.

14

If it was what the doctor ordered for Kit, it wasn't a good prescription for Lily. But, she was growing used to their peculiar way of making love, and she didn't expect much else. It was the one area of their marriage that she felt she could put up with, until all of the other differences were straightened out. Still, she did hope that someday Kit would understand that even so-called *ladies* could be allowed to enjoy lovemaking without being looked upon as loose women.

The next morning during breakfast, Kit asked Pia if she would like to accompany him to several stables in the area, to purchase a horse for her. Needless to say, she was thrilled. Kit had already spoken to Howard, and told him about Pia. Kit said that he wanted her to be taught to be a fine horsewomen. Naturally, Howard concurred. So, Pia and her father set off with Edward driving them. Lily was very pleased that they would have some time alone, to grow more familiar with one another. Win was off to school, and Lily had the morning to herself. She decided to go out for her own horseback ride. Howard saddled Taffeta, and off she went into the trails. It was not a warm day, and not particularly a good one for riding, but she enjoyed the fresh air, and the time to think. She was very happy with the way

Kit had promised to try with Pia, and she even believed that in time Mother Claybourne might come round.

Lily rode over to the tenant's houses, and stopped to have tea with a Mrs. Gatewood. The poor dear had her hands full, with six children. That was another thing Lily was trying to help the wives with. Their husbands didn't use anything to prevent pregnancy, and some of them had babies nearly every year. Lily started teaching them lessons about various ways that pregnancy could be prevented. Most of them had never been taught anything about their own bodies. Each time she left those homes, Lily felt that she had helped in some way.

After her ride, she went through some of her jewelry, and choose a few, simple pieces that she thought would be appropriate for Pia. Lily had the pearls that her own parents had given her when she turned sixteen, and she decided to give them to the newly arrived sixteen year old in her life. She also found some pretty gold bracelets, small pearl earrings, and a pretty gold and pearl ring. When Pia returned, Lily planned on taking her shopping, and then stopping by John's office to make an appointment for him to see her and to introduce her to Gena.

It was amazing when Lily looked at the calendar, to realize that the Holidays would soon be upon them. She knew it would be the nicest Christmas she had spent at Claybourne Court, what with Pia and Win to buy gifts for. Also, it would be the first time she'd ever planned the Christmas Eve Gala. She wanted it to be especially lovely this year, as it would serve as Pia's introduction to the village and to any friends who came from further away. She sat down in the library and compiled a list of people who would be invited. She decided to word the invitation in a bit different manner. She worked out something she liked much better:

> *"The Earl and Countess of Gloucester*
> *Request Your Presence at their Annual*
> *December 24th Dinner*
> *To Celebrate Our Savior's Birthday*
> *And to honor the arrival of their daughter*
> *Miss Pia Sabina Claybourne*
> *Eight O'clock P.M. Claybourne Court*

Lily leaned back in her chair, placed her pen in the ink well, and admired her work. Laughing aloud, she thought to herself that the invitation would set the village awash with gossip. Lady Cynthia would be mortified, but Lily knew that Pia would be thrilled. The date was still about six weeks away, but it was not too early to order the invitations and begin addressing them. By the time people began receiving them, many in the village would already know the entire story of Pia's arrival, so it would only be a surprise to those who lived further away, or who didn't know much about what went on at Claybourne Court. Lily thought it a perfect way to introduce Pia to society, as well as to her new home. There were always many titled people on the guest list from all parts of England, but also included were the lesser sorts, who Lily actually enjoyed much more. Naturally, her dear fiends Maddie and Poppy would be there, as would Tom Holiday, who had saved Kit's life during the war. She planned on dropping the invitation off at the engraver's on the way to the village shops that afternoon.

Lily then picked up the telephone and rang her mother. Elisabeth answered on the second ring.

"Hallo, Mum, it's me, Lily. How is everything and everyone?"

"We're just fine, dear. I'm just sitting here drinking a cup of tea. In fact I was thinking of you, and hoping we might get together soon." Elisabeth Morris answered.

"Yes, indeed we will. I have some smashing news to report. I think you're going to be knocked for six, but knowing you as I do, you'll think it's as fabulous as I do."

"Lily? You're making me curious. You aren't going to have a child, are you?"

"No, Mum, not that. But, very similar. Kit and I already have a new child. A lovely daughter, who was born in Italy, named Pia Sabina. She's sixteen years and breathtaking."

Elisabeth was stunned. Of course she wanted every minute detail, and Lily explained everything very thoroughly. Unlike Lady Cynthia, the other new *Grand'Mere,* this new *Grand Mummy* was filled with joy.

"Oh, Lily, how perfectly lovely. How dear of you to bring her into your home, and make her a part of your family. Of course, I cannot imagine you doing otherwise. She *is* a Claybourne, after-all. There wouldn't have been any other choice. And, you say she walked all of the way from Rome, Italy. Lily, I've never heard of anything so pitiful in my life. I don't quite understand why she didn't have access to Kit's telephone, or certainly his address, so she might have rung him, and he could have collected her. Did he not know of her?"

"Oh, yes Mum, he knew of her. But, she was not spoken of in the family, and his father had paid off Pia's mother when she was born, so that she would never contact Kit again. I get so angry when I think of the entire muddle."

"Lily, you know that the aristocracy views that sort of thing in a different way than we might. I'm sure they view it as a scandal of the worst order," Elizabeth said with a chuckle.

"Oh yes. But, no matter. I've set them straight on my point of view and even threatened to leave here and take Pia to London, if there is any argument about how she'll be treated. I don't think Lady Cynthia has come round yet, but Kit is trying very hard. He's taken her to look at horses this morning. I made it plain that she's to have anything that Win has been fortunate enough to own."

"I'm sorry to hear that you had to go to such an extreme, dear. But, you are, without a doubt, right. This poor child didn't ask to be brought into the world and to grow up with no father."

"Absolutely correct. I'm already very fond of her. I'm anxious for you to meet her. We're going to go shopping in the village this afternoon, to buy her a wardrobe. Poor thing arrived with only the frock on her back. If I knew with certainty when she and Kit would be back here, I'd arrange for us to meet you for tea."

Why don't you ring me when you leave there? Then, we'll see what time it is and take it from there?"

"Wonderful idea, Mum. I'll do just that. So, let me ring off for now, and I'll talk to you later."

With that, Lily went down to Kit's library and took a large book from the shelf. It focused on English schools. She needed to find a good school for Pia. After an hour of reading, she finally zeroed in on the *King's School* in Gloucester, which appeared to have all of the elements she wanted for Pia. It was coeducational, with a very old heritage, dating to the time of Henry the

Eighth, and it was either for boarding students or day students. There was no question that Lily wanted Pia at home with the family every evening, so that she could absorb what she needed of English life in a country house. She made a note of the location, and looked it up on a map. It seemed ideal. Gloucester, she knew, was a nice sized city, and was famous throughout England for its lovely, ancient cathedral. There was excellent bus connection to *Claybourne-on-Colne*, which had only recently begun, but Edward would certainly be able to drive her back and forth each day, just as he did Win to *Beaudesert School*. Both locales were to the west of Claybourne Court. She decided to discuss the school with Kit, and to schedule a day trip to visit, taking Pia along.

She heard the door open and close, and sure enough Kit and Pia had returned. It was not quite noon. She went quickly down the stairway, and saw Pia grinning from ear to ear. They must have bought a horse. Lily asked, and was told that indeed they had – a lovely, black mare, with a white streak on her nose - 15.2 hands high, and very gentle. Her name was 'Starlight'. She would be delivered to Claybourne Court in two days. Pia couldn't believe everything that was happening to her. She must have felt like she had awakened in Wonderland. Lily knew how she must feel, and she nearly broke into tears when she saw the happiness on the young girl's face.

"Pia, I'm going to ring your other Grandmother – my own Mama - and we shall meet her for lunch in the village, if you would like. I just spoke with her a bit ago, and she asked me to call her back when you got home, so we could possibly meet in the village. We can have lunch with her, and then go shopping. You will need a riding habit now, too," said Lily.

"Of course, I should love to meet your Mama. That would be so lovely," Pia replied.

Kit was still standing in the hall, thumbing through the day's post. Pia turned around, and put her arms around his neck. "Oh, Father. I never thought anyone would buy me such a gift. Thank you so much. I will treasure my pretty horse, "she said. Then, she kissed him on the cheek.

Lily laughed to herself, because Italians are so much more effusive and not a bit frightened to show affection. Kit must have been stunned. But, he didn't show it and while not able to muster up enough emotion to kiss her back, he patted her gently on the back, as he disengaged from her arms.

Then Lily told them both about the school she'd discovered and said that she was going to ring them and make an appointment for a tour of the campus and an interview with the headmaster. Pia beamed and Kit said that was just fine. Pia excused herself, and scampered up to her room, where she changed frocks, and appeared back downstairs within fifteen minutes. She looked precious in the sailor-Midi dress that Lilly had worn on that Christmas when she helped her mother entertain Will Morris and his son David. The outfit was darling on her. She had pulled her hair into a pony tail, and scrubbed her face. She looked very young, and doe-eyed. Lily rang for Edward, and he brought the car back around to the front. Lily kissed Kit goodbye, and they were off to meet Elisabeth Morris in the village. Lily had rung her while Pia was upstairs, and Elisabeth was thrilled that they would be able to meet. It was turning out to be a very busy day.

Lily and Pia met Elisabeth at their favorite tea shop on the High Street. Elisabeth stood up when the twosome entered and put her hand over her heart, as she was wont to do.

"Oh – I'm speechless. What a beautiful creature you are. I simply must give you a cuddle," Elisabeth smiled.

Pia hugged her back, and they all sat down at a corner table. "Now then, start from the beginning. How are we so fortunate to have you enter into our lives, you precious girl?" Elisabeth asked.

Lily did start at the beginning and brought her up-to-date on everything that had transpired. Elisabeth had heard it on the telephone, but she nearly keeled over when she heard the entire story of Pia's journey from Rome to Claybourne Court. Elisabeth kept raving about how absolutely gorgeous Pia was, and there was no doubt that her impressions were totally accurate. Lily was so glad that her Mum was praising Pia to the heavens. The girl needed a lot of love. She'd never had a family, after all.

After they finished a splendid lunch, the three of them started at the best shops the village had, and began to purchase items for Pia. They had such fun, and Pia was in a daze. Fifteen frocks of every sort, from simple day-wear to lovely tea gowns, and also skirts, pretty blouses, and tunics to go with them were bought. Then, nightwear was added and some lovely underclothing. Shoes, gloves, hats, stockings – all of the items that a well-dressed female needed made up the wardrobe. The final addition was a beautiful riding habit, in a lovely, dark blue, with elegant boots and appropriate hat. By this time, Pia was nearly overcome with the enormous amount that was being assembled. After the shopping expedition, Elisabeth took leave of them, with hugs, kisses and promises to see them soon, and Lily took Pia to a salon to have her hair washed and trimmed neatly. She had such beautiful hair – thick and nearly jet black. She did not want to have it cut shorter, and Lily agreed, but the ends needed cleaning up, and the cut shaped. When they emerged, Pia's head was shining and her cheeks were glowing from happiness. What an exciting, wonderful day it had been for her, and it was only the start of a remarkable new life.

The next thing of major importance was enrolling her in school. The very next day, Kit, Lily and Pia had Edward drive them to Gloucester to see *The Kings School,* so that Pia could look it over and interview for a place in the proper form. She had attended *Marymount International School* in Rome, a well-thought of private, catholic institution and she had done very well. Her transcripts had been received very quickly, since Kit telephoned the headmaster. Apparently her mother had used a good bit of money seeing that her daughter received a fine education. It appeared that she was up to snuff when it came to placing her into an English Private school. When she left Rome, she'd been in 'scuola *scecondario di secondo grado'*, which lasts five years, from ages fourteen to nineteen. So, she probably had two to three years left to complete her undergraduate education. When they reached the city of Gloucester, the three of them climbed out of the automobile and strolled about the town. It was quite large, when compared to their own, small village. The highlight was the spectacular Gloucester Cathedral, which could be found on the school's campus. Pia loved the setting of *The King's School,* and was excited to enroll. They went to their appointment in the admissions office, and the Head Master spoke with her for some time. He went over her transcripts from Rome, and was duly impressed. After that, he showed her about the various classrooms, and sporting fields. He felt that she would undoubtedly benefit from additional English classes, so he arranged her schedule to reflect that need. In place of art history, which she had been exposed to extensively in Rome, she would take another English class for those who didn't speak fluently. The decision was made that she would begin classes after the Christmas break, at the beginning of the New Year, when many newcomers entered. That way she wouldn't feel like the odd one out. The date was only a bit over a month away.

Pia had gone through so much change, in such a short time, that both Kit and Lily agreed it would be wise for her to have time to settle into her new environment, before tackling a new school too. She would also need uniforms for *The King's School,* and Lily learned where to order them. The car was rather silent on the way back to Claybourne Court, since there had been non-stop chatter since morning, and everyone was a bit worn out. When they arrived back at the Great House, both Lily and Pia went to their rooms for a lie-down. Kit collected the post, and went to his library to read his letters.

The first thing he noticed was that there was a letter from the Evans in America. There had already been a 'thank you' note from them, as well as a lovely gift of hand embroidered sheets and pillow cases. They were, however, continuing to write letters to Kit on a regular basis. He opened the recent one and scanned its contents. This one was also meant for Win, rather than Kit and Lily. It made mention of the proposed trip to America the following summer, and spoke of stables, horses, races, and camp -outs. Kit feared that they were going to have little choice but to send Win, if he still wanted to go. After looking through the rest of the post, he noticed the list for the Christmas party and the practice invitation that Lily had left on his desk.

When he read the invitation he was nearly apoplectic. It was obvious that Lily was going to announce to the world that Pia was a Claybourne. He felt nauseous. Oh God, what would his mother say? He remembered what Lily had said about his having allowed his mother to rule his life, and he knew there was truth in those words, but he also *did* agree with Lady Cynthia when it came to many points of view. This was one of them. He put his head in his hands. Why, oh why, couldn't Lily just let things take their natural course? Why did everything need to be so rushed and out in the open? When it came to the Christmas Gala, couldn't they simply have introduced Pia as a relative from Italy, whose mother had passed away, and to whom they were offering a home? Did Lily have to put 'daughter' into writing? The subject would be the talk of the town, and it would spread to London rapidly. It would be obvious that Kit had fathered this child out of wedlock. While that same thing had certainly happened to a good many young Englishmen while sowing their wild oats, it simply wasn't spoken about. Lily was breaking a hard and fast tradition. Kit thought for several moments, and then decided he needed to speak with Lily, before he told his mother about his wife's decision. Perhaps he could convince her to alter the wording of the invitation.

Before he started to climb the stairs to Lily's bedchamber, he took down the book of etiquette written by Emily Post, which covered every conceivable social quandary. He meant to see if he could find a written rule about such a thing. Unfortunately, the closest he could get was a paragraph which made it abundantly clear that there was only one way to treat such a conundrum, and that was to do the moral and correct thing. So, in essence, Emily Post was in total agreement with Lily. Perhaps that would sway his mother. When reaching for the book, a piece of paper floated to the floor. He reached down and retrieved it, and realized that it was a letter. It appeared to have been written by Eleanor, and the date was right before she'd left Claybourne Court for the London Townhouse, after Kit's return from the war. It was dated June, 1915. Apparently, she'd never posted it. It was addressed to Win. Kit smoothed it out, and read;

"My Dear Son,

I'm writing this letter because I have no idea when or if I shall ever see you again. I want you to understand when you're old enough, why I disappeared from your life and left you with your father. It wasn't because I didn't care for you. I did, as much as was possible for me to care for a baby. You see, Win, it's a difficult thing to admit, but I am not a 'baby' person, and I don't seem to have been blessed with the proper temperament one needs to raise a child. I'm a very nervous sort of person, and to be honest, as a baby, you did get on my nerves — dreadfully. I really had no training in how to raise a child. I suppose it comes naturally to some mothers, but it didn't to me. I was very young when I married your father, and didn't really want a child. But, along you came, anyway. You were a very sweet baby, and everyone adored you. But, I was still very young, and I wanted more out of life than being confined to Claybourne Court, having to look after a baby. Besides, we had Barton, and she absolutely worshipped you. I'm assuming that since you're grown, you still are keenly aware of who Barton was, and that you're probably still in contact with her. She would have made a much better mother for you.

You may have heard from your father, or others, that I wasn't always kind to you, and I have to admit that's true. When trying to discipline you, my primary means was to pinch you. Not terribly hard – just enough to let you know that what you were doing was unacceptable. I think sometimes I overdid it a bit, though. For that, I'm sorry. But, your father refused to spank you, and I could think of no other way to manage you. When your Gran Mere, father and Granmummy found out my method of discipline, they were very angry. One would have thought I'd been beating you with a strap. I did kick you one time, but it was simply a momentary lack of judgment. You'd angered me by spilling a full glass of champagne all down the front of a very expensive gown that I was wearing. It was very naughty of you.

I'm off to London now, and then I hope eventually to return to my original home in the United States, which I never should have left. When you're reading this, you will be old enough to understand things, and then perhaps we can be friends. As long as I don't have to do things for you, like feed you, dress you, change your nappies, or read you stories, I think I might like you.

Goodbye for Now.

Your Mother,

Eleanor Evans Claybourne"

Kit was absolutely appalled. The letter brought back horrific memories of his former wife. It reminded him of the letters he'd received from her when he was fighting in France during World War I. His first impulse was to throw the wicked piece of paper into the fireplace. But, then he stopped himself. First, he thought Lily should read it. She had great common sense and might see a reason for it to be kept. So, he trudged up the staircase, with the letter in his hand, along with the invitation to the Christmas Eve Gala, and the proposed guest list. When he came to Lily's doorway, he knocked and she told him to come in. She was lying on the bed, but she wasn't asleep.

"Excuse me, Lily, but I have a couple of things that I think we need to discuss. Is now a good time?" Kit asked.

"Yes, its fine, Kit. What do you have in your hand?"

"A letter I just found in a book in the library. It's from Eleanor to Win, to be read when he was older. I don't know if she changed her mind, or just what, but it wasn't in an envelope, and had obviously never been posted." Kit handed the letter to Lily. She silently read through it and then placed in on her night table.

"Well, there's certainly no question that it was written by Eleanor," Lily smiled sadly. "Only she could write such a horrifying letter to her own son."

"The question is, what are we to do with it? My first impulse was to toss it into the fire. But, I wanted you to read it and give me your opinion, "said Kit.

"Oh no. I'm glad you didn't do that – burn it, I mean. I think it should be put into the safe and saved. I would hope that the day never comes when we wish Win to read it, but one never knows. Those America grandparents of his are going to fill his head with a lot of nonsense about his true mother. I feel certain of that. If we ever feel that it's necessary to prove that she was not a good person, there it is in black and white."

"Excellent idea, Lily. I'm glad I asked your opinion. It will go into the safe today."

"You said that you had a couple of things you needed to talk to me about. What's the other?"

Kit sat down on the corner of the chaise lounge. He hated bringing up the next topic. "Darling, I found this practice invitation to the Christmas Eve Gala, along with the invitation list on my desk in the library. I'm a bit troubled over the wording of the invitation. I think we should discuss it."

"That's fine, Kit. What do you want to discuss about it?"

Oh, Lily. I'm not certain how to word this without our becoming embroiled in an argument. But – well – I absolutely cannot believe that you would even think about sending out an invitation practically shouting to the world that Pia is my illegitimate daughter," Kit said, as his voice rose an octave.

"Not that she's your illegitimate daughter Kit, but that she's your daughter. I despise the word illegitimate. It's placing a label on an innocent child. It would be better to say that you're her *bastard* father, than that she is your *bastard* child. Did you really intend to have Pia present at the party and not introduce her correctly? What did you have in mind as an introduction?"

"Lily, I thought perhaps she could just be introduced as the daughter of an old friend, who passed away, and that we have agreed to bring her into our family, and raise her as our own. After all, that really isn't a lie."

"Kit. Please don't try to make such an argument to me. You know as well as I do that it indeed would be a lie. Surly you realize that you're stretching the truth to a fair-thee-well by saying that her mother was an 'old friend'."

"Well, I suppose, but I think it would save Pia a lot of embarrassment," Kit argued.

Lily was silent for a moment. Then she spoke. "Kit, which do you think Pia would prefer? To be introduced as your daughter, or to be introduced as the daughter of an old friend whom we are bestowing our kindness upon by taking her into our home as a foundling?"

"Well, of course, when you put it like that . . ." Kit answered."

"Isn't that what you're implying? Let me propose this, Kit. Why don't we ask Pia which way she would prefer to be introduced? We shall tell her that it's entirely up to her, and that we want to do whatever pleases her the most, and makes her the most comfortable. "

"Oh, Lily, you know what her answer will be," Kit said.

"No, I don't actually. Perhaps you're right. Perhaps she would feel embarrassed with everyone knowing the truth. I certainly would never intentionally hurt her. So, let's leave it up to her."

Kit felt like he was between a rock and a hard place again. Of course, he had no choice but to agree with Lily. He thought about suggesting that they speak with his mother about what to do, but that would probably only make the situation worse. So, it was decided that when Pia woke from her lie-down, the question would be put to her, with no inkling of which way either Kit or Lily was leaning.

15

Which would you prefer, Pia?" Lily asked, as she sat on the edge of the bed in Pia's room. Kit stood, with his arm on the mantle over the fireplace. He was smiling and trying to act as if her answer was of no consequence to him one way or the other.

The exquisite Pia sat up in the bed, with a pillow propped behind her shiny hair. One side of it was swept behind her ear, and the other hung down the front of her gown. Her doe-eyes looked back and forth from Kit to Lily, trying to gauge whether or not there was a correct answer to the question that had been put to her. Neither of them gave any hint that one response would be better than another. She sat very still, clearly thinking it over very carefully. Finally, she looked up, with her great, long lashes touching the bottom of her perfect brows. "Yes. Well . . . I think I should prefer to be known as Pia Sabina Claybourne. That truly is my proper name, isn't it? Shouldn't people know who I am, and that you are my Papa?" Unless, of course, you feel the shame for me?" she said, innocently. She looked over at Kit, with an adoring smile on her face. "You see, Father, I never had a man to introduce me as his daughter. I used to cry when I was *piccolo ragazza*- a small girl- because all of my friends had Papa's and I had none. I am so happy to have a Papa, and I do want everyone to know." Lily put her arms around the thin girl.

"Then we have our answer. I shall leave the invitations to the party as I have already written them. I think it will be a lovely way to introduce you to our friends and acquaintances." Pia hugged her back, tightly and tears spilled from her eyes.

"You are so very good to me Lily. I loved my Mama, but truly, you are better. I love you."

Now, Lily had tears in her eyes too. Kit's heart melted at the sight of those two women – one his own flesh and blood, and the other his wife, who he adored more than anyone in the world. He walked across to where both of them were still holding one another. Bending over, he put his arms round them and said he was glad that Pia had made the decision she had.

"I never dreamed that I would be fortunate enough to have such an incredibly beautiful daughter, along with a beautiful wife. I'm very proud of you, Pia, and I *do* wish everyone we know to meet you and see for themselves what a lovely girl you are. I'm equally proud of you, Lily, for being the sort of wife who loves so easily.

Lily was overtaken with happiness. She really had not expected such a gesture from Kit. He was generally so much more reserved and, while she had held strong hope that he would eventually come to feel the way she did about Pia, she hadn't expected it to be so soon.

Kit kissed his daughter on the cheek, and they left her to change her clothing. She was taking a riding lesson that afternoon from Howard. Lily and Kit went back to her room. They both stood and looked out the window where they could see in the far distance the gently rolling Cotswold Hills and the massive forest of trees, with only a few remaining autumn leaves. Autumn and winter generally made Lily a bit sad, for it was the season of dying, and she so loved spring and summer. But, she was completely thrilled with Kit's response to Pia's assertion and her happiness painted everything with a warm glow. The only remaining fly in the ointment was Mother Claybourne, which Lily did not look forward to. At first, standing there looking over their magnificent estate, she thought that perhaps Kit should simply deal with his mother alone. But, then she knew that she wasn't being fair if she asked that of her husband. She knew he had a difficult time going against her wishes, and Lily suspected she could make it easier on him. She told Kit her feelings, and they decided they needed to face the formidable

Dowager Countess immediately. Kit rang the Dower House and told his mother that they were dropping by for a chat.

Of course it didn't go well. They'd known it wouldn't. It was a very good thing that Lily had accompanied her husband. Lady Cynthia was what could easily be described as 'fit to be'tied.' "Surely you cannot be serious," she shouted. "I absolutely forbid such folly. What has gotten into your heads? You will not shout this to all of the land. Don't you understand that this is the worst sort of scandal? The absolute worst. Why, in my day, this girl would have been kept far away from Claybourne Court, and only a very few people might have been privy to the secret. One's barrister, perhaps, or solicitor. This is not the done thing. You are well aware of that Kit. I should much prefer that this young lady be sent to visit somebody or other during the Holidays."

"Just who would that 'somebody or other' be, Mother Claybourne?" Lily asked.

"I haven't any idea. Surely there are places one can put a person for a period of a few days. Let her go home with one of the servants who iss leaving for the Holidays."

"Mother. You can't mean such a thing. Pia is a lovely girl. I'm very proud of her. I felt the way you do at first, when I was shocked at her arrival, but I've gotten over that now. I'm not ashamed of her. Quite the contrary. I wish I could count the number of boys with whom I went to school that this sort of thing happened to. Half of those poor children were aborted, because the boy's wealthy, aristocratic parents made that decision and paid for it. At least my father didn't take that route. Lily has made me aware of what is morally correct in such a situation. If Maria, her mother, wished to keep her, then I should have been a participant in Pia's life. What harm would have come from my having visited her from time to time to make certain that she was doing well? That poor child just got through telling me fifteen minutes ago, that she used to cry when she was a young girl because she didn't have a father."

"Indeed. That is certainly tragic. I feel dreadful myself that the poor child was ever born. She didn't ask to come into this world in such an unwanted manner. But, that is what happened. There's no sense going back and saying what could or should have been done. The point is, it's not too late to stop this madness. Kit, you are going to ruin our reputation. Simply ruin it. Your father and I worked long and hard to keep the Claybourne name impeccable. Even when you got yourself involved with that Italian woman, we stood by you, and paid her money to leave you alone. Now, after all of these years, you're going to let something you did when you were eighteen stain the Claybourne name forever. This scandal will never be forgotten. Lily, I don't expect you to understand, but Kit should. From here on, when the family is listed in Burke's Peerage, and Debrett's, details about his illegitimate child will be recorded with zeal. You will not be welcome in polite, English society."

"Oh, bother Mother. I think the world is changing. I don't believe any of my true friends' are going to snub me because of something so ridiculous. Perhaps in your day that was true. But, this is the Twentieth Century. And, to be honest Mother, if anyone is so small minded, then I don't wish to associate with them."

"Kit, I believe you've lost all of your dignity."

"No, Mother Claybourne," Lily piped up. "Kit has *found* what honor and dignity really mean. The absolute core issue here is that there is a lovely girl, who did not ask to be born, who needs her father and a family in order to grow up with her own dignity. We can either give that to her, or break her heart, and God knows what would become of her. I will not be a party to such treatment of a fellow human being."

Lily, I never expected this of you. You aren't the least bit like the young girl who came here to interview, and who Kit hired to be Eleanor's nurse and ladies 'maid. You have very independent ideas, and really quite wild thoughts. One would think you were an American, or one of those suffragettes. I don't feel as though I know you anymore. I expected that Kit would mold you into the perfect Countess for Claybourne Court. I thought you understood that both Kit and I would guide you in the rules of etiquette common to the aristocracy. But, you seem Hell bent on destroying all of our age old traditions."

Lady Cynthia was very angry and Kit was uncomfortable with the turn the conversation had taken. At first the subject was Pia, but now his mother was pointing the finger at Lily.

"What do you mean, you and Kit thought you could mold me?" Lily asked.

"Just that, my dear daughter-in-law. You know that I was one hundred percent in favor of your relationship with Kit, even while he was still married to Eleanor. The fact that you came from a lower class was not a concern to me. In fact, I thought it would be a good trait. Because you were not of the aristocracy, we both thought that you would be happy to have us to teach you the ways of nobility. Instead, you seem bent on laughing at our rules and treating them as if they should be left behind in another era."

Lily was astounded. She turned to look at Kit. "Tell me if what your mother is saying is true," she demanded.

"Oh, Lily. Yes, of course there was some of that thinking. And I think you've done very well listening to my instructions about how things should and shouldn't be done. I've listened to you, as well. So, in that regard, I believe we've helped one another. I understand what my mother is saying on this point about Pia, but I also understand what you feel. Because I've grown fond of Pia, I want her to be a part of our family. But, I must say, Mother is correct about *Burke's Peerage* and *Debrett's*. Anyone who ever wants to look up our name in either of those esteemed volumes *will* know immediately that Pia is illegitimate."

Lily's eyes were filling with tears. "Oh, for God's sake Kit. Who gives a damn? There is no one on earth whom I care to socialize with, who would make judgments about us because of something so inane. If that sort of thing is what your life is built around, I made a horrible mistake when I assumed you were an upright, decent, honorable man." Lily was crying and screaming.

"Now, you calm down this very minute," shouted Lady Cynthia. I'll not have this going on in my home. You're beginning to sound like Eleanor."

"Like Eleanor? The entire focus of my life is caring for other people – helping those who need it – looking at everyone equally. And you have the nerve to equate that behavior with Eleanor's?"

"No – not as far as your generosity of spirit," Lady Cynthia replied. But, I'll not stand by a second time and let a wife of Kit's belittle him, just because he happens to be gentleman of the old school."

Lily gave up. She just shook her head, and said "You will never understand. You aren't capable of understanding. Do whatever you will, but I am still the Countess of Gloucester, and Claybourne Court is my home. As long as I am the wife in this family, I shall continue to treat Pia as a daughter, just as Win is treated as my son. There is no difference between them in my mind. Act however you wish. You'll only be making a fool of yourself in my opinion." With those words, Lily turned and left the Dower House.

A month went by. Lily and Lady Cynthia spoke as little as possible. She allowed Kit to deliver messages to his mother. She also began to assume more responsibility in the big house. She began to plan a redecoration project after the New Year, and she did not seek Lady Cynthia's opinions regarding what should and shouldn't be renovated. Instead, she leaned on Pia for advice and found that the girl had fine artistic and creative abilities. Nothing could get underway until after the Christmas Gala, but Lily had all of the fabrics picked out, as well as wallpaper samples and paint. She was really intending to undertake a rather massive redo. There would be few rooms unaffected. While Claybourne Court was a magnificent old mansion, there was no question that it needed freshening. Lily would never have considered changing the interior to something terribly modern, but she knew that old, stained wallpaper that was peeling from the walls, and cracked ceilings needed to be repaired. Not to mention the filthy and stained fabric on sofa and chairs, rugs that were so worn that they were bare in spots, and draperies which were much too old and heavy for the rooms, mostly dark velvets. She had always hated Eleanor's treatment of Win's nursery, and she intended to include the boy himself in choices for his room. She would do the same thing with Pia. Lily had no idea if Kit had told his mother of her project, and she didn't care a whit. If Lady Cynthia had anything to add, of course Lily would listen, but she was not going to be treated like a child.

For the time being, the Christmas Gala took precedence over everything else. Win was doing very well at school, and Pia would not start until after the New Year. Lily's redecoration would start at the same time. So everything was lined up appropriately. Kit was even extraordinarily busy with his plans for new plantings and the raising of sheep. He was also having the blueprints drawn up for a Mill to produce fine woolens. The walled, brick garden that Lily had longed for was finally complete, and it was the culmination of a dream for her. It was going to become her own sanctuary, where she could sit on the marble bench in the spring and summer, and even warm fall days, and read her beloved books. It sat where the gazebo had once been. With very high brick walls, to keep out all but those Lily wanted to visit, it was a nice size. It was planted with roses throughout. Benches were scattered about, and there was a lovely fountain in the center. An arched, wooded door led into it, and it truly would become her refuge. Butterflies could be seen in profusion, and didn't seem the least frightened when Lily brought her book, and sat down to read. She had one favorite, a white one, with a tinge of yellow in places. Whenever she entered the garden it seemed drawn to her. Often, while reading, she would look up and see the gracious, lovely butterfly sitting on one of the roses, directly to her right. She loved to study it. Butterflies were such magical creatures – beginning life as something rather ugly, and then going through the metamorphosis that transformed them into one of the earth's most graceful and charming creatures. They reminded Lily of her own life – of the enormous change that had taken place in so short a time.

The invitations were sent out, as originally designed by Lily, and Pia asked for one to be framed, so that she could hang it on her wall. Lily gladly complied. Responses poured into Claybourne Court. It seemed no one wanted to miss this year's festivities. Obviously, the wording of the invitation had raised curiosity. Many people in the village of *Claybourne-on-Colne* already knew about Pia, but there were many people from farther afield who hadn't the slightest notion to whom the invitation referred. A month before the Gala, Lily took Pia on a train day-trip to London, where they shopped for a spectacular dress for her to wear that night. At a small boutique on Bond Street they found the perfect dress. The sleeves were cap, with a rounded neckline, and it was styled with one of the newer dropped waists. There was lace trim around the neckline and on the scalloped hemline, and ribbons wove in and out of the skirt, separating squares of velvet from taffeta, all in shades of baby pink. Pia looked ethereal in it. She chose a wide, gauzy headband, which was tied into a magnificent bow at the side of her face. It was reminiscent of Lily's bridal headpiece. Velvet Mary-Jane shoes completed the look. Lily thought she looked like an angel.

Lily, herself, also selected a pure white, drop-waist frock, with a tiered skirt of silk and lace. Her dress was sleeveless, and also dipped quite low in the back. She knew that she would be wearing a diamond tiara for the Gala, so she didn't have to bother about headwear. She and Pia had an absolutely wonderful day. It was the first time that Lily had returned to London since her rather dreary wedding trip, and though it seemed unkind to admit it, she had a much happier time on the second visit. Pia was spellbound. Although she had grown up in Rome, one of the world's most beautiful cities, she had always heard of London. This was Lily's opportunity to see all of the historic landmarks she had wished she could visit before. They made a day of it, and missed almost nothing. On the return ride to Claybourne Court, Lily told Pia how she had once dreamed of becoming a physician –attending school in London. Pia didn't know that such a thing was possible for women. Lily told her about the London College of Medicine for Women, which had been founded by Elizabeth Garrett Anderson, among others, in 1894.

"Do you still dream of such a thing?" asked Pia.

"Only occasionally, Pia. There is no question that medicine is my passion, and I do wish I could have realized such a dream. But, one cannot have everything. I had to relinquish that dream when I married into the Claybourne family and became a Countess."

"What does this 'relinquish' mean? Pia asked.

"'Relinquish' means to 'give up something', Pia. I had to give up my dreams of becoming a physician."

"That seems very unfair. Why can you not do both?" Pia questioned.

"Oh, Pia. Someday I think women *will* be able to do both. But, in this day and age, a Countess must be only a Countess. I don't particularly like it, but that's the way the world is organized."

"It seems very silly to me," laughed Pia. "When I am grown and married, if I want to be someone else too, I shall do it."

"I pray that you're able to, Pia. What do you think you would like to do, besides being a wife?"

"I want to be a model, she answered, stretching her legs out in front of her in the small compartment.

"Well, you would certainly make a lovely one, Lily answered. "But, I think you'll need to grow taller. Most models are quite svelte and tall. You're certainly svelte enough. You just need more height."

"My Mama was quite tall. She could have been model. She had offers. But, it has to be done correctly, I know."

"Yes, I would surely think so. If that still interests you when you leave school, we'll look into it further. Are there any other careers that interest you?

"I would like to work in the very big department stores. Like Harrods, which we just saw."

"Oh, I see. Do you want to sell goods in a shop, then?"

"No. No. I want to have important position in big store, like Harrods-create interesting displays to show off merchandise to sell in store."

"Yes, I understand now, Pia. It might be necessary for you to go to school for such a position. I believe they are called Managers of the Display Department", or some such thing.

"Yes. Then I shall go to school. That will be no problem. I am very smart."

Lily laughed to herself. Pia was not being cheeky or bragging. What she said was true. She was very smart. Her school grades from Italy proved that. Lily didn't for one moment think that if Pia set her mind to anything she couldn't do it. After all, this was the sixteen year old girl who had walked from Rome to Claybourne Court in five months

16

The Gala was a huge success. There wasn't one person who didn't absolutely adore Pia. And not one person said an unkind word, or asked an improper question about her origins. Pia looked like an angelic lady out of a *Renoir* painting in her pink confection gown, with the organdie headpiece, which called attention to her nearly black, doe-like eyes. Win, in his new Eton suit, looked like he'd stepped out of a *Gainsborough* portrait, with his apple-cheeked smile, and his tawny blonde hair. Lily greeted guests, along with Kit, and the two children stood next to her. Unlike Eleanor, she did not need to resort to pinching in order for Pia and Win to be beautifully behaved. Kit wore white tie and tails and was his usual genteel, elegant self, and Lily glowed in her white gown and diamond tiara. The house was filled with red and white roses and green pine garlands. The traditional tree adorned the drawing room, decorated with all of the Claybourne family, heirloom ornaments. As usual, the food was divine, and the footmen circulated through the rooms offering crystal champagne flutes and silver egg nog cups. Lily offered the children cranberry juice mixed with sparkling water with a cherry on a toothpick.

Lily employed a small chamber music quartet, and they played wonderful Christmas music all night long. Win's new nanny, Emma, who they all adored, watched over the children, and Will, who was going on five years, promised that he too would make certain that the little ones were all safe. The yearly children's tree decorated the Great Hall, and as always, gifts hung from every branch, individually tagged for each child present. The same was true for the drawing room tree, except that the gifts were stacked underneath, gaily wrapped by Lily and Pia and hand selected by them, since Lady Cynthia abandoned that task. Lily thought it great fun. She made a list of every person who was invited, and then made a notation about them – their personality- their occupation – their likes and dislikes. It made buying the proper gift much easier. What wasn't particularly easy was learning something about every guest, but she managed, by trotting in and out of shops on High Street, and surreptitiously snooping into people's lives. Just enough to ascertain what sort of gift would please someone. Kit helped Lily and Pia with the knowledge he had about many people. At any rate, it was accomplished, and Lily felt that a very good piece of work had been done. After everyone opened their gifts, there was a great show of appreciation. This year, Lily had engaged a professional photographer, and anyone who wished could have their photo made by the lovely tree. Children were photographed by their own tree in the Great Hall. There was also dancing for the first time. Lily had the ballroom decorated beautifully, with poinsettias, amaryllis, pine boughs, and roses. After the food was served, the musical quartet moved upstairs, and many of the guests either waltzed to lovely, traditional tunes, or tried their hand at the newer dances which were all the craze in London, especially the Charleston. Lily's dear friends Maddie and Poppy came from London, and of course, Gena and John were there. Neither Poppy nor Maddie had found the right man yet. They weren't in the least in a mad rush, and said they were having far too much fun to settle down yet. Lily promised them that she would make it a point to travel to London more often in the coming year to lunch with them.

Only one person didn't attend. That was Lady Cynthia Claybourne. Kit did everything in his power to convince her to attend the party, but she refused. It was she who missed out on all of the splendor. Kit felt rather guilty that his mother wasn't present, and several guests inquired as to her whereabouts. All he could answer truthfully was that she hadn't felt up to attending. Naturally, everyone thought she was ill and no one bothered to correct them. While Kit felt guilty and sad, Lily felt a bit angry. Lady Cynthia was the same person who had been so terribly put off by Eleanor's childish pouting and sulking, and now it was she who was playing that role. Neither Kit nor Lily told Pia the reason for her absence. She was always polite and decent when she encountered Pia anywhere on the premises, but she did not go out of her way to be terribly friendly. She never joined the family for dinner anymore.

A little after midnight, one by one, the guests departed, assuring Kit and Lily that it had been the best Gala ever, and telling them that they had the most beautiful family imaginable. Lily wished Kit's mother could hear the compliments about how Pia was captivating and bewitching. The marvelous bit about Pia was that although she had to have known that she was indeed beguiling, she was not in the least full of herself and instead had a demure quality.

When the door closed for the last time, the entire family threw themselves onto the sofa and chairs in the drawing room. They spent a good hour going over everything that had taken place, telling each other tales about this guest and that. Kit and Lily laughed about how many of the young, unattached men present had been rather google-eyed over Pia. She didn't seem in the least interested and thought it all quite amazing. Win asked if there had always been a Christmas Gala at Claybourne Court.

"Yes, Son. As far back as I can remember, and I think long before that. It became a tradition for the family in this house to entertain those of the village and the tenant farmers on the estate."

"Not very many of them come," Win answered.

"The tenant farmers?" Kit replied. "No, I'm afraid they might feel a bit out of place. Most don't have the proper clothing and so forth."

"Then, don't they *ever* get to come up to the big house?" Win continued.

"Oh, yes. Of course. During the war we did away with the agricultural fair, but we'll bring it back again this year. That's when prizes are given for everything from the loveliest rose grown to the biggest pig raised. We try to make certain that everybody gets a prize for something."

"Why don't I know any of the tenant people? They must have some boys about my age."

"I imagine they do, Win. But, you would have very little in common, besides age. I believe they would be frightened of you."

Why is that Kit?" Lily asked.

"Well . . . you know, Lily. We just live in a completely different world from theirs."

"Ye-e-e-s. But, Kit, if it weren't for the rent they pay, and the farming they do, we might not be able to have everything we have," Lily murmured.

"All right, Lily. I know that. But, let's not discuss this tonight. You and I don't always agree on topics like this."

"But, Daddy, I don't see why I couldn't play with the boys, if there are any," Win continued.

"Win, I don't want to discuss this anymore. There are just certain things that people in our class do and don't do. Our children do not *ever* play with the tenant farmer's children." Kit said it in such a manner that made it clear to Win that he had better not continue questioning his father. But, he could tell that Lily didn't think the same, and he wasn't going to forget it. He would ask her more about these unknown boys, who might live on the Claybourne property, at a later time.

Christmas Day was lovely, and even Lady Cynthia came over to the Great House for dinner and gift opening. No one acted like there was anything amiss, and she was a bit less aloof then she had been. Perhaps having missed the Christmas Eve party had brought her to an awareness of how much she needed to have her family near. Or, perhaps it was just a desire not to spend Christmas alone. There was certainly no question that she adored Win, and *he* adored Pia, so if she was to enjoy Win's company, she would have to warm up toward her new granddaughter.

They all opened gifts, and it looked like everyone had gone a little bit overboard. Lily was somewhat surprised, as the economy was horrible, and showed no signs of getting better. Ever since the war there had been a stubborn recession that went on and on. Businesses were having a difficult time, and unemployment had hit ten percent. The coal miners were striking, and the Irish Republican Army were starting trouble. Of course, women continued to march for equal rights. Although the children at Claybourne Court weren't aware of the difficulties within their country, adults still worried. That was one of the reasons Kit wanted to expand and diversify his holdings. For the first time in his life, he put quite a large sum of money into the American stock market, since it appeared to be booming, and America was the only country where the economy was very good. But, whatever monetary difficulties existed, or even if they existed at all, at Claybourne Court things went about as usual. Christmas gifts were lavish – perhaps even more so than in years past.

Since the first of the year was fast approaching, Lily was busy readying Pia for entrance to the *King's School*. She was excited, but a bit frightened, which was natural. Her uniforms had been purchased, as had new ones for Win and school supplies such as writing paper, pencils, erasers and a dictionary placed into haversacks, so they were completely prepared. Win was such a sweet brother to Pia. He tried to give her an idea of what to expect, as if she had never attended school before. He was certain that English schools were entirely different from Italian schools. Lily and Kit weren't worried about Pia. She was a very bright girl and had a winning way about her. That, combined with her breathtaking beauty and rather bashful personality was certain to make her school days happy ones.

When the day finally arrived, Win had Edward drive him, as usual, but Kit and Lily took Pia. This would not be the normal routine, but they thought she might feel a bit less anxious if they were with her on that first day. When they arrived at *The King's School*, the three of them walked to the Headmasters office, and announced Pia's arrival.

Everyone was very warm and friendly to her, and Pia seemed at ease. The Headmaster put a girl in Pia's same form in charge, and told her to take Pia to all of her classes, eat lunch with her, and spend time with her during any free hours throughout the day. The girl he assigned seemed lively and sweet, and it was clear from the start that they would be friends. They both kissed her goodbye, and told her that Edward would be there to collect her and not to worry if he were a few moments late. He would also picking be collecting Win. She waved goodbye to them, with her lovely smile and those precious doe-like eyes, and disappeared into the imposing, old building which served as the main building of the school.

Kit and Lily signed when they got back into the car. How their life had changed in one short year. They had been married in April of 1919, and now it was January of 1920. It was amazing how much could happen in less than a year. Compared to their wedding day, Kit had mellowed and seemed more ready to accept her more liberal ideas, particularly when it came to letting go of the age-old traditions that had been drilled into him forever. Lily knew that it wasn't easy for him, and she did try to be conscious of that. She was extra loving and dear to him. While their sex life hadn't improved but a smidgeon, Lily still felt that there were more important issues than that to put her energies toward. She still had not lost her feeling of wanting to be more fulfilled. It had only been pushed to the back burner, when Win's grandparents had arrived on the scene, followed in quick order by Pia. There was no need to even think about the wild difference that had occurred with Pia's introduction into the Claybourne family. But, there was no question in Lily's mind that the difference was nothing but wonderful. Kit still held some quite rigid ideas about class differences, as witnessed by the conversation about Kit playing with tenant farmer's children. Lily *did* understand his viewpoint. Even her own mother, Elisabeth, although a simple doctor's wife when Lily was a young girl, and now a Chemist's wife, would probably not have been pleased if Lily had brought home a playmate whose father was a tenant farmer. But, she did not want Win to get into his head that a child of such an up-bringing was any less than he was, in terms of being good or decent.

They both rode along in silence, and once or twice Kit reached over and patted Lily's hand. He was being more than usually affectionate. Lily suspected that he was looking ahead to a whole day of quiet, without the children underfoot, although Pia mostly stayed in her room reading. The girl was an absolutely voracious reader, and it turned out that she had taught herself all of the English that she knew. She had asked for two books on 'Learning English' for Christmas, and her nose had been in one or the other since that day. Still, it was a nice thought to have the house all to themselves, but for the servants, who always knew to knock gently before entering a room.

When they arrived home, Kit garaged his auto, and came into the great hall briskly. He put his arms about Lily, and kissed the back of her neck. "What do you think, my lovely wife? Shall we celebrate our own day of freedom?"

"I have nothing on my schedule, Kit. The whole day is yours, dear."

"They walked up the stairs arm-in-arm, and headed straight for Lily's bedchamber.

In a matter of moments, they were unclothed, and lying on the crisp linen sheets. Kit was kissing her tenderly, and she had her arms around his neck. Lily had memorized by now the way the procedure went. First the kiss, then the clothing, then a few feeble attempts at what he would probably have termed foreplay, and then Kit leapt on top of Lily and pumped away until he was finished. Then, there would always be one final kiss and a mention of his gratitude. This time was no different than any other, and since Lily had come not to expect more, it bothered her less than it had at the beginning. At least there was no pain anymore.

He fell asleep, and Lily went into the adjoining bath. She ran a nice tub, and enjoyed relaxing in it. It was hard to believe that she would be welcoming her second spring and summer at Claybourne Court, and before long, it would be their one year anniversary. It would also be Win's fifth birthday. They would have to think of something special for his birthday. Reaching for a scented bar of lavender soap, she thought about the nanny and ladies' maid. Most of their introduction to the regimen at Claybourne Court had been left up to Mrs. Briggs, but Lily wanted to make extra certain that Will got along well with Emma. She felt quite confident about her ladies' maid, Ruth, and there was no question that things were running more smoothly at Claybourne Court with their two additions to the staff. She had given them both this day off, since she knew things would be in flux with the beginning of school.

The extra help had enormously ironed out wrinkles that were present before. Lily realized that she should have added those two positions when she first married Kit, but she had been certain that Win would rebel against a nanny. She still believed he would have now, but he was fast becoming a little boy, and didn't mind so much giving up Lily's full - time attention. He was more prone to follow Kit round. Also, he was being such a dear about Pia. It was more than she might ever have hoped, and Pia adored Win. Neither had ever had a sibling, so it was a new experience, and one they both thought quite special.

Two months went by without Lily getting her monthly. There was no question in her mind of the cause. It had been exactly that length of time since they had taken Pia to her new school, and had come home to an empty house and lovemaking. She wanted to be absolutely certain before she told Kit, so she made an appointment with John, as soon as she could get one, which turned out to be three days later. She had every symptom that she knew was associated with pregnancy. Of course there had been no monthly, and Lily was very regular; she felt nauseous in the morning, and had begun to keep soda biscuits by the side of her bed, to nibble when she woke; her breasts were tender, and seemed to have enlarged, and her usual perfect skin had a few small breakouts, which had never happened before. She was excited – she couldn't imagine any woman not being excited – but also frightened. How would Pia and Win accept a new baby? Would she find herself confined, like Eleanor had been? She doubted that, because Eleanor's was a special case. Of course, there would be no more horseback riding, which she would miss, particularly in the summer months. She thought that if this were true, she would ask Kit to have a small pony cart built for her. She thought she might ride about the grounds in more comfort, and with no worries about the baby. She counted to herself. If she had conceived in January, then it seemed likely that a baby would be born in October. What a difficult thing to comprehend. The timing was good, because Lily wanted to present Pia to society as a debutante in the spring of 1921, and the baby would be about seven months old by then. She'd been thinking of a large ball at Claybourne Court, and of course, the usual Court presentation to the King, probably at the May garden party at Buckingham Palace.

Lily was Hell bent upon making certain that Pia had the absolute best up-bringing possible, and if there was any hope of her marrying within the landed gentry, she would need to be presented. That would be another issue that was certain to send Lady Cynthia over -the -moon. She would deal with it when the time came. Certainly Lady Cynthia's stamp of approval would go a long way toward allowing Pia to enter the vast sphere known as the aristocracy. Kit had told Lily that she, too, was eligible to be presented, since she'd married an Earl, but she had no interest in doing so. The whole thing seemed rather ridiculous to her, but if that was the way the game was played, then she would play it for the sake of Pia. She personally didn't give a whit who Pia ever married, or even *if* she married, but, she didn't want her to be treated second rate by anyone. Thus, Pia would, indeed, have her Season. Lily already had plans to take her to the Claybourne Townhouse in London. Since Lily had seen it, she had fallen in love with it and couldn't think of a more posh or elegant venue for Pia's debut. Anyway, that was where she and Pia would stay during the Season, and Kit could visit on weekends. Or come to London during the week, as well. Win would be off in America by then, which she detested thinking about. His first summer in America would be coming in six months, June, 1920. She dreaded the prospect. Perhaps having a baby would take her mind off missing him.

Three days later she was up early, bathed and dressed before Kit ever lifted his head off the pillow. That was what she had hoped for. Her appointment with John was for eight o'clock, and hopefully, Kit would just be ready to think about breakfast when she arrived back home. She rang for Edward, and he was in front of the house at once. If he was surprised at her early appointment, he said nothing. She gave him directions, and he took her straight to John Garrett's cottage practice. Gena was not at the desk that morning. It was a different nurse. Gena had told her during their last long chat that John was going to hire a new person so that Gena could concentrate on re-doing the house. Lily wondered if she was going to have to put her plans to redecorate Claybourne Court on hold until after the baby. She hoped not.

Soon she was asked to step back to John's examining room, where he greeted her jovially.

What are we going to discuss today, Lily? You're looking very fit?" he said.

"I suppose I am, except that I have some breakouts on my skin, which never happens to me," she answered.

"My dear Lily, you aren't going to tell me that you've come to see me about a spot on your face? That doesn't sound like the Lily I know," he laughed.

"No – not that, John. I suspect I might be pregnant. I've waited until I missed two monthlies and I seem to have all of the other signs. Will you be able to tell me definitively?" I should be able to. We'll have to take a urine sample and sent it off to a lab, but at two months, I should be able to manually make a diagnosis."

"Well, then let's get to it," Lily smiled. "I'm very eager to know."

He went about examining her thoroughly and took some blood as well as urine samples.

After he was finished with the physical portion of the exam, he smiled and said "Congratulations."

"Oh, do you mean it? I'm really going to have a baby? Oh, how very, very splendid. When do you suppose the child will be due?"

"When do you think you conceived," he asked.

Probably January 2, 1920," she replied.

My estimate would be October 9," he answered.

"That's about what I thought," answered Lily.

John was sitting down on a stool in the examining room. "So – how do you think Kit will receive the news?"

"Oh John. He'll be over-the-moon. It's been such a strange year in so many ways – now we're adding pregnancy to the muddle. It will be fun," she laughed.

Of course it will. You're ending up with a lovely family, aren't you?

"Indeed, John." Of course he knew all of the details surrounding Pia's entry into the Claybourne family, and was pleased that Kit had done what he considered the 'right' thing', instead of the tried and true 'done thing'.

Lily left John's office loaded down with a book on pregnancy, as well as a box of prenatal vitamins, and instructions for things she should not do in the early months of pregnancy. She read it over and didn't see anything that worried her. She had last drunk alcohol on New Year's Eve, before she became pregnant; she didn't smoke anymore; she had always eaten a healthy diet, and drunk plenty of water. All in all, everything looked perfect.

17

When she arrived back at Claybourne Court, Kit was dressed and sitting at the breakfast table, reading the *London Times* while eating. She kissed him on the cheek, and sat down across from him. Her own cheeks were very rosy, and anyone who saw her would have known that she was excited and happy.

"Where have you been off to so early this morning?" Kit smiled.

"I had an appointment with John at his office," she answered.

Lily, you aren't ill are you?" he said in a concerned voice.

"Not in the least. I'm fit as a fiddle. In fact, I should say that *we* are fit a fiddle, since there are two people sitting in this chair." She smiled a catlike smile.

"Lily, darling, are you saying what I think you are? Are you expecting a baby?" His face drained of all color. Then he got up and rushed around the table, and put his arms about her. "Oh tell me that's the truth, Lilly. I can't believe it, Well, I knew it would happened eventually, but now it has, and I'm so enormously happy,"

"So am I, Kit. It hasn't quite sunk in yet. The baby will be due in October – probably the ninth, according to John. I think that's a good time. It means that by the time Pia's presentation and debut arrive, the baby will be about seven months and can either come to London with us, or be left for just a short time with the nanny."

Kit looked astounded. "Pia's presentation and debut? Are you daft? Pia isn't going to be brought out nor is she going to bow to the King." There's no precedent for such a thing."

"Kit, let's not ruin a lovely day bickering over Pia."

"No – I don't want to either. But, Lily, you must erase those thoughts from your mind. I would be made a laughing stock." Kit had now turned ashen.

"Like you were made a laughing stock at the Christmas Gala? You and your mother made such an uproar about that, and no one said an unkind word."

"This is completely different. This is practically flaunting my misbehavior in the faces of all aristocracy. I can't do that. I'm not certain mother wouldn't cut me off completely over such folly."

"Kit, it isn't for me or anyone else that I wish Pia to be presented. Do you or don't you care if Pia makes a good marriage? If you do, the only way that can happen is if she's presented and takes part in the Season. Pia is a glorious girl. She will attract an enormous amount of attention. She could easily marry someone with a title. Wouldn't you like that?"

"Of course I would, Lily. But – but- she was not born on the right side of the blanket for such expectations. It can't be done."

"I'm sorry, Kit, but it *can* be done, and it will be done. I shall sponsor her, and I am the Countess of Gloucester. It would be nicer if both of her parents brought her out. I think you should think on this dear," Lily answered. And Kit, I absolutely want you to start adoption proceedings for Pia just as soon as possible. Then there will be no question about her presence in society. She will legally be a Claybourne."

Kit muttered something about his mother, but Lily pretended not to hear. Would you like me to invite Mr. and Mrs. Poindexter, your barrister and his wife, to dinner sometime next week? That would be a nice time to bring it up. They both met Pia at the Christmas Gala and thought she was stunning," Lily went on.

"Lily. Please give me just a bit of time to digest all of this. Here you've presented me with wonderful news about a child, and then you knock me for a loop by saying what your plans for Pia are. I need time to let it all sink in. And, whether you are in favor of it or not, I must speak with my mother" Kit replied.

"Absolutely. I think you should speak with your mother. She needs to know that we're expecting a baby, and she needs to know the debut plans. I also want to know her plans. Unless she stops her foolishness, and accepts Pia as a full, beloved granddaughter, I should not have anything more to do with her. That includes the new baby's Christening, and any other events that would normally include the entire family. I'm fed up with her behavior, Kit."

"Lily, I never thought you could be so hard," he cried.

"I don't want to be cold. I want us to be a warm, loving family. But, I'm not going to be satisfied with her pretending in front of others, and then acting emotionally unavailable when she is with her family alone."

"This will be an incredibly difficult conversation for me. I feel that I'm telling her that I don't care about her anymore, now that I have a family."

"Kit, that's rubbish, and she knows it. Now let's talk no more about this. I'm feeling quite tired, which I think is a normal part of the pregnancy. I'd like to have a lie-down. Perhaps your mother is available for a visit with you."

Kit dreaded it, but he knew Lily was right. He did need to talk with his mother. Instead of ringing her ahead of time, he broke with tradition and walked down the winding path to the Dower House. Fortunately, she was in the garden, tending to her roses.

"Hello Mother. It's a lovely day, isn't it? What are you doing? I can't believe you're fooling with your roses during the winter months."

"Yes. Well, I'm cutting them back. The gardeners didn't do a very good job in the fall, and then we had so many warm days this month, that they began to leaf out again." She took off her gardening gloves, and said "Kit, it's so good to see you alone. We never have the chance to chat like we used to. Why don't you come in for a nice cup of tea?"

"I'd enjoy that, Mother. Lily's having a lie-down, so it's a perfect time for me to visit with you for a while. We have wonderful news. Lily is expecting our first child."

"Well, you're becoming a regular rabbit hutch over there, Kit," she laughed.

"Mother. That's a tad unkind of you. Surely, you're as over- the-moon as we are?"

"Yes, Kit, of course I'm happy. I am just beginning to worry about Lily's mothering skills. She seems to be rather filled with strange, improper ideas."

"I really feel Lily is a splendid mother. I know you don't agree with some of the decisions she's made, but you have different points of view – that's all. She is much more liberal in her thoughts about child-rearing. But, she's fair and willing to listen to reason. I've come to realize that she's very bright, and that listening to her is smart of me."

Lady Cynthia rang for some tea. She kept sliding her wedding ring off and on, as though thinking about her own marriage. "Kit, I worry that some of her radical ideas are going to permanently ruin the image of this family. We're going to become known as 'Those Eccentric Claybourne's'. It could even lead to our being ostracized from the aristocracy."

"Mother, you worry too much. None of Lily's ideas have come close to anything like that. She is very broad minded, and cares a lot about the feelings of others. I believe she was brought up that way. At any rate, she just has an enormous amount of kindness. She also has strong belief in doing what's right, regardless of people's opinions. I rather admire her courage – wish I had more."

"That is pure rubbish, Kit. Lily wasn't raised in the aristocracy. She would have learned soon enough that courage is best left to the battlefield and not the drawing room. In our world there are time-tested traditions. They have worked well for hundreds and hundreds of years. Those traditions are to protect people from unseemly acts and mistakes that take place in the world. Such as the birth of illegitimate babies. I certainly agree that Pia is a lovely child, and I have no wish to cause more difficulty in her life. God knows she's had enough. But, for heaven's sake, allowing a sixteen year old to attend a fine boarding school is hardly contributing to her difficulties. I'm not at all certain I understand why she must be swooped up and made a member of the family overnight, like a stray animal.

Mother, as Lily made me understand, Pia had never even been away from her home before. She wasn't, in any sense of the word, prepared to go off and board at a school where she wouldn't have known anybody. She needs the help that we can give her as a family. She's very bright. There's no doubt of that. The only thing she needs is more confidence and help with learning our language better. Of course, she also needs love. She lost her mother, and there was no one else in the world to love her. Do you honestly believe that I should have turned my back on my own flesh and blood when she was in need? Lily and I can help Pia. She is such a lovely girl. With a bit of finishing, she'll be ready to take her place in society." Kit reached for the cup of tea."

"Oh Bollocks, Kit. Forgive my language, but I've just about had enough of hearing Lily's words spewed out of your mouth. Before you married her, you never spoke like this. We always agreed on everything. Now, you parrot her with every sentence. She isn't a mental giant you know, but even if she were, she knows nothing – nothing- about our way of life, and its standards. Really. How could she be expected to? She was raised by a very small town physician and his wife, who is a sweet person, but who began life as a Ladies' Maid. Lord Kit. She seems to enjoy forging new paths, and completely upsetting the traditional way we have always lived, which served us perfectly all of our lives."

"Did it really Mother? Would Sebastian be dead today if he'd simply been allowed to follow his own instincts and announce that he was a Conscientious Objector? I think he would. But, he couldn't do that, because it would have marred the family image. So instead, he killed himself, in a most gruesome manner. Instead of white feathers thrown at the house, we got sympathy cards and bouquets of flowers. That was more acceptable wasn't it? In my opinion, I lost my brother to your so-called societal expectations."

"Kit, I truly believe that if Sebastian had actually entered the military and fought like a man he would have learned the value of honor and sacrifice for his own country. He would have matured, which is what he needed." Lady Cynthia commented, sipping her tea.

I believe you're dead wrong. I think Sebastian would have gone AWOL and been hung"

"There's no point in discussing this further. Sebastian is gone, so we'll never know what might have been."

"I agree with you there. But, Mother, Pia is very much alive, and I, for one, am very proud of her. I'm not proud of the circumstances surrounding how she came to be, but I certainly am glad to be able to call her a daughter now."

"The next thing you'll be telling me is that you really intend to let her have a Season after she finishes school," Lady Cynthia's mouth became a thin, straight line.

"Yes, that's Lily's hope. I'm starting adoption proceedings, so she will legally be our daughter – Anyway. Maria put my name on the birth certificate.

"Well, Kit, I can't stop you from doing something so foolish. All I can say is that I'm terribly embarrassed and ashamed. Certainly, I shall not attend any of the parties or balls, and certainly not the presentation to the King."

"Have it as you will, Mother. It's still A year and a half away. I'd like to see Pia marry well – into the aristocracy. That's entirely feasible, with her appearance, and now a fine education. Why in the world shouldn't Pia have the same opportunities in life as Win?"

"Because it simply is not the 'done thing' Kit, and you know it. Before you married a ladies' maid, there would never have been a thought of such a thing."

Kit stood up. He was hurt and confused. A part of him understood his mother's viewpoint. After all, it was the same point of view that he'd been raised with. Tell the truth, he had never questioned it before. As his mother so elegantly put it, it was simply the done thing."

"You're right, Mother. I probably wouldn't have thought of it." He walked to the fireplace and fooled with the various artwork that was displayed there "But, I've thought of it now, and that's the difference. Lily is dead set against anyone saying that Pia cannot have a debut. I don't intend to lose Lily over something so absurd."

That remark completely ruffled his mother's feathers. "What do you mean 'lose Lily." Is she holding you hostage to her wants and wishes? If you don't do as she says, is she threatening to leave you?"

Kit, still standing by the fire, looked down at the floor. "She has indicated such," he murmured.

"Oh for God's sake, Kit. How did a son of mine find himself in such a predicament? Both your father and I raised you to understand that the man is always the head of the household - that he makes the decisions, and the wife follows them. Period."

"Yes Mother, and for the most part that is the way our marriage operates. Lily isn't a rebellious shrew. She just has her own opinions, and some are very strong, and she has a basis for them, besides 'that's the way things have always been done'. Her heart is very loving Mother. I've learned from her. Sometimes it's a good thing to have fresh eyes look at age-old ideas. Suddenly one realizes that the ideas have outgrown their use."

"Just like I have, I suppose," she quipped.

"Of course not, Mother. You could be such a wonderful person for Pia to learn from. As you know, Lily didn't have the privilege of a presentation and debut. You did. Think of the things you could teach her."

Oh, Kit. Please go. And do not come back here trying to appease me by throwing a crumb to me, trying to convince me that I could be the one to make Pia into a paragon of Society. I have no interest in doing so. This conversation is futile. Things will simply have to continue as they are."

"Mother, what in God's name would you have me do?" Kit asked, as he strode across the room to where his mother sat. "I love my wife. I love you. And I love my children. I came here to tell you of the joy I'm feeling about a new baby coming. Can't you even be happy about that news?"

"Yes. I'm happy for you. But, I suspect that the child's head will be so filled with foolishness about Britain's class system, that he or she will completely ignore all of our traditions. If that's the case, I wish Lily were not expecting."

"My God, Mother. I never, ever thought you could be so cruel. Do you mean to say that unless you see that our new child follows and believes all of the edicts set down by Queen Victoria, you would rather the child not even be born?"

"That's exactly what I'm saying, Kit. The family name is the most important thing in the world to me. Your father left it in my care, asking me to promise to make certain the name Claybourne continued down through the generations in its same pristine, well thought of manner. I am trying to keep that promise. I never dreamed it would be so difficult."

"I'm begging you to reconsider your viewpoint, Mother. Promise or no promise, people's feelings are on the block here. I love you and I need you in my life. But, I also love Lily and need her in my life too."

"When I see that you've taken hold of the reins and begun acting like the head of a household should act, then I shall decide what I'm going to do, and how I'm going to feel about Pia and your new child," Lady Cynthia answered.

When Kit returned to the house, Lily was awake. He asked her how she was feeling, and she said she was doing fine. "No morning sickness of any magnitude, thus far," she smiled.

He sat down on the edge of the bed, and took her into his arms. "Lily I hope you understand how very pleased I am that we're going to have a baby. A symbol of our love for one another. You've brought great happiness to Claybourne Court."

"Kit, I really haven't done anything. Everything that has happened has been an expression of love. Pia, my adoration of Win, my love for you, and now a new child to be brought into the world."

"Yes, but Lily, you brought the love. I've just returned from speaking with Mother. Lily, she's just hopeless. I won't go in to all she said, but I see no possibility of change in her attitude anytime soon. Eventually perhaps. She feels that you don't conduct yourself like a Countess should. She's wrong, of course. I'm afraid she wants you to 'toe the line' a bit too much. She believes I've lost all control and am not the head of the household anymore."

"Kit, how foolish. She makes me out to be a child who isn't minding her p's and q's. Not obeying the rules, and keeping out of mischief. All she thinks I should be is an ornament for Claybourne Court to bring out at balls and dinners, to hang onto your arm and simper. That's not who I am Kit, and I never want to be. Of course you're the man of the house. I rely upon you for nearly every decision that's made on these premises. And, I know I still have much to learn. But, I've gone by instinct up until now, and I feel that those instincts have served me well. Kit, you know I'm not a religious fanatic, but I do strongly believe in the Bible. The most important lesson to be gleaned from that book, I believe, is that of love. What do you think our Lord would have done if someone like Pia had shown up at his family's door? Of course the answer is that he would have loved her- and accepted her wholly into his family." She cleared her throat, and reached for a glass of water. "That is the test I apply to any decisions I have to make of that sort. Of course, my own heart tells me what to do, but if in doubt, I use that simple test."

"I didn't know that, Lily. I would like Mother to know that, but I doubt that it would change her views. I never realized that she is so stubborn."

"You never gave her anything to be stubborn about. You always obeyed and bent to her way of thinking. You didn't have a real identity of your own. Her identity was your identity. As long as you agreed, and didn't form your own opinions, what was there for her to become stubborn about?"

"Lily. You have such incredible insight. I would never have thought about that, but it makes perfect sense."

"That, Kit, is because my parents allowed me to find out who I was, and what my own inner feelings and beliefs were. Of course they taught me right from wrong, but not this 'faux' right and wrong that has come about from societal expectations. All of that is simply a way for a class of people to use silly rules to keep outsiders away from their charmed circle. I truly believe that undoubtedly the nicest people on earth are those who don't have to try to be something they aren't. Honesty Kit. Just, plain honesty is the key to so much. Don't you ever wonder why some people are born to a life of poverty and suffering, while others come into the world with everything they could ask for?"

"Yes. I believe it's partly because of the family we're born into, and partly because our class is endowed with more intelligence and desire to work hard."

"And so, if someone like Pia isn't fortunate enough to have been born into the right family, or the so called right family rejects her, no matter how hard she's willing to work, and no matter her intelligence, she has very little chance of rising above the position she started out with?"

Kit moved over to the small stool by her bed, and Lily put another pillow behind her back. "You know, Kit, let's take as an example, the question Win brought up on Christmas Day. He asked if he could play with the tenant farmer's children, and you very firmly let it be known that he could not. Now, I'm not wanting an argument. But, really Kit, why can't he? Simply because they were born with less than Win was?"

"Oh Lily I think you understand why. It's always been that way. Various classes, at least the very high and the very low, just don't mix."

"But, Kit, isn't that really rather silly? What harm would come to Win if he were to learn that children from lower-class backgrounds are really no different than he is, except for their way of speaking and the amount of material goods their family owns? I think it might be a good lesson for him to learn. Up until now in his life, all he knows is that nicely dressed, good-looking people visit our home and, go to his school. Shouldn't he understand at some point that isn't all there is to the world? A sense of caring about others, and of generosity, should be formed inside of Win. Certainly you've heard the term 'Noblesse Oblige'? And of course, all that means it that those of us who were blessed with an abundance in life, should help those who are less fortunate."

"But Lily, we do. I contribute large amounts to the church, and we give old clothing to the jumble sales. I give quite large amounts to various charitable organizations," Kit answered.

Lily laughed, but not unkindly. "Yes, and that's quite good of you. But Kit, it's really only a beginning. What about sending a child to school who shows early promise, even though he or she might be a tenant farmer's son or daughter? And more precisely, what about letting Win play with those children? I believe that all of the children would gain something from that. The poorer children would learn that there *are* aristocratic people who are kind, and don't believe that any harm can come from innocent children from different classes knowing one another."

"I'm sorry, Lily. I see your point, I really do. But, I think allowing such a thing would be opening up a can of worms. What happens when these children grow older? My God, can't you see how fraught with danger such a policy could be? Would you want Win to marry the daughter of a tenant?"

"It wouldn't be my first choice. No. But, if she's a nice girl, and has learned the things she needs to know –proper speech and so forth, then I wouldn't care. At any rate, yes, it could open a can of worms, but Win were taught simple principles that I believe should apply to all marriages, and man-woman relationships, I doubt it would happen.'"

Such as . . .?

"Such as the fact that marriage is terribly difficult even when people come from the same backgrounds and are raised to have similar beliefs. But, when a couple begins adding in cultural differences, or social class differences of a wide divide, it makes a relationship much more difficult. Not impossible. But, I think there has to be a lot more work to make the relationship able to survive."

"Are you referring to us when you make that statement?" Kit asked.

"Not only us, but I suppose we're a good example of that theory. I do believe that our marriage has been made more difficult by the wide gap between our upbringings – and social class. When you think about it, that topic permeates all of our arguments."

"It's a very complex thing, Lily. And I do see what you're saying. But, I don't want Win to be associating with such children. It might work out fine, but it might not too. Why take a chance?"

"All right, Kit. We won't speak of it anymore. If that's how you feel, I'll acquiesce to your wishes. I don't think it's terribly important to Win, anyway."

18

It was June. The children were out of school for the summer months and Lily was five months along in her pregnancy. Win had turned five years old in April, Lily and Kit had marked their first anniversary the same month, and Win would be spending July and August in America with the Evans. Pia was going to have private English lessons. She had already made great headway with her classes at the *King's School*, and it was felt that one summer of private lessons would bring her up to a very fluent level.

The weather was quite warm, and Lily was enjoying a short stroll around the grounds each day. John told her that exercise and fresh air would be good for her and for the baby. Win, of course, rode his pony every day and had a wonderful time playing in the woods. Kit had asked Eden (Howard) to build Lily as cart that she could hitch Taffeta to, and ride about the grounds, so she didn't lose one of her favorite activities, yet made certain not to harm the baby. Kit was still working on his sheep project, in addition to the Mill. People in the village of *Claybourne-on-Colne* were most excited at the thought that so many new jobs would be available. The woolen Mill would employ over one hundred workers, at decent, livable wages. Kit was a bit worried that some of his tenant farmers might decide to seek employment at the *Claybourne Mills*, as of course the work would be not so back breaking. It wasn't completed yet though, so he was a bit ahead of himself on such worries.

Lady Cynthia continued with her polite, but aloof treatment of Pia, and actually, this was the attitude shown the entire family, but for Win, who had the ability to melt her heart. She was quite devastated that he would be gone for such a long spell in the summer. His nanny, Emma, was very excited about the upcoming trip. She was already working on packing their large trunk, filling it mostly with play clothing for Win, as well as his riding gear. Since she had never been to America, she had no idea what to expect, but Dorothy Evans wrote and said that the weather was very similar to England's, except for the rainfall, so she packed simple day frocks, and cardigan sweaters for cool evenings.

Everything was progressing according to plan, and then a huge kerfuffle began. It involved Win, and when all was said and done, it was probably a very good thing that he was going away for the summer. On a lovely summer day, at about half after eleven, Win came running up to the house, with a little girl by the hand. She was a pretty, little thing, with dark curls and a sweet face. Neither Lily, nor anyone else at Claybourne Court had ever seen her before.

He was rather out-of-breath when he introduced her. "Mummy, this is Susan Gatewood. She lives in one of our tenant houses. I was riding my pony down by the stream that goes through the woods, and she was sitting by the stream, throwing rocks into it. We threw them together to see who could go the farthest and I won. We made a bargain that whoever won, would have to have the other one eat lunch at their house," Win smiled, looking for all the world like he had just won an Olympic Medal.

Oh Lord, Lily thought to herself. Kit would not be pleased at all about this. But, what was she to do? She most certainly wasn't about to hurt the little girl's feelings, so she did what she considered the proper thing. She told her that she was most welcome to have luncheon with the Claybourne's. The table was just being prepared for lunch, and Win took little Susan up to his nursery, to show her all of his things. She trotted along behind him, like a little dog. Mrs. Briggs and Lily rolled their eyes at one another, but didn't say anything. Lily expected Kit to return most any moment, and she secretly hoped he would be delayed. He was at his Land Agent's office, and sometimes those meetings went on and on. Of course, she knew the Gatewood's. At least, she knew Mrs. Gatewood. She was the woman who had so many children and needed help to learn how not to have any more. Lily had never met any of her children, but she could see the resemblance between little Susan and the mother. She hoped nothing would be said about Lily's visits to the tenant farms. Kit would be livid.

She heard his step on the front path, and soon the door opened into the Great Hall. He was smiling, and seemed to be in a fine mood. Throwing a light jacket he'd worn, in case of unexpected rain, on the hall tree, he gave Lily a kiss. She was wearing a white, cotton voile maternity gown, with her hair swept back very neatly. She looked lovely, as always. The lunch gong rang, and Lily and Kit made ready to go into the dining room.

"Where is Win?" Kit asked.

"He's upstairs. Now, Kit don't get into an uproar. He's brought a little friend home to eat with him."

"Why should I get into an uproar about that?" he asked.

"Because the friend is a sweet little girl from one of the tenant farms. She's awfully pretty. Apparently Win came upon her throwing rocks into the stream that runs through the woods. They made it a contest, and whoever won took the other home to lunch. Of course, Kit won." Lily smiled, but was a trifle worried.

Kit frowned. "He knows how we feel about this sort of thing. I'll not embarrass the girl, but I certainly mean to have a talk with Win. He's not to do this again."

"That's fine Kit, but to be honest, I think letting him think he's upset you dreadfully might make him wonder what is so awful about playing with Susan. He's likely to seek her out another time."

"Not if I have anything to say about it," Kit answered. "Anyway, he'll be leaving for America soon."

"Yes, that's what I was thinking. Perhaps better for the entire house, if we just let it pass. Two months in America will make him forget all about her."

"All right, Lily. I hope you're right."

Just as he finished the words, the two children came into the dining room, hand in hand. They had each washed up, and little Susan was quite presentable. She wore a nice, if somewhat faded, play-dress, in a pretty cotton plaid, and she had Mary Jane shoes with anklets on her feet. In addition to her curls, she had very pretty, large blue eyes – very dark blue.

"Daddy, this is Susan Gatewood. She lives down where the tenants are. Her Dad works a farm on our property. Kit knew who the family was. They were decent people, as far as it went, but certainly not who he wanted his son to be mingling with. However, Kit had vowed to be kindly.

"Hello, Susan. It's very nice to meet you. I understand that you and Win had a rock throwing contest, and Kit won".

"Yes, Milord. I weren't me best today. Sometimes I can throw really far. Maybe next time I'll throw longer than 'e does."

"Perhaps," answered Kit, trying not to cringe at her English pronunciation, and hoping there wasn't a next time.

"Do you go to school yet, Susan?" Lily asked. "You look about Win's age."

"Yes, Milady. I go to the public school in the village. I be the first one to go to school in my family, ever, she announced proudly."

"That's really quite lovely, isn't it," Lily replied.

"Yes. Me Mam and Dad are proud of me."

"I'm sure they should be. How old are you, Susan?" Kit asked.

"I'm just now six. Me Mam and Dad had a party for me. Me very first," she smiled.

She tucked into the lunch with zeal, slurping the first course soup as fast as she could. Next came a lovely Shepherd's Pie, and Lily could tell she'd never seen one.

"These are so good Susan. All filled with lots of good things, like chicken and peas, and carrots in gravy. Just dip your fork in, and break the crust, and you'll see what's underneath."

Susan did as instructed and looked with awe at the lovely gravy, meat and vegetables beneath.

"Umm. This is yummy. I can't wait to tell me Mam and Dad about having lunch here. They always say that the people in the big house are toffs, and not our kind, but I think they're wrong. You're very nice and not posh at all."

"Well, thank you very much, Susan," Lily answered, smiling and glancing over at Kit. He too was suppressing a smile. "We're happy you could join us, Susan, "Kit replied.

"Yes. Specially cause me brother is down with the typhoid and nobody's gettin much to eat at me cottage," she blurted out.

Lily's face grew pale. "Your little brother is down with Typhoid?" she repeated. "Has the doctor seen him?"

"No. Doctors cost lots of money. Mam knows what to do. She washes everything real clean, and makes us all do the same. She says it's from the water. We got drain problems."

Lily looked over at Kit again. "I want you to have Henson check on this at once. That's a terrible, deadly disease. She's right about the water. We need to put in new drains, she whispered."

Kit frowned deeply, and got a very angry look on his face. Now it was more than just the little girl having luncheon with them. He was terribly annoyed at Lily's giving him instructions about the tenant's cottages, which he felt were none of her business. Lily knew exactly what had turned his countenance into that of a frightening landlord, but she didn't care. As soon as the children left, she would tell him how she felt.

They mostly ate the rest of the lunch in silence. Win and Susan chattered among themselves, and seemed to enjoy being together. Poor Win really had no friends to play with, except when he was at school. It was no wonder that he was looking forward to his trip to America. She blamed herself for not having thought to organize some sort of play group for him, so that he knew more children. Naturally he was thrilled at finding a child his own age on his own property. It was bound to happen.

Lunch ended, and Susan was very polite. She curtsied to Lily and to Kit, and said "Thank you Milord and Milady." Then, both children put their napkins on their plates, ran to the back of the house, and out of the kitchen door.

Lily turned to Kit. "Oh Kit. I I'm very thankful that you weren't away somewhere. We should go over to the Gatewood cottage at once. It's down by St. Paul's church; you know, that gruesome wet place, under the footbridge, with the front covered in Morning Glories? If it's true that one of their boys is sick with Typhoid, the drains should be removed and replaced.

Otherwise, all of the other children could get it. I believe there are six children." Lily spoke quickly, too engrossed in what she had to say to notice Kit's expression. He just sat there silently, twisting the napkin in his hand.

"Lily, how do you happen to know where this 'Gatewood' family house is, in addition to knowing how many children they have." he asked her, in a voice like his mother when she was speaking to someone in a lesser class.

"Well, to tell you the truth, I've been there," Lily answered.

"You've been there? Yourself? To a house where there's typhoid fever? Pregnant? Lily . . ." His lips went into a thin line, just as his mother's did when she was angry.

"You don't understand. I wasn't there when the typhoid was present. I rode my horse in that direction one day, and stopped to chat with Mrs. Gatewood. She's a very nice person. There's nothing wrong with my state of health. I feel just fine, really I do. And you know the doctors have ordered me to walk and ride my pony cart every day.

"But, not to go and sit with Mrs. Gatewood in a house filled with disease."

"But, Kit, I have to do something. There's no one to see about them. And if the home is filled with disease, it's the fault of the Claybourne's. They've no nurse nor anybody to help the mother, or tell her what to do; that child needs a doctor."

"Is it your idea, Lily, that I should provide every cottage on my estate with a doctor?" Kit asked sarcastically.

"Well, I wish you would. At least there ought to be a nurse on call, and a doctor ought to see free patients every day; and the drains – Kit, you have to come with me right now and smell the drains," cried Lily.

"If your intention is to bring Typhoid Fever to Claybourne Court, I can't imagine a better way of doing it," he began. "But, perhaps you don't realize that the doctors are by no means sure . . ."

"Oh, but they *are* sure. Just ring John and ask him. Typhus comes from bad drains and infected milk. It can't hurt us in the least to go down there and see what's happening at the Gatewoods'; and we have to do it, because they're our own tenants. Please come with me now? Howard will be glad hitch the horses on the cart."

"Lily, I do wish that you wouldn't call Eden by his Christian name. I've already told you that the groom is always referred to by his surname."

"Kit, what *can* it matter? I call the servants by their surnames, but I never can remember about the others. And the only thing that matters now . . ."

Kit walked over to the bell, and rang for one of the footmen. When he appeared he told him to pass the word to Eden in the stables that no one would be needing the pony cart today.

"Is that your answer?" she shouted, once the footman had disappeared. Her breath was coming very quickly.

He smiled at her. "Lily, don't look so pathetic. I'll speak with Henson. He'll look into the drains. But, please try to remember that this is a small concern. It's not my concern at all. It's Henson's. And, it most certainly isn't the slightest concern of yours. My mother was very much respected and looked up to here at Claybourne Court, and it never occurred to her to interfere directly with the agent's business, except regarding Christmas festivities, and the agricultural fair. You might do better to follow her example."

Lily stood staring at Kit, without saying a word. She couldn't believe that words that were coming out of his mouth. She had a strong feeling that he was parroting his mother.

"You ask me to be careful about my health and, in the very same breath, you say that you can't be bothered about these poor people, and their child who is undoubtedly dying. She fell back into a chair, hiding her head in her hands. Kit looked at her without speaking. He honestly didn't know how to deal with her. He went over to her and laid his hand on her bent head.

"Lily," he said.

She jumped to her feet. "Leave me alone," she screamed. He heard her cross the hall and go up the stairs in the direction of her room. He sighed, and decided to let her be alone for a bit. He would go to his library and do some work. He had no idea what to do other than let her calm down, and cry it out. He certainly wasn't going to take a pregnant wife to a cottage where there was a child with typhoid fever.

He spent a goodly amount of time working on his papers, and rang Henson, asking him to look at the drains in the Gatewood house. When about an hour had passed, he went up to Lily's room, and knocked on the door. There was no answer. Thinking that she must have fallen asleep, he very gently opened it. Lily was nowhere to be seen. He began to search the house. He could find her nowhere. It had begun to rain outside, and was quite cool for June. Kit became concerned about her. Surely she couldn't have left the house? And, even if she had, she would return when the rain began. Wouldn't she? He slipped into his Burberry and walked to the walled garden. She wasn't there. Then, he became even more concerned. He walked in the direction of the stables.

Arriving there, he asked Eden if the Countess had been to the stables in the past couple of hours. He said she had, but that he had orders from the Great House not to rig up the pony cart. She had thanked him and gone on her way. He thought she looked as if she had been crying.

Kit asked Eden to saddle two horses, one for himself and one for Kit. He explained that they were going to ride the estate, in the direction of the tenant's cottages, to try to find Lily. Night had fallen, and because of the rain, it was very hard to see. A fog had rolled in as well. After well over two hours of riding they came upon Lily. She was lying on the ground, curled up in a ball, trying to shelter herself under a big Oak tree. Kit got down and carefully put her on his saddle in front of him. Then, they proceeded back to Claybourne Court. Kit rode straight to the front door, and took Lily in that way. Eden had rung the house from the stables, so all of the servants had been alerted. Mrs. Briggs followed Kit as he carried Lily to her room. She was soaked clear through, and was shivering all over. Worse still, there was blood on her skirt in the back. No one needed to ask what it was. Clearly she was miscarrying. Her eyes remained closed, but she was breathing. Every now and then she would let out a cry of pain, surely from the cramping she was having because of the baby. She awoke just one time, as he was placing her into her bed and placing warm blankets around her. She looked up into his face, with raindrops still on her eyelashes, and said "The Gatewood child died. He never had a chance. Now we will pay by losing our own child." She didn't speak another word, but fell into a very deep sleep.

Kit was crushed. If he had only gone to the Gatewood cottage. If she'd only felt everything that could have been done, had been done. He knew she would blame him all the rest of her life. But, before he could think about that, he had to think of her health. God help him, he was not going to see three deaths that night — the little Gatewood child, his own baby, and Lily too. John Garrett was called and came at once. He examined Lily thoroughly, and then met Kit in the library. John refused a drink, as he said he never drank when he might have to deal with a very sick patient.

"What exactly took place here tonight?" John asked.

Kit told him the entire story from start to finish. Half of the time he had his head in his hands.

John listened without interruption, but he had a frown on his face. When Kit was finished John spoke. "Kit, this doesn't even sound like something you would do. I hope you realize that Lily was right. You do have the death of that poor child on your conscience. Of course Typhoid comes from infected water and dirty drains. Good God, man, with all of the money you're worth, why shouldn't the people who work on your land have decent housing. By that I mean indoor plumbing and toilets, fresh running water, and solid roofs, as well as a heating system, beyond a mere fireplace. Would you live the way you expect them to?

I think not, Kit. My God. This is the twentieth century. How can you have told Lily that what was happening at your tenant's house was none of her concern? Of course it was her concern, just as it was yours. Well, I hope you've learned a damned good lesson from this. Lily will be fine. Of course, as you already know, she's lost the baby. I attribute that to her walking for miles in a cold rain. You should have known Lily well enough to know that if you forbid her to take her pony cart, she would simply walk to the cottage. I'm sorry to be so angry, Kit. But, your ridiculous stance contributed to the loss of your child. Lily will recover. In body. But, I can predict that she'll go through a deep depression. Her hormones will be affected, and the way this baby was lost when it never needed to be, will cause her to be deeply irate. Don't try to win her over with gifts or promises that you have no intention of keeping. Let her recover at her own pace. I hope this doesn't end your marriage."

"Oh my God, John. You can't believe that. Lily is a strong girl. She knows I would never have dreamed my actions would bring this on. She's very forgiving. I can't imagine that it would cause her to not want me any longer."

"Kit, I need to tell you that Lily has been unhappy for quite some time. She has had a very difficult time adjusting to the way of life in the aristocracy. She doesn't believe in half of the foolish things that go on. Your mother's attitude toward Pia has been difficult for her to accept. Now there's this thing with the tenant farmers. Lily has a very different outlook on life from yours and your mothers. Frankly, my own opinion is that you are both decent people, but that Lily had no understanding of what she was doing when she married into a noble family. She is the kindest and most giving person I have ever had the privilege to know. She cares deeply for her fellow human beings. She doesn't understand this class distinction nonsense, and she doesn't want to. She believes England is moving toward an entirely different way of life, and she wants to be a part of that. You and your mother, on the other hand, are holding on to the old traditions with iron grips. Something is going to give, Kit, unless there is a change."

"But, John, don't you realize how difficult it is to change overnight? I have tried with Lily. But, sometimes I feel like she asks too much. I'm caught between my mother's views and Lily's. I don't even know what my own are."

"Then, I think it's time you learned, Kit. You know, I come from a noble family, too. But, I thank God that I was a second son. I was able to follow my own path. I became a physician, and married Gena, who also comes from a noble family. We both want no part of all of that claptrap. We are as happy as any two people could be. You could be too, but I warn you, you cannot have Lily and your ancient ideas about what is and isn't correct."

19

After long weeks of illness, a new Lily emerged. This Lily never again spoke of the child she'd lost. She also never spoke of the future. She buried herself in the activities of her children, Pia and Win, which did not always bring satisfaction or reward. Win in particular, became a terrible problem.

While she was ill in bed, with the miscarriage and a terrible bout of bronchitis which lasted for weeks, Win and Emma, his nanny, boarded a ship for America. She was too frail to see them off, but Kit accompanied them to Liverpool, from which they sailed. Lily had Win sent to her room before he left, and kissed him goodbye. He clung to her, and told her he loved her. Lily's illness had frightened him, and left him with feelings of guilt. His Mummy never would have known about the Typhoid that had caused so much sadness, if he had never brought Susan home to lunch. Lily assured him that wasn't true – that she would have learned it on her own, and that if anything she was glad she had found out, for now his Daddy was doing something to make the situation better for all of the tenant farmers. That certainly was true. Kit had followed John's advice, and had completely renovated each of the tenant cottages, putting in modern plumbing and wiring, as well as indoor toilets, and heating systems. Lady Cynthia was furious beyond words, but Kit didn't let her get in the way of his plans.

Thus, Win sailed for America with a lighter conscience. It was very quiet in the house with him gone. Lily definitely missed him. Often, when she was up to it, she strolled down to the stables, and petted his pony, so the poor animal wouldn't feel abandoned. Pia continued with her English lessons throughout the summer, and the progress she made was nothing short of remarkable. She was beginning to speak fluent English without the trace of an accent. She was developing into an even prettier young woman. Her legs grew longer, and she took on a graceful elegance. Her dreams of becoming a fashion model looked like they might become reality.

Near the end of the summer, Lily turned her attention back to re-decorating Claybourne Court, which had long ago been placed on the shelf, due to so many other happenings in her life. She was feeling very dissatisfied with life in general, and thought that perhaps a decorating project might help to calm her need for self- fulfillment.

She didn't ask anyone's advice. Not Lady Cynthia's, and not Kit's. Only Pia acted as her confidant.

They pulled out the original swatches of fabric and paint colors they had planned on using before, and decided they were still what be appropriate. Lily wondered if she really had the courage to sweep away all of the silly, little family mementos which covered the walls, from postcard-like views of Mount Etna erupting, to very poorly painted still-life's by the Dowager Countess's great-aunts, as well as ghastly locks of hair from dead relatives, framed on faded moiré, and photographs in ancient frames of noble relatives, horses, and students grouped around sporting trophies. She would only know if she tried it.

So, with a ladder that reached practically to the ceiling, and Pia holding it at the bottom, Lily took every single beastly item down. If the Dowager Countess wanted them, she could hang them in her own Dower House. She left the walls mostly bare, except for some really excellent paintings done by old masters. Lily was partial to antique furnishings, and had no great desire to re-furnish the house in the Art Deco that were coming into their own about that time. So, most of the lovely old furnishings were retained, but all were re-covered in lovely, bright fabrics of silk stripes and chintz. She put many of the figurines of little shepherd's and their mates in the large box that was to be delivered to Lady Cynthia. She replaced some of the not-so-good knick-knacks with pieces of crystal, Lalique, Waterford, and Baccarat. Draperies were hung in lovely colors – mostly pastels, or pure white taffeta. The old carpets were stored in the attic, and Lily purchased new Aubusson for all of the downstairs. The woodwork in Kit's library was lightened and pickled. She also had all of the baths modernized, with new fixtures, and pretty wall coverings. Pia's room was re-done in toile wallpaper with matching spread and drapes, and Lily's own room became a palette of white, with touches of pink in bed pillows and the chaise.

When it was completely finished, she stood back in amazement at the transformation in the house. Her mother-in-law had not seen a whit of it, as she had gone on a trip to Bath to take the waters, and while Kit knew what was underway, he didn't say a word, for fear of upsetting Lily. Naturally, the servants never commented, except for Mrs. Briggs and Ruth, who said it was all a delightful change. At about the same time that the last wallpaper was hung, and the last paint was dry, Lily packed up all of the items that were to be delivered to Lady Cynthia's and rang for the footmen to take them to the Dower House. She knew that Kit's mother had returned from Bath just a day before.

Lily was lying in her bed, reading and Pia was in her room studying an English lesson, when the front door opened and Lady Cynthia roared into the Great Hall like an angry bear stomping out of the woods. "Who is responsible for this desecration?" she screamed. She stood stock still and surveyed all of the changes that had occurred. "Lily, did you do this? Kit, where are you? You had no right to make changes to this lovely old home. It hasn't been altered in over seventy-five years."

Lilly, still lying on her bed, smiled, and thought to herself 'I can certainly believe that.' It was easy to hear Lady Cynthia going from room to room, shouting obscenities, and acting like the house looked like one of the tenant farmer's.

Kit finally emerged from the rear terrace, where he had been smoking a cigarette and enjoying the warm day. "Mother, for heaven's sake, you can be heard all over the village. What is the matter with you?" he asked.

"What is the matter with me? Are you daft? Look around you. Did you give your permission for this – this – defilement?" she shouted.

"Mother, calm down. No, I did not give my permission for the redecorating. But, if you recall, it was discussed long ago, and Lily finally felt up to taking on the task. I take little interest in such things, and I'm glad Lily was kept occupied by it."

"You have lost your mind, Kit Claybourne. That woman has made this lovely home look like an American noveau riche mansion. Are you telling me that you're in favor of this? She's removed every old, priceless treasure in the home. She had them all delivered to the Dower House this morning."

"Well, it seems to me that it was decent of her to send things to you. Then, you can put them on the walls of the Dower House," he answered.

There was silence for a moment, and Lily couldn't make out what was taking place. Then she heard the sound of breakage occurring, and she knew it was the crystal that she had so lovingly purchased. "Mother, stop that this instant. You are acting like a child," Kit yelled.

"Not nearly as much as I shall be," she shouted back. There was more smashing, and then Lily heard draperies being torn down and fabric being ripped from furniture. She got up off the bed, and ran to the railing that overlooked the Great Hall. It looked like a mad woman had roared through it. All of her hard work, and hours of decision-making had been destroyed. Lily was beyond furious. She ran down the stairs and grabbed Lady Cynthia by the arms.

"This is my house, and I'll decorate it the way I choose. What business do you have coming in here and destroying everything?" Lily sank down on the sofa, which had a large tear in the upholstery. She put her hands over her face, and began to sob. It made no impact on her mother-in-law who continued to rant and tear things up.

If she had turned around, she would have glimpsed Pia creeping down the stairway, dressed in a white summer dress, and wearing her white scarf over her head. She disappeared through the baize door to the downstairs level. Kit walked through the rooms surveying the damage, which caused his mother to stop her rampage. Instead, she followed behind him pointing out what she termed 'the horror' that had been made of their lovely home. Kit was terribly upset. The truth was, he didn't particularly care for the new decoration either, and he could understand his mother's upset. He was awfully used to the house being a certain way, and even if it was a bit shabby, that was the way English country houses were supposed to look. Lily obviously didn't understand that. Lily continued to sit in the drawing room sobbing. She was waiting for Kit to take up for her.

After making a complete tour of the house, both Kit and his mother returned to the first level. Kit walked into the drawing room, and sat down next to Lily.

"Lily, why didn't you speak to Mother before you made all of these changes? I do think that you went a bit far. Of course, I'm no expert, but it looks different from any country house I've been in. It's lost it's old, charming appeal. Those rugs you took up were very, very old Orientals, purchased in China. You've chosen draperies that are far too modern for this sort of house. In addition, you've removed treasured mementos from the walls – things that have been in the family for generations. I hate to do this, Lily, but I'm going to have to side with Mother here. She is going to come in and bring it back to its original look. There are some things that can be kept. I think the new baths are a nice touch, and the bedrooms can be left intact, but almost all of the rest has to go."

Lily stood up and looked at Kit in amazement. "I was told that I could re-decorate this house. You told me that before we were even married. I remember sitting in this very room talking to Gena about it. I believe your mother was present too. She never said a word then about how the house should be decorated. Now, after weeks of enormous effort, you have the audacity to tell me that it's all wrong?"

Lady Cynthia came into the room. "Yes, it's all wrong Lily. Just as many of the ideas you have put into effect since marrying my son have been and are. It will be put back to the condition it was in before, I can assure you of that. There will be no more meddling with things you don't understand and have no business trifling with."

She had her hands on her hips. What had happened to the lovely person Lilly had thought her to be at the beginning of her marriage to Kit? And, what had become of the Kit she once knew? Lily brushed her hand over her hair, and pushed it behind her ears. She knew when she was beaten. With a great deal of disappointment and sadness, she left the room and went to her walled garden. She settled herself on her favorite marble bench. Tears were still falling from her eyes, and she felt hopeless. Then, her favorite butterfly landed on the pink rosebush next to her. Lily sat there and studied its gracefulness and freedom. Suddenly it dawned upon her that her life could be compared to butterflies. She'd certainly gone through a similar change from the person she once was. The difference was that butterflies only lived for about a year. But, during that year, they were free to do whatever they wished. She needed to be conscious of using the time she had in life in a meaningful way. The horrible mess that had just occurred was not productive, and had accomplished nothing.

"Come Hell or high-water, I'm not going to live like this much longer," she whispered to herself.

Win returned from America two days later. Of course the house was still in shambles, but Lily didn't care. Pia had crept back to her room when all of the screaming calmed down, and she stayed there as much as she possibly could. Both she and Lily were glad that Win would be coming home.

However, when he arrived, it was a totally different Win. He had sprouted up quite a bit over the summer, but that wasn't really the change. His hair had been cut into a very short style, if it could even be called a style. It was combed back away from his face, and there was oil on it. Lily was appalled. He was dressed in something called 'blue jeans', which he said all of the American boys wore, and he had picked up some positively rude ways of speaking. Instead of saying 'yes', he said 'yeah'; Instead of referring to a male friend as a 'fellow' or a 'mate', he called them 'guys'; and, he went around clearing his throat and spitting. Lily was overcome with amazement. Where was her darling Win?

She decided to let it go, thinking it was obviously remnants of behavior he had picked up on his Grandparent's ranch. It wasn't worth another row in the house. But, when they sat down for dinner on his first night home, he crossed the line.

Turning to Pia, he smirked and said "Did you know that your mother was a whore?"

Pia dropped her fork on her plate, and Lily turned ashen. Kit kept right on eating, and acted like he hadn't heard the comment. Apparently because he hadn't got the response he was looking for, Win decided to move his bad behavior up a notch.

"Mummy, did you really steal my Daddy away from my real Mummy by doing nasty things to him that weren't proper?"

This time, Lily dropped her fork. She stared at Win for a moment, and then answered. "No Win, that is not what happened. You are not to speak like that again at this table – neither to me nor to your sister, is that understood?"

"You aren't my real Mummy, and Pia isn't my sister. Her mother was a prostitute, and you were nothing but a housemaid. I don't have to listen to anything you say."

Kit looked up, and said "Now son, enough of that." Then, he turned to Lily. "Pay him no mind. He's only a boy. I'm not going to go through any more shouting in this house. So, don't trouble yourself to get upset, Lily. I think it's time I took back the reins. Things have gone out of control here. I've let everyone think they can say and do whatever pleases them, without any repercussion from the head of the household. I excuse Will, because he's still such a young boy, but from now on, I make the rules, and I expect them to be followed. Is that understood?"

There was quiet at the table, and then Lily excused herself. So did Pia. They both went upstairs, and Lily called Pia into her room.

"Pia, how would you feel about moving to London with me?" Lily asked.

"Oh, Lily, I would love it. But, what about my father and Win?"

"Your father and Win can sit here in this mess of a house, and let your grandmother have what she wants. To be the Countess of Gloucester, and Lady Claybourne again."

"What about my school?" Pia asked.

"We shall find you an excellent school in London. As a matter of fact, I'm going to return to school too. Remember when I told you that I'd always wanted to be a physician? Well, I'm going to do it. I wrote the *London College of Medicine for Women* months ago, after I lost the baby. Rather on a lark, but now I'm very serious. They replied with a very nice letter saying that from looking at my grades from my last school, and reading my letter, they felt quite certain they could find a spot for me in their fall class."

"Lily! Pia smiled broadly and looked very happy. I would love to see you realize your dreams. You have done so much for everybody. It doesn't seem like you are appreciated. I love my father, but I don't like the way you are put second in this house. Maybe even third or fourth, behind Gran Mere and Win."

"What position do you feel that you hold, Pia?" Lily asked.

"Oh, I am fifth, for certain. But, that is all right. I never had a family, so I should not be first or even fourth. I have to work my way up."

Lily grabbed her and hugged her. "Well, darling girl," you have just moved into first place with me. We are going to have an equal household. No ones and two's. I, too, love your father, but I am not certain that I can live with him anymore. I need more in my life than being a Countess who isn't allowed to make a move without asking her husband or her mother-in-law. I need to be the best I can be, and to do something with my life. I have always wanted to be a doctor, and I shall be. We'll go to London, and live in the house there. It's lovely and large, and in an excellent neighborhood, convenient to lots of things. You will be presented at Court, with my sponsorship, and you'll have a debut party, even if it isn't as grand as it might have been here at Claybourne Court. The London house isn't a tiny cottage. It could well accommodate such a celebration. We'll take Ruth with us, and hire a cook and whoever else we need in London. You're going to need your own ladies' maid before too awfully long. Win may choose to do as he wishes. From his nasty comments tonight, I suspect that he'll remain with his father. We can write him letters. I'll speak to him before we leave. Now, go and pack your things, Use the big trunk. Take clothing for all seasons. Take everything."

"All right, Lily, but aren't you even going to tell my father?" And what about your mother? And Gran Mere?"

"I shall write Kit a long letter. Perhaps he'll understand better when he reads it, after we're gone. I'll ring my mother tonight and tell her what is happening. Pack a separate small bag for tonight and tomorrow. We shall spend the night with my mother and step-father. As far as Gran Mere is concerned I owe her no explanations. Tomorrow, we shall take the train to

London. I'll get the key to the London house from the hook in the kitchen. Now hurry along. If anyone comes to your door, except me, don't answer. We are through talking, Pia, and there will be no more insults thrown our way."

Pia kissed Lily and skipped to her own room. Lily sighed, and began packing her trunk. She heard the front door open and close, and saw from the window that Kit and Win had gone over to Kit's mother's house. Lily picked up the telephone and rang her mother. She only briefly related her tale of woe, and asked that Will come to fetch them. He said he would be delighted. An hour later, two trunks were ready to be sent to the rail station, and two figures walked to a car that had pulled up in front of the house. They got into the auto. In the backseat of the car, Pia asked Lily,

"Will you divorce my father?"

"No. Not yet," Lily replied. "Unless, of course he wants me to. He may come to London to visit if it pleases him, but I have no intention of returning to Claybourne Court until I am dressed in the white coat of a physician, and they will have to call me *Doctor* Lily Claybourne.

Just then she spotted that same white butterfly floating about the place where the car stood. Lily was certain that it was a good omen

Other Books By Mary Christian Payne

The Somerville Trilogy

Willow Grove Abbey: Book 1 of the Somerville Trilogy
St. James Road: Book 2 of the Somerville Trilogy
Serendipity: Book 3 of the Somerville Trilogy

The Claybourne Trilogy

The White Feather: Book 1 of the Claybourne Trilogy
The White Butterfly: Book 2 of the Claybourne Trilogy
White Cliffs of Dover: Book 3 of the Claybourne Trilogy

The Thornton Trilogy

No Regrets: Book 1 of The Thornton Trilogy
No Gentleman: Book 2 of the Thornton Trilogy
No Secrets: Book 3 of the Thornton Trilogy

ABOUT THE AUTHOR

Mary Christian Payne was highly successful in several management positions in Fortune 500 Companies, in New York City, St. Louis, Missouri, Orlando Florida, and Tulsa, Oklahoma. Her work included Grant writing, and designing and writing Training Manuals for Executive Training Programs.

She left the corporate world, and became Director of Career Development at the Women' Resource Center at the University of Tulsa, where she designed a program that enabled hundreds of adult women to return to college and better their lives. She received the Mayor's Pinnacle Award in 1993 for this achievement. Mary left that position when the Center closed, and then opened her own Career Counseling Center. She retired in 2008.

Mary Christian Payne became a successful, best-selling author at the age of 71, with the help of her publisher, Tom Corson-Knowles. All of her life, she had wanted to write, and had received accolades for her unpublished work. She was encouraged in college, and writing was a significant part of the various jobs she held.

In 2013, she read Tom Corson-Knowles' book about publishing on Kindle. She wrote to him and he telephoned her. The rest is history. Since that time, she has published nine books, with more on the way.

Mary lost her husband in June, 2015, after 33 years of marriage. The grief process brought a lull to her writing, but she found that putting words on paper helped immensely. She is now in the process of writing her second novel since his death. She lives in Tulsa, Oklahoma, with her two beloved Maltese dogs.

Sign up for the newsletter to get news, updates and new release info from Mary Christian Payne:

http://bit.ly/MaryChristianPayne

ONE LAST THING...

If you enjoyed this book, I'd be very grateful if you'd post a short review on Amazon. Your support really does make a difference and I read all the reviews personally.

Thanks again for your support!